Praise for *Paris in the*

"Another crime adventure from the Pulit[...] [...] Butler. Set in Paris during the First World War, it is infused with the life of this special city, with its aromas, cafes, and fascinating and interesting people walking the streets amid its own unique architecture. . . . A fun read."   —*New York Journal of Books*

"Written in a hard-boiled, staccato style, *Paris in the Dark* is an intelligent, stylish thriller, and so atmospheric that the pages reek of Gitanes and coffee."   —*Times* (UK)

"Pulitzer Prize-winning novelist Robert Olen Butler continues to deliver a gripping blend of historical fact and detective fiction."
                                        —*Minneapolis Star Tribune*

"A morally complex and beautifully written thriller with a delicately portrayed love story at its heart. A cut above."   —*Mail on Sunday* (UK)

"*Paris in the Dark*, Robert Olen Butler's fourth in a series of historical spy thrillers, starts with [a] literal bang and doesn't let up . . . a satisfying, stylish thrill."   —*Tampa Bay Times*

"The parallels here are as much Graham Greene's *Quiet American* and the earliest days of the Vietnam War as they are early 20th century Europe or 21st century everywhere . . . Butler skillfully paces the narrative, balancing deception, misdirection and reveal with historical realism, quality writing, and insightful modern perspective."
                                        —*Electric Lullaby*

"The award-winning Robert Olen Butler once again shows his mastery of the historical thriller with this striking novel . . . *Paris in the Dark* is not only shot through with a keen intelligence rare in the genre, but it is also couched in elegant prose."   —*Crime Time*

PARIS in the DARK

Also by Robert Olen Butler

The Alleys of Eden

Sun Dogs

Countrymen of Bones

On Distant Ground

Wabash

The Deuce

A Good Scent from a Strange Mountain

They Whisper

Tabloid Dreams

The Deep Green Sea

Mr. Spaceman

Fair Warning

Had a Good Time

From Where You Dream: The Process of Writing Fiction
(Janet Burroway, Editor)

Severance

Intercourse

Hell

Weegee Stories

A Small Hotel

Perfume River

The Christopher Marlowe Cobb Series

The Hot Country

The Star of Istanbul

The Empire of Night

PARIS in the DARK

A Christopher Marlowe Cobb Thriller

ROBERT OLEN BUTLER

The Mysterious Press
New York

A portion of this book originally appeared in *Narrative* magazine.

Published simultaneously in Canada
Printed in the United States of America

This book was set in 11.5 pt Janson MT
by Alpha Design & Composition of Pittsfield, NH.

First Grove Atlantic hardcover edition: September 2018
First Grove Atlantic paperback edition: October 2019

Library of Congress Cataloging-in-Publication data available for this title.

ISBN 978-0-8021-4770-7
eISBN: 978-0-8021-4646-5

The Mysterious Press
an imprint of Grove Atlantic
154 West 14th Street
New York, NY 10011

Distributed by Publishers Group West

groveatlantic.com

19 20 21 22   10 9 8 7 6 5 4 3 2 1

For Kelly.
It just gets better and better.

1

In the dark above Paris, in the deep autumn of 1915, there were always the Nieuports flying their patterns, like sentries walking a perimeter. The new, svelte Model 11—called *Bébé* by its pilots—operated above the high-flying Zeppelins, poised to drop on them in a column of searchlight if the Zepps got by the guns at the French forts to the east.

On a November night I sat beneath the Nieuports at a table outside the Café de la Rotonde. The weather had been unpredictable. It snowed last week but tonight it was almost mild. It might as well have been April and that hammering of engine pistons up above might as was well have been French worker bees going after chestnut blossoms.

My drink was a Bijou—the greenery taste of the chartreuse fitting right in with the bees in the night—and I was surrounded by people I couldn't actually see, just vague shapes and spots of cigarette flame. But I knew who they were, the assorted male denizens of the Left Bank. Artists and professors; students furloughed for six days from hell; students furloughed for good by a stump of an arm or an empty pants leg; the old, the infirm, the foreigners.

The conversations—at turns hopeful, fearful, or miffed—had been low, as if the Zepps would hear us, and I'd sat away from them, near the street. I had my own brooding and ranting to do, which I kept to myself.

But now a voice rang clearly in the dark.

"Monsieur. You will like one Bijou more?"

I looked up at the shadow hovering above me. He'd spoken in English but wallowing the words in his mouth as the French do. He was old enough to have grandsons in the trenches.

"Thank you," I said. "That is just what I need."

I'd replied in French. My French was pretty good. My actress mother, who took on my education in all subjects, knew French well from playing Racine and Corneille in her two long, triumphant tours of the Continent in the mid-nineties. And from a beau or two of hers along the way.

Before the waiter moved off, I said, "Henri, isn't it?"

"Yes that is me," he said. "Have I forgotten you, to my shame?" He was speaking French to me now.

"Ah no," I said. "I heard someone address you."

"Thank you," he said.

I said, "I always like to know the name of the man who will help me become more or less drunk."

Henri laughed a faintly suppressed laugh.

"I'm Kit Cobb," I said.

"Monsieur Cobb. You are American, yes?"

"Yes I am."

"You are here." He paused. I grew up in the theater. I knew how to hear subtext. Here meaning Paris. Meaning Paris deep into the Great War. His silence said: *Though your countrymen are not.* Then he finished formally, courteously. "I am grateful to you."

"Plenty of us will be here," I said, addressing the thing he'd left unsaid. "To fight. The day is coming."

He lowered his voice. "There are too many professors."

I shot him a smile, though I doubted he could see it. He knew his clientele here amidst the universities of Paris on the Left Bank. And he knew our American president.

"I share your distaste," I said. Then, so he knew I knew what he was really saying, I added, "For Professor Wilson."

He chuckled, and I could even make out his shrug. "But still your countrymen will come?" he asked.

"Yes."

"I pray it will be in time."

"So do I."

"And you, sir? What do you do in Paris?"

Ah, how to answer that.

I was a reporter. A war correspondent. But hobbled, thanks to Henri's government. And part-time, thanks to mine. I was also a spy.

But I said something that surprised Henri, and surprised me too: *Je suis poilu.* I did not know how to explain other than to lift my arm and tap myself on the heart. I hoped he could see the gesture. I am a poilu.

The public—everyone in France—called the French infantryman *le poilu. The hairy man.* As a reporter of wars, I'd known a great many hairy men under various flags in my life.

He did see the gesture. Or he already understood. "We must all be poilus," he said.

"Yes," I said. Emphatically. *Bien oui.* "Your boys will hold on. I am sure of this."

"*Vive la France,*" Henri said, almost in a whisper.

I said it too, and as I did, I realized that he'd whispered so his voice would not crack from emotion.

He was gone.

Three or four searchlights flared up now and scraped around against the ceiling of clouds, and then abruptly, quietly vanished again.

I knew the sound of Zepps and there was none of that. Only the buzz of the Nieuports.

I drained what was left of my present Bijou and it burned its way up into my nose and all through my head.

There'd be no Zeppelins tonight. The German command had lately shifted their attention to the more vulnerable London. I knew something about all that, had even exerted a bit of influence on those operations during a challenging week at the end of August, when I'd no longer been Kit Cobb at all but a man who existed only in phony documents and a scrim of lies, sneaking around Germany for my country's secret service.

I'd done well enough that I'd been able to insist on a couple of months' break from being a spy so I could be who I really was.

As if that were actually possible in this wretched war.

My own quiet café rant, as a war correspondent, had to do with one of the nasty advances of this so-called Great War. Strictly codified censorship of the news. A parallel war against a free press. We could not get into the battle-line trenches where the bodies of the husbands and sons and fathers of Europe were being savaged, countless tens of thousands of them, just forty miles from where I sat. We could not even follow the battlefield advances and retreats until the events were reviewed and adulterated by the generals and the politicians. All in the name of public morale.

At least I'd gotten clearance from the French War Office of Muckety-Muck Press-Suppression to write what might become a decent story. Might even get me close to the action. A feature on the American volunteers driving ambulances to and from the Western Front. The French approved, I figured, because it might give Woody Wilson a kick in the butt, a big story in the U.S. papers about all these American college boys and farm boys and mailmen and store clerks finding the guts that the American president can't find, to come to France and stand up to Kaiser Willie.

Henri returned with my third Bijou, my intended last, for I would be working tomorrow.

He set it in front of me and said, "Perhaps soon the British will be of more help."

I thought I heard his subtext: *Since America won't likely be.* But as clearheaded as Henri could be about us, he was buying the propaganda about the Brits. He immediately said, "Perhaps from the meeting something good will come."

Adjoining the war ministry's office for the suppression of news was the office for manipulating the news. These mugs were doing a lapel-grabbing sales job about a meeting in Paris in a week and a half. General Joseph Joffre and General Archibald Murray, the chiefs of their respective general staffs, were coming to a local hotel. Old Archie, as he was called, was the third such chief since the beginning of the war and the Brits still hadn't gotten their act together. Short on artillery shells. Short on men. Doing little enough in the war to worry the hell out of the French.

But Henri was hopeful. The power of the press, even if it was in the back pocket of a government.

"Let's hope," I said to him.

I figured Henri had his unspoken doubts, however, as he had no further hopeful word to add beyond, "Enjoy your drink, Monsieur Cobb."

He slipped away.

I looked into the dim expanse of the Boulevard du Montparnasse. I sipped my Bijou.

Five streets converge around La Rotonde and two of them were over my left shoulder. I did not have to turn to recognize the sound that was swelling along one of them. I heard it in this quarter of the city often. The iron-rimmed wheels of a fiacre and the iron-shod hooves of its horse, hurrying this way with a fare, the sound of metal on cobble drumming up another sound beneath it, from deeply beneath, a cavernous sound found in no other city in the world. This whole area sat upon the Catacombs, the ancient limestone quarries that now held the skeletons of six million dead, the cemeteries of Paris disgorged more than a century ago.

The carriage rushed past. *Dim as a ghost*, I thought. Or: *As if chased by the ghosts it was summoning up.* I itched to type my byline and plow into a story on the Corona Portable Number 3 that waited for me on my desk in the small hotel up the Rue de Seine.

Soon there would be some Americans to talk to. At least that. From the American Ambulance Hospital of Paris, in the city's adjacent *commune* of Neuilly-sur-Seine. A hospital full of volunteers. I turned my thoughts to them. Nurses in white caps. Guys in khakis. Americans.

And from off to the west the air cracked. The sound brass-knuckled us and faded away.

A bomb. Awful big or very near.

All around me the shadows of men had risen up and were retreating into the bar. They had the Zepps in mind. I jumped up too but stepped out onto the pavement of Boulevard Montparnasse. The fiacre had stopped cold and the horse was rearing and whinnying.

It wasn't Zepps. I'd have heard their engines. And the crack and fade were distinctive. Dynamite. This was a hand-delivered explosive. I looked west. Five hundred yards along the boulevard I could make out a billow of smoke glowing piss-yellow in the dark.

I made off in that direction at a swift jog.

My footfalls rang loud. Nothing was moving around me in the dark. Or ahead in the glow. I pressed on, and ahead I recognized another convergence of streets, the Place des Rennes, before the quarter's big railroad station, the Gare Montparnasse.

As I neared, there were sounds. Battlefield sounds just after an engagement. The silence of ceased weapon fire filled with the afterclap of moaning, of gasping babble. Nearer still I heard the approaching fire-engine hooters and police whistles, and I saw figures dashing across the boulevard from the station.

I entered the Place des Rennes.

There were lights now. Gas lamps from the broad, two-storied front facade of the train station; tungsten beams of gendarme flashlights; incidental fires in the wreckage.

Someone had bombed the ground-floor café in the Terminus Montparnasse Hôtel, reduced it to the twisted ironwork of the sidewalk canopy, the shredded and smoldering canvas of the awning, the fragmented clutter of what had been tables and chairs.

I stepped onto a trolley island halfway across the *place*.

A long-hooded Renault ambulance brisked by in front of me and turned sharply right, stopping in front of the hotel.

The police were wading into the bomb site now, abruptly bending forward, crouching low. To bodies I could not see.

I took a step off the island and onto the cobbles. My foot nudged something and I stopped again. I looked down.

A man's naked arm, severed at the elbow, its hand with palm turned upward, its fingers splayed in the direction of the café, as if it were the master of ceremonies to this production of the Grand Guignol. *Mesdames et messieurs, je vous présente la Grande Guerre.* The goddamn Great War.

I lifted my eyes once more to the Café Terminus.

Not one detail I was witnessing—not a bistro table in the middle of Boulevard Montparnasse, not the severed arm at my feet—would ever make it past the news censor's knife.

As for me, I'd seen enough for tonight.

I turned.

I walked away.

And I realized I'd left something undone.

I walked quickly on.

At La Rotonde, some of my previous drinking companions had reemerged, mostly the wounded and the furloughed. A couple of the soldiers who were still whole were on the sidewalk looking in the direction from which I came. All the rest had resumed their seats.

I turned in and entered the café. The civilians—the professors and the elderly and the routinely infirm—were holding on, but they were inside now, at the marble-topped tables.

I stopped and looked to do what I needed to do.

Henri was turning away from the bar. He saw me and crossed to me.

I pulled money from my pocket.

He nodded to me gravely.

"I hope you didn't think I was running from my bill," I said in French.

"Of course not," he said. "Did you see?"

"A bomb at the Terminus Hôtel."

Henri cursed. Low. "The Barbarians," he said. Meaning the Germans. "They are among us."

2

The next morning I was in a horse-drawn fiacre, its iron wheel-rims ringing on the cobblestones, its four-seat cabin smelling of chilled mildew, its leather seats brittle from age, a vehicle of the sort resuscitated into Paris use to replace the motorized taxis, most of which—along with every last motorbus—were now off plying the roads to the front for the French army.

We crossed the Seine at Pont Royal and skirted the Tuileries. The figures moving among the garden's chestnut trees were mostly men on crutches and women in black. I wondered if they went there with the intention to meet, these two constituencies of a grim wartime social club, to find consolation in each other. Beyond the gardens we headed west on the Champs Élysées at a surprising trot for a bay horse starting to dip in the back and go bony in the withers. The old boy was another resuscitation project, a good French horse relinquishing retirement, pitching in. Soon he carried us out of Paris at the Porte Maillot and into Neuilly.

All this way, I noted the passing scene only idly, the journalist in me collecting details to describe the city for my readers in Chicago. My mind was out ahead of my resolute old horse, devising questions for the superintendent of the American Hospital, the American nurses in the ward, the French soldiers in the beds, and, of course, the boys who might get me near the action, the American ambulance drivers, though my initial time with them wouldn't be till tomorrow, at day's end, at the New York Bar on the Right Bank.

I noted our turn north. I moved my eyes to the window of the fiacre. We negotiated our way through a large intersection and, shortly thereafter, a smaller one. The hospital wasn't far now. Then we passed a line of road-roughed recent refugees that stretched across the front of a homely, Gothic-revival Protestant church, through the churchyard, and into a heavy canvas shelter tent next door.

Henri bent near in my head and repeated himself. *The Barbarians. They are among us.*

And the thought occurred to me: *This is how.*

Unarmed, bedraggled, seeming to flee the carnage, anyone could enter the city and vanish and then reappear in the dark with a bomb, the Nieuports above powerless.

And then there were the others who were coming to Paris from the carnage. An hour later I stood before such a man. Only his eyes were visible. A poilu. The rest of his face was hidden beneath bandages. What face there might have been.

He lay in one of the dozens of nine-bed wards at the American Hospital, in a space built as a classroom. To the "American Warriors of Mercy"—I was phrasemaking already in my head for my readers in Chicago and across the country on the newswires—to these volunteer Americans, the French government had turned over a newly finished but still unoccupied school building, the Lycée Pasteur. A massive four-story French Renaissance quadrangle of red brick and white stone facings built around a courtyard. The doctors and presiding ward-nurses were from American university medical schools. The nurse "auxiliaries" were young women with guts and independence and, among the ones who stuck it out, strong stomachs for hospital dirty work. Assorted women. They were actresses and typists and shopgirls, tenement girls and society girls. One was even Secretary of the Treasury McAdoo's daughter.

At my side was a Harvard doctor, talking with a tinge of compulsion about head and face and foot wounds from the trenches. About compound fractures from collapsing buildings. And about the shrapnel wounds. On these he paused, as if searching for a word, and then said, "These are hard to describe, in their terrible variety."

I turned to the wrapped face before us. The eyes were shut.

"The random tumble of metal through torsos," the doctor said. "Parts of faces blown away."

The eyes opened and moved to the doctor.

The doctor did not notice. His tone wasn't clinical. But neither was it empathetic. Perhaps it was ironic. He was middle-aged and until a few months ago had been a university teaching-doctor for American Brahmins. The shrapnel tumbled through him, as well, a hundred times a day, with the savage irony of his dealing with these shards of war in a school building. His detached tone was a wrap of bandages around him.

I returned to the poilu and he'd shut his eyes again. Had he understood the English?

"Ah, Louise," the doctor said.

I looked toward the door.

She was all in white linen. Her nurse's cap had a black stripe across it, near the crown. She was pale as her linen but her eyes were gray as shrapnel and they were sorrowful as a pup's. The cap stripe signified a senior rank, though she was young, this Louise.

"Nurse," the doctor said to her, with a corrective stress on the word as if his use of her name had been a breach of protocol.

She arrived.

She nodded at the doctor.

On this morning, she still smelled of lilac water, not yet of wound-drain and carbolic acid. Touching, really, given the professionally hardened look in her lovely large eyes, given her senior status in a tough trade, touching to me that she would splash this parlor-and-parasol smell onto her body before a day of wounds and death.

She nodded at me. And she let her gaze fix unwaveringly on mine as the doctor spoke my name, fully, Christopher Marlowe Cobb, and hers, Supervising Nurse Louise Pickering.

I offered my hand.

She took it with a man's grip. A smallish, bookish man perhaps, but a meet-you-more-than-halfway man. I'd known a few suffragettes pretty well and was increasingly fine with that.

She seemed willing to shake a moment or two more, but I let go.

"The American newsman I spoke of," the doctor said to her.

"I assumed," she said, directly to him, and then she turned and assessed me for a few moments as if I'd just been carried in from the back of an ambulance.

The doctor excused himself. "I leave you in the capable hands of Nurse Pickering," he said.

We watched him go.

I said, "So he's a Harvard man, the doctor."

"Yes," she said.

"And you?"

"I'm not a Harvard man." She said this with no smile, no twinkle. She was either drily witty or contemptuous of newsmen. Or a natural copy editor. I'd spoken ambiguously, after all, though I'd tried for drily witty.

So just as smileless and twinkleless, I asked, "A Radcliffe man?"

She paused for a breath or two. I held mine, in sudden regret for proceeding on the assumption she'd been bantering. I didn't need to banter with her, even if she had wonderful eyes and smelled of lilacs. I had a story to write. I was more interested in the drivers, but she was important for background on this whole operation.

"Not Radcliffe either," she said. "My liberal arts were bedpans and sponge baths. Which I studied at Massachusetts General."

"You've come far," I said, tentatively relieved.

"I have," she said, and whatever playful thing it was that seemed to have begun between us seemed now to have ended.

And so we had some time together, Nurse Louise and I, and it was all business between the two of us. But inside the wards I encountered the wreckage of men like men I'd encountered before, in Nicaragua and Bulgaria, in Mexico and Turkey. Most of the others I'd been with were in their nakedly wounded state, at the site of the clash of arms.

Here the men were washed and drained and reassembled and swathed. Here they were—to a man, among the ones capable of talking to me—calm and bucked up and cheerfully brave in their sunlit rooms. With these who were aware, I made sure to leave each of them with a firm touch. A hand taken up to shake, a shoulder squeezed, from one man who knew war to another.

Between the wards, as we moved along the hardwood hallways of this intended school, Nurse Louise spoke to me of the hospital's various new machines, made for X-rays and ultraviolet sterilizing and magnetic removal of shell fragments from wounds. She spoke of four hundred beds soon to become six hundred. She spoke of sepsis and gangrene and tetanus, how infection was the nearly universal state of these men's wounds when they first emerged from the ambulances, spoke of how it was dealt with.

And as she spoke through the tour, she rarely looked me in the eyes, in spite of the close scrutiny she'd given me when we first met. Or maybe *because* of that scrutiny. Perhaps she'd seen all she cared to see. She spoke to me coolly, clinically, even as she offered her own warm asides—toasty greetings and pillow-fluffings and shoulder-pattings— to the men in the beds.

We ended in the administrative wing, where she stopped me several paces short of the hospital superintendent's office. Her back was to a high, bright, mullioned window.

I'd been taking notes all this time. Mostly out of courtesy, because for the story I had in mind, the real stuff was still to come. I put my notebook in my pocket. I offered my hand.

She began to shake it again.

Softer this time, it seemed to me. I softened too. Now she was looking at me again, the gray eyes gone nearly black with the backdrop of daylight.

"Thank you, Supervising Nurse Pickering," I said.

She pinched her mouth to the side. I'd certainly intended to needle her just a little with the formality, but I didn't expect her to do a mouth-pinch.

Whatever that might mean.

But it seemed to me that it meant *something*.

She kept shaking my hand softly for a moment more and said, "Good luck, Mr. Cobb."

"Kit," I said.

"Ah," she said. "As your namesake."

"Christopher Marlowe. Yes."

She let go of my hand.

Now that things had softened between us a little, I didn't want to let go quite yet. I sought more talk, but not clinical, not chilly. She knew her Elizabethan playwrights. I asked, "Were you a theatergoer in Boston?"

"When I could occasionally afford a narrow place in an upper balcony."

"Did you ever see Isabel Cobb?" I didn't make a practice of invoking my mother in order to small-talk a beautiful woman. But Mother had a salutary effect on certain kinds of beautiful young women. Ones, particularly, who had inner resources enough to shake a man's hand as an equal and seek out a war.

Louise briefly cocked her head at me, with narrowed eyes. It was a how-did-you-know look. She said, "As a child I saw her every day."

It was my turn to cock my head. As in: Are you pulling my leg?

She smiled faintly, the first smile she'd shown since I met her. She said, "My father smoked Duke's Honest Long Cut. He had lithograph cards of Isabel Cobb and Lillian Russell on our mantelpiece for years. His two favorites."

"I know her Duke's card," I said. "Is she wearing a Welsh-crown hat covered in bird plumes?"

"Yes. Her eyes are raised. I thought, when I was a child, that her look was sympathetic. Rather regretful. As if she were watching the flight of the plucked bird."

I hemmed at this. I did not want to point out how unlike my mother that would be. Isabel Cobb may never in her life have sympathetically noticed a bird, plucked or unplucked. In the look on her face that was stuffed into all those tins of tobacco, there was only a keen consciousness of her own beauty. She kept that same tobacco card on her dressing table for years afterwards, even when her fame far exceeded early-career recognition by Duke's of Durham.

I said, "So did you ever see Isabel Cobb in person?" I stressed the surname ever so lightly for her.

I watched her suddenly fit two things together. She cocked her head again. "Cobb," she said. "Is she related to you?"

"She's my mother."

At last the composure of Supervising Nurse Louise faltered a little. She was impressed.

She actually sighed. "I saw her once. We lived in Gloucester till I went off to become a nurse. During my time in Boston I never had a chance. But my father brought me down to the city once for your mother. When I was sixteen. She played Medea."

"She was a good Medea."

"Very good."

We fell silent, Louise Pickering and I. Not knowing what to say next. Mama had taken over the stage, as she was wont to do. Though, to be fair, it was I who'd spoken her entry line.

But before I could figure out how to induce my mother to exit stage left, Louise said, "I have to go, Mr. Cobb. Superintendent Pichon is expecting you."

"Thank you for your help, Nurse Pickering."

I expected her to turn away, but she hesitated a moment more. I watched her eyes upon me, which were intent, as if making a parting assessment. Then she said, "You seemed genuinely to care about them."

I didn't understand.

"The wounded," she said.

She'd noticed that in the wards. Now she'd skipped over the mother-banter to go back to it. I liked this Louise Pickering.

"I've seen a lot of them," I said.

"So have I," she said, very softly, as if it were a secret between us. And with this, she turned and walked briskly away.

3

At nine o'clock the next morning I stepped out of my hotel on the Rue de Seine to find a massive American automobile sitting at the curb. Even as a beautiful woman passing by might have riveted my attention while a rogue chimney pot plummeted toward my head, I stopped to ogle a maroon-bodied, black-roofed, closed-cabin Model 48 Pierce-Arrow, its famous fender-molded headlights bug-eyeing the street ahead, making this two-ton beauty seem always yearning to rev up and dash off.

Then the chimney pot.

A familiar voice. It said, "Kit Cobb."

A familiar face. This was framed in the open rear window of the Pierce-Arrow's passenger vestibule, with a clean-shaven and pugilist-square chin, brilliantined black hair, dark eyes as unwavering as a sharpshooter's.

James Polk Trask had come for me.

Not me. Not the me I came to Paris to be. Came, no doubt, for the agent of his secret service.

I hesitated.

He waited.

Trask's driver, with a muscleman body straining at his serge suit, popped out of the driver's compartment and opened the vestibule door.

I stepped in and sat beside Trask, who said to his man, "Drive along the river."

The door thumped shut.

"Nice automobile," I said.

"The Ambassador's," he said, and he turned his face to the window beside him.

I figured he knew what I was going to say next. Which I said: "But I was supposed to be the one to get in touch. When I was ready."

He was looking at my modest, newswriter-cozy hotel. He craned his neck to take in its upper floors and said, "We could have done better for you."

As if I'd have gone straight back to spy work for the sake of a better hotel room; as if he'd even have sent me to Paris at all instead of Sofia or Baghdad or Pinsk. This declaration came from what I had come to understand as J. P. Trask in a playful mood. His own special brand of playful. Say a pointed thing without a direct transition from what preceded it. Couch it in the commonplace. Let *you* fill in the skipped steps buried in the subtext.

I played it back to him: "Were you waiting long?"

We pulled away from the curb and he returned his face to me. When we first started working together—what seemed like a long, long time ago but, in fact, was less than two years—he would have continued to show me nothing in his demeanor, even as I joined him in his game. Now he gave me a fleeting smile, the eyes never wavering. "You keep regular hours."

He'd been watching me. Of course he had.

After a brief beat of silence he added, "How's the story going?"

"At its own necessary pace," I said.

The driver braked and used the Klaxon on something in our way. Neither Trask nor I looked to see what.

The game now was not to flinch first.

As if that would decide whether I did my story or worked for him.

Neither of us was giving in.

We were accelerating again, though we were still in the tight confines of the Rue de Seine.

"How are things in Washington?" I said. Back there, Trask had but to lean a little to speak directly into Woodrow Wilson's ear. Though that privilege was still doing less good than Trask wished. He and I had the same assessment of Woody's backbone. But at least the president was giving his secret service a more or less free hand to stay involved over here. As long as we did our work quietly.

Trask replied, "One year from tomorrow, fifteen million men will elect two hundred and eighteen representatives, thirty-five senators, and one president of the United States."

"So things are jumpy," I said.

"Darwinian," he said.

"Can he be beat?"

"If France and England were voting, no doubt."

"As for our fellas?"

"I don't know. So far the Republican contenders are just a bunch of favorite sons. But then there's Teddy."

"As a Bull Moose?"

"His third party only succeeded in giving us Wilson last time. He knows that. There's talk he'll come back to the Republicans."

"We'd be rough-riding into France the day after his inauguration," I said.

"That's sixteen months away." He said it almost offhand. Willfully so. A Traskian show of emotion.

We both fell silent.

I could hear him thinking: *So in the meantime we've got our work cut out for us.*

I doubt if he heard me thinking: *Not till I finish my story.*

Outside, the run of building fronts abruptly yielded to a pocket park and then a glimpse of the baroque dome of the Institut de France. Trask followed my gaze, turned to look out the window.

Our little preliminaries were through. The Pierce-Arrow emerged from the Institut complex. We slowed to tourist speed along the cobbled quais of the Left Bank of the river.

Trask turned back to me and said, "There was some trouble in your neighborhood last night."

"I was at the scene in about ninety seconds," I said.

He cocked his head.

I told him where I was, what I saw.

He listened without comment, and after I was done he nodded once, slow and deep, as if it confirmed some point he'd previously made. He said, "There's no hiding from this war."

"Which is why I'm trying to get to the front lines to report."

"That's not the war you and I are fighting."

My turn to shrug. Which I did.

Trask said, "In this town the Zeppelins are just theater. It's all searchlight show and the home-team flying machines. But a bomb in a bistro and body parts on the street are another matter. The boys I know in this government assume last night was just the beginning. They're seriously concerned about public morale."

A legitimate fear. The government boys Trask ran with no doubt had their own morale at stake as well. The French people had a track record in dealing with their failed ruling and managing classes. From the head-chopping of the Revolution to the barricades of the Paris Commune.

Trask said, "If the Germans can bring the battle to the restaurants and the theaters and the front doors of the Parisians, if they can turn women and children and boulevardiers into bomb fodder, they might make some progress in this war."

I wagged my head in disgust, feeling like an old codger living in the past. "War used to be for soldiers."

Trask said, "We need the French to hang on, Kit. The Brits are still not ready to wage an effective war. The Germans may not have broken through, but they've had a good year in the field. We're going to get into this scrap one of these days. It's only a matter of time. We don't want the German flag flying over Paris when we finally do."

I heard Trask making a case for this bombing being a mess we needed to quietly stick our noses into. Quietly but urgently.

"Would they let us in on this?" I asked.

"The French have always been very adept at spying on the French. Forget the playwrights and novelists; this country's greatest literary form is the *dossier secret*. But those files are mostly about the French financiers and politicians and clerics. The actors and artists. The jockeys and boxers and dudes. Not to mention the mistresses and fancy men of all these. That's the work of the First Bureau of the French secret service. Spy on everybody in the public eye. The Second Bureau makes a little more sense to you and me. They've always watched the ports and the train stations and the border entries for suspicious outsiders, the radical socialists and the communists and the anarchists and all that rabble. Those, they know how to deal with."

I could see where Trask was heading. I already arrived there yesterday morning.

I said, "But who's watching the refugees? The German saboteurs sneaking in with them."

I do like to surprise Trask. He thought he'd be giving me that idea himself. I elicited my second ephemeral smile of the morning from him. "Just so," he said.

"They can't handle this?"

"They're a bureaucracy, set up for a different sort of world."

"Do they even understand the need?" I offered this hopefully. I couldn't see us doing this entirely on our own.

"I have a smart, well-placed friend amongst them."

"Too bad."

Trask ignored this, saying, "The situation calls for a certain rare set of talents. He has no one among his operatives even close."

"*Gott im Himmel*," I said, playing the exasperation of the oath, angling my face away from him to look out the vestibule window.

I could guess at the talents. Convincing actor for a cover story. Fluent German—field-tested—along with pretty good French. Handy in a fight. Certified proficiency in killing a man.

Trask said, "Even *Gott* isn't right for this job."

Across the river the Tuileries were passing. The cripples and widows over there were no longer made safe by their wounds or their losses. The Hun from last night could put a satchel beside a garden bench on a mild November afternoon and nip a bunch of compensatory romances in the bud.

I looked squarely at Trask again and said, "Only if I can continue to work on my news story."

He didn't show me a thing in his eyes.

And he wasn't talking.

The fact was, I was still officially a newspaper reporter. This other Kit Cobb worked on the side. There was no binding contract for either spy or government. I worked from patriotism. From a pleasing stimulation of the nerves and a true-bred reporter's curiosity with the world. Not from the hotels and the walkaround money and the visceral privilege of killing bad guys.

I said, firmly, leaning a little toward him, narrowing my eyes against his blankness, "Whatever's to be done, I'll juggle it in my own way."

He pushed his lower lip upward ever so slightly.

He continued to keep quiet.

I said, "You know, James, I really like my little bijou of a hotel. It has everything I want and need right now."

And Trask said, "Underlying that rare set of talents I referred to is trustworthiness."

Characteristically affectless, Trask paused after this declaration, almost as if he were exhausted from the praise, even though he still had not overtly attributed any of this to me.

Then he said, "Very well then, Kit. Do it your way. We'll all be fine with that."

Not quite all of us. Not me.

4

The Ambassador's bespoke Pierce-Arrow had a speaking tube and Trask unhooked it, brought it to his mouth, and said two words to his driver. "The island."

Then he turned to me. "You need to see a Frenchman," he said.

The island was the Île de la Cité, home to the Palais de Justice complex. As we approached it from the Right Bank, I figured the French secret service was somewhere inside its walls. But instead we turned onto the Pont Neuf, and halfway across, we entered the enclosed, triangular Place Dauphine, at the island's western end. We stopped before one of its contiguous six-story row houses of brick and limestone and slate. This wasn't the *Palais*. The door bore no sign. But it was indeed the French secret service.

Stepping with me out of the car, Trask said, "His name is Henri Fortier. He appreciates your help. A tough guy. You'll like him."

With no more words, Trask accompanied me to the second floor and into a high-ceilinged front office, bright from the casement French windows. At the shadowed far end of the room was a massive oak desk facing this way and a man rising behind it.

Trask held us up for a moment, but the man waved us to him. We approached. Trask fell back a step as we arrived and said, from over my shoulder, "This is Cobb. The man you've been expecting."

Henri Fortier offered his hand across the wide desk, meeting mine in the middle. His grip was tough-guy firm, firm enough that I had to quickly ratchet up my own to match his. Which I did, while we looked each other steadily in the eyes.

A little test from a guy that a guy like Trask would admire for his toughness.

Fortier was not young. His pomaded hair and waxed mustache were storm-cloud gray and his face was creviced and weathered. But there was nothing jowly or flabby about him. A tough guy, as Trask said. No doubt.

After one last, enhanced pump of my hand he let go and pointed to a chair before his desk. "*S'il vous plaît*," he said.

I sat and thanked him in French and told him I was pleased to meet him. He liked my French, giving me a brow-lifted smile and a nod, which he then gave to Trask, as well. I was as advertised.

"I will leave you, gentlemen," Trask said, and his footsteps began to recede.

During the little exchange between these two I let my attention drift to the wall behind Fortier's desk. I'd been focused on the man so intently that the display there startled me now. In the middle hung a long, sleek, walnut-stock, bolt-action military rifle with a big cat's-eye of a trigger and guard. A Chassepot from France's last war with the Germans. I figured it was once the young Fortier's weapon, which put him at about age sixty-five.

But he'd been using it since. To the right of the rifle hung a mounted boar's head. To the left, the head of a wolf. A big one. My eyes were on the wolf, thinking how its face was almost identical—except in its magnified size and posed ferocity—to some American farm boy's sheepdog.

"The wolves are mostly extinct now in France," Fortier said, still in French. We were to speak his language together. That was fine with me.

"Did you shoot him with your Chassepot?" I asked.

"Ah, you know the weapon, do you?"

PARIS IN THE DARK

I turned my eyes from the wolf to the man. "I've never fired one," I said.

"Perhaps someday. I take it down now and then. I will invite you."

"I'd like that."

"The answer to your question is yes," he said. "I put twenty-five grams of lead into its heart."

"One round."

He gave me an approving smile. "One round."

I looked back to the wolf. The taxidermist had bared its teeth, as if it were about to kill.

Fortier said, "In Brittany. Nearly forty years ago. They savaged anything made of flesh. Livestock. Children. These beasts were a scourge of France. Merciless. We hunted them until they were all dead."

I looked back to the man. I sensed he was no longer simply speaking of wolves.

I said, "Now they've come to the streets of Paris."

He gave me another approving look. This one was not quite a smile. It was an I-can-do-business-with-this-man look.

"They have," he said.

"How can I help?" I said.

"You heard of our event two nights ago?"

"I saw your event."

"Saw it?"

"I was sitting outside the Café de la Rotonde."

"Very near."

"Very near."

"Did you go?"

"At once."

"Any thoughts?"

"Just before, I'd been watching your aviators on patrol. The Zeppelins wish to be the wolves. But you stop them. Better than the British."

"Machines." Fortier nearly spat the word.

"The wolves are flesh and blood," I said.

"Just so," he said, and he looked away, as if to control his rage. A moment later he returned to me. "We have fifteen months of war. Now suddenly the sabotage in the capital. We ask ourselves where these saboteurs have been. Some Germans were already existing in our country, of course. Immigrants."

He paused ever so slightly after this word. He had given it the same expectorant inflection as *machines*.

"We have been dealing with them," he said. "But there is only so much we can do. They are here. We do not have the wherewithal to put them somewhere else. And many of their second generation have become French citizens, technically speaking. But your President Roosevelt—would he were still the president of your country—he understands about hyphenated citizens. He spoke only recently. Do you know?"

I'd read about his speech in the American papers. He'd given it just last month in New York. On Columbus Day.

Fortier went on: "Your President Roosevelt said, 'There is no room in our country for hyphenated Americans.' He meant the Irish-Americans. The Italian-Americans. The German-Americans. All of them. He said, 'A hyphenated American is no American at all.'"

"I do know," I said.

"We understand. In French we do not allow our hyphens to serve that sort of purpose. But it is hard to call these Goths among us French-men. They may have papers of one sort or other. But they are not French. We do not melt them in a pot in this country."

I thought: *At least Teddy would banish the hyphen to make the assimilated German a fellow American. Not to preserve a vision of his own purity.*

But as Americans we had no hyphens for allies, either. I was now the American ally of this Frenchman before me, so he was one of my own.

I said, "I had another thought yesterday, the morning after the event. About saboteurs."

"I would be interested to hear."

"The refugees."

I had more to say on this, of course, but I'd already struck a chord in Fortier. He pushed back in his chair and rose to his feet.

I didn't continue. He wanted to take the floor.

"Mr. Cobb, we have separately come to the same conclusion. It is no longer a matter of keeping our eyes on a managed flow of outsiders through the ports and borders. These refugees come now huddled together in great numbers. Many of them, of course, are our own brethren displaced within our country by the Huns. So Parisians have opened their hearts. Others are our legitimate allies. The Belgians, for example. These we wish to care for. This is who we are. We put our refugees wherever we can. Church halls and warehouses. The old seminary of Saint-Sulpice. The arena of the Winter Circus. And still they come. The compassion is admirable. The security is disastrous. There are no papers for these people, no eyes to watch them. The conditions are such that these others, the wolves in immigrant clothing, can blend in and sneak through. Each of them is a potential weapon far more effective than any Zeppelin."

He finished his point. Stayed standing. Seemed to be waiting for my assent.

I said, "Why throw a bomb into the dark from ten thousand feet, when you can personally deliver it to the center of a restaurant in a handbag."

Fortier laughed, a sharp, guttural sound worthy of either of the heads flanking him on the wall.

With that thought I glanced briefly at the wolf. Fortier saw the look, turned around and reached up to the Chassepot, saying, "Would you like to hold it?"

He lifted the rifle from its mounting hooks and turned to me.

I rose from my chair. "Of course," I said.

He gave me the weapon.

It was lighter than I'd expected for its era. About the weight of the Mauser 98 I'd handled in Mexico a couple of years ago. I put it to my shoulder and sighted into a dim corner of the room.

Fortier let me hold the rifle in silence, though when I lowered it and turned to him, he was smiling at me like a proud papa.

The rifle had been far superior to the German infantry's comparable breechloader, the Dreyse.

"The Prussians feared it," I said.

"They did. Greatly." Fortier said this with his pride nowhere to be found in his tone. The Chassepot's war, the war of Fortier's youth, was lost by the French emperor and his politicians and generals.

Fortier took the rifle from me and put it back on the wall. He motioned me silently to my chair and we both sat.

He stewed for a moment more.

It could be argued that the present war actually began with the French failures in their War of 1870, which ended up uniting the German states and emboldening their military.

Then Fortier rolled his shoulders and steeled his face and said, "I understand you were in Germany a few months ago."

"I was."

"Not as yourself."

"As a German-American newspaperman."

"Is he still of your acquaintance?"

"He can be."

"We asked ourselves where these possible saboteurs, who make themselves like refugees and come into our capital, where they will go."

He paused.

"After the circus," I said.

"Yes."

He waited some more. As if he were still measuring me, testing me.

I said, "The immigrant Germans in Paris, the ones you dealt with but only so far. Are they scattered? Or do they have a neighborhood?"

Fortier lifted his hand, his forefinger pointing to the ceiling, and then he dipped the finger at me. "Exactly so," he said.

"Josef Wilhelm Jäger," I said.

I paused and waited for him this time.

When he realized I was saying no more, he lifted his brows a little, then gave me a slow smile. "That is you."

"I relinquished my hyphen in America and became Joe Hunter. But I am still German. You understand. I would like to find the true Germans, the loyal Germans trapped in Paris, so I can tell their story to their counterparts in America."

Fortier smiled again. "You are very convincing. As Mr. Trask promised." He opened a drawer, removed a number-ten letter envelope, saying, "He tells me you are good at figuring out what to do next." He closed the drawer, reached partway across the desk and laid the envelope down. "The neighborhood," he said.

He had even more of these small, subtly destabilizing power moves than Trask. He used one of them now only from long habit, I figured; his smiles at me felt genuine, but he was making me reach.

I leaned forward in my chair and picked up the envelope.

I did not give it a glance. I put it in my inner coat pocket.

Fortier said, "You will also find a man's name and his address. He is German, living amongst them. But he works for us as an informant. We have been of help to him, and he has reason to safely preserve his place in France. In his case, do not present yourself as Herr Jäger or Mr. Hunter either one. He expects a man at his door who will greet him with *Gott strafe Deutschland.*"

God punish Germany. I'd heard the original version of this often in the streets of Berlin this summer: *Gott strafe England.*

Fortier said, "He is to answer with the same. This will give you a chance to watch his eyes, hear his voice. Mr. Trask says you are adept at reading these things. I would be interested if you find any trace of discomfort in him as he damns his home country."

Fortier paused.

"He has information for me?" I asked.

"He does. He has recently become credible to us."

"But you're still assessing him."

"We are always assessing."

I said, "How do you assess the timing of his information? Am I right you've suppressed mention of the bombing in the press? I haven't seen anything."

"For the moment the newspapers are patriotic. The German bomb is meant to explode more than a restaurant. The confidence of the people of France is the real target."

"So how did your informant go to work on this so quickly?"

A pair of furrows popped up between his brows.

I got it.

"He warned you beforehand," I said.

Fortier didn't answer. But the furrows remained. He'd been warned well before, but he did not give it credence. The informant's present credibility was determined two nights ago.

I decided not to push it. I said nothing more.

The silence lasted long enough that Fortier unfurrowed. He even gave me a little nod. I'd proved my smarts and I'd proved my discretion.

He pushed back in his chair.

We both stood up, though one crucial question remained.

He said, "Someone will answer our door downstairs at any hour."

Which only hinted at it.

I suspected I knew the answer. But I was curious to hear how he might tell me.

I said, "And if things come to pass that I am, let us say, *confronted* with a man or men I think to be German saboteurs? If I have no effective way to apprehend them?"

"I leave that to your discretion," he said. "You have a free hand."

No wink. No nudge. No fleeting smile. No inflection to his voice other than the flatness of it, which I took to be a clear inflection of its own.

I was known by this liberty now. I was free to kill.

He offered his hand, and this time I made his grip ratchet up to mine.

5

Trask's driver was waiting for me when I emerged from Fortier's row house. He handed me another envelope, a larger one, and opened the Pierce-Arrow vestibule door for me. Trask was not inside.

"Where to?" the muscleman asked.

"Just a minute," I said.

I got in, sat down where Trask had been sitting, looked inside Fortier's envelope. It held a small, folded map cut from a larger map. The German Quarter straddled the 9th and 10th arrondissements south of Rue Lafayette. Not as remotely isolated as I thought it would be. An easy walk from the Folies Bergère. There was also a letter identifying me for free access and full cooperation, typed on Préfecture de Police de Paris letterhead and signed by Émile Marie Laurent himself. My command over the police if I needed them. And there was a handwritten note with details about the man I was to meet. I didn't read it.

I glanced into Trask's envelope, as well, and was not surprised to find the Joe Hunter credentials I'd used in August. My two spy masters had figured from the jump that they had me. I put Fortier's envelope inside Trask's and laid it aside.

I unhooked the speaking tube and told the driver to take me back to my hotel. The secret services of two countries would have to wait till tomorrow. Today I was a reporter for real.

However.

I soon found myself simply standing in the center of my small, top-floor room, the casement windows and their outer shutters open to the mansard roofs of the Rue de Seine, which were still dim in mid-morning shadow. My Corona sat on the desk, its platen centered in the paper guide, a stack of blank bankers-bond typewriter paper beside it, the corners carefully squared, awaiting words. A horse and cart rang hollowly by in the street below. An alarm clock ticked on my nightstand.

I could type up my notes from the hospital yesterday. But I'd finish before the sun lit the rooftops across the way. And tonight there would be more notes, better ones, full of the words of the ambulance drivers themselves. Moreover, I found that my morning encounter with the secret service boys had riled up that other Kit Cobb. I had a chunk of the morning and a whole afternoon ahead of me.

So I sat at the desk, closely read the German informant's details, and afterwards burnt the notepaper in the ashtray. He was Bernhard (which he now spelled as Bernard) Lang. Fifty years old. He'd lived at number seven, Cité de Trévise, third floor rear, since 1910. Worked as a maître d'hôtel at a prominent German restaurant in the neighborhood, now closed. Informing for money.

I put my own papers into the false bottom of my Gladstone bag, pocketed Josef Wilhelm Jäger's papers and the map of the German Quarter, and strapped my Mauser pocket automatic pistol into its leather holster beneath my coat, at the small of my back.

I realized, with a minor shock, that it was as simple as that, my transformation. As simple as that, to change from Cobb the reporter into Cobb the spy. It grew simpler each time.

I went out of the hotel.

The street was empty and the Metro was nearby, and after a few minutes' walk I was beside the thousand-year-old, porch-towered Abbey of Saint-Germain-des-Prés. I paused at the top of the steps leading underground. Only for a moment, to shake off the sense of impending tight enclosure, the incipient clamp of my chest, clutch of my throat. Just a brief moment. It was a rare thing, but persistent. From my backstage childhood. For a long while—not long, actually;

long only by the pulse of my fear for the few minutes it had actually lasted—I'd been trapped in a trunk backstage at the Lyceum Theatre in New York, playing a foolish child's game.

But that was a couple of decades ago and I'd flexed through this scar tissue many times since. So I went down the steps, deep into the ground, and I was fine. The barrel vault of the train hall lifted the last little bit of oppression from me. The beveled white tiles of the station caught and held the cheddar light of the carbon lamps, and then I was inside a swell Sprague-Thomson train car with a passel of Parisians, and in less than ten minutes I was stepping out of the car and into a sweet, autumnal burning smell from the train's wooden brake shoes. Still, when I emerged from beneath the ground into the expanse of air and sunlight of Rue Lafayette and paused between the Metro's twin, art-nouveau, orchid-stalk lampposts, I felt something release in me that had not fully ceased until this moment.

Cité de Trévise was a cobbled street not even ten yards wide, canyoned between neo-Renaissance row houses. Number seven was just beyond the street's central, circular *place*, where a fountain plashed softly above the heads of three gossamer-gowned stone nymphs holding hands.

The floors I climbed were quiet. It had been a rough sixteen months for many of the residents of Cité de Trévise no doubt. They were German, no matter how long they'd been here or what their papers said. Where could they flee? Many were behind these doors, lying low.

I knocked at the apartment at the rear of the third floor. There was stirring inside, briefly voices, more than one. I had acquired a reflex in the past two years. Pistol awareness. I made no move to it, no gesture to suggest it was there, but I became keenly conscious of the Mauser leaning heavily into the small of my back.

The voices stopped.

Footsteps approached.

Then silence.

At eye level was a peephole. A shadow moved on the inner side of its small glass lens.

I held still, waited.

Then a bolt was thrown. Then a chain lock. Then a twist lock in the handle.

Bernard Lang was a man afraid.

The door opened.

He was a big guy, thick-necked, walrus-mustached, as upright and commanding and smartly authoritarian as you'd expect from a maître d' of a prominent German restaurant, even with the top half of his ribbed-wool union suit taking the place of his ex-officio tuxedo shirt. His suspenders stretched tight over his barrel chest holding up his blue serge pants that had gone a little loose at the waist from the hard times.

His bearing was fine but his eyes had lost their maître d' command. He did not examine mine, though he focused on them. He was ready to flinch. Ready, always, to be taken away.

I said, low, "*Gott strafe Deutschland.*"

He exhaled sharply. His eyes softened. What Fortier would have me look for was not here. These were not the reflex responses of a German loyalist pretending to be an informant. His breath was a release of fear. His eyes saw an ally. And he said, just as low but with what sounded to me like conviction: "*Gott strafe Deutschland.*"

We said no more for a moment.

I then lifted my chin to indicate the space behind him. "Shall we talk inside?" I put on my best German.

His eyes widened a little, no doubt at hearing me continue in his native language.

"Yes. Please come in," he said, also in German.

He turned and led me down a short corridor, past two closed doors, past another corridor going to the left, and into a parlor at the back of the apartment. Its windows looked out on a narrow courtyard and across to the shuttered windows of other apartments.

I chose a chair at a right angle to the windows, with my back toward a wall with a piano. Lang accepted my choice, sat in a facing chair. Beyond him was an open door to a dining room and, straight on, another open door to a kitchen.

Even as the kitchen registered on me, a woman appeared there, moving past, but her face turned to the parlor, and she drew up at my seeing her.

She was a Valkyrie of a mate for an imposing maître d', big-boned and wide-shouldered, a middle-aged Brünnhilde-at-home, wearing a flowered bathrobe with a tasseled cinch, her hair braided into a long, thick rope. She'd squared around now to look at me, since I was looking at her. The robe was only loosely wrapped and she was showing a wide expanse of her ample chest rising from a lacy something she was wearing underneath. This she quickly realized but only slowly remedied. More defiantly than slowly, really. She took her time pulling her robe together.

I realized that one of the voices I'd heard through the door had been a woman's. A deep-pitched, shield-maiden of a voice.

Lang said, "You are German?" Not quite a question. Ready to believe a *Ja*.

I focused on him. "I am from German parents," I said. Joe Hunter's story.

"Perhaps I knew there was something," he said.

"Perhaps I have an American accent."

"American," he said with a faint twist of what might be admiration in his voice. He had already made himself an immigrant. Perhaps he had a further ambition.

"The accent is only small," he said. "Not even worth mentioning. Very small."

"Thank you," I said.

"You have been sent," he said. He raised the volume of his voice. This was not simply a confirming declaration directed at me. He was informing the woman in the other room.

"Yes, I've been sent," I said, raising my voice enough for her to hear, lifting my chin a little in her direction, to let them understand I was wise to them. If Fortier had known about her, he'd have mentioned her in his note. But I had no problem if Lang's woman was part of his operation.

"What do you have for me?" I asked.

"A dangerous man has entered France as a refugee," Lang said, leaning toward me, his hand rising from his lap, twisting palm upward. "He crossed at the Belgian border."

"When was this?"

"I'm not sure. At least two weeks ago."

"And how long has he been in Paris?"

"For ten days now."

It took a little effort for me to show nothing in my face. Fortier and his boys had certainly muffed it.

A moment of silence passed between us. Lang was making an effort with his face, as well.

For a similar reason. He said, "I told them right away."

He was anxious for me to know about the timing. Had he heard of the bombing? Nothing had been in the papers, but this was the second day after. The rumor of a thing like that would get around pretty fast.

"They should have listened to you," I said.

He shrugged. But his hands moved to his knees and gripped them hard.

He'd heard.

There was movement behind Lang. I looked beyond him. His woman had arrived in the doorway to the parlor.

She leaned against the jamb.

I said, "Is he still in a processing center?"

Lang huffed faintly. It was harder now. "Too late for that," he said.

"Do you think he's here, in the German Quarter?"

"I am told he is." Lang's hands rubbed at his knees, as if both palms had suddenly begun to itch.

"Were you told where he might be found?"

"There is one place where he may go. This is new information. A cellar bar. Once *Le Rouge et le Noir*. Closed now, to the French eye. The sign is gone, the windows are shuttered. But men of the Quarter still drink there. He would perhaps be among them. Number nineteen, Rue des Petites Écuries."

"Will they let me in?"

"At the door you will be asked your name. You must first reply, '*Et le Blanc.*'"

The Red and the Black. Ironic to start with. Then speaking the white that was always there unspoken, turning the Stendhal novel into the flag of the German Empire. These boys were the thinkers in the community.

"Their politics?" I asked it more rhetorically than for information.

"As you might imagine," Lang said. "They favor Berlin."

"How did I learn their password?"

"Not from me."

"Of course not. That's why I'm asking."

He thought for a moment, began to speak and then didn't. Now he thought again, and then asked, "Whoever you will be to them, could you know a waiter at Café de la Paix?"

"I could."

"His name is Dieter. He would tell you this."

"And how will I recognize our refugee?"

"He is a gaunt man. Clean-shaven. About my age. There is a scar like so." Lang put his forefinger high up on the center of his forehead and drew it down at an angle toward the outer edge of his left eyebrow.

The woman suddenly appeared directly behind Lang. Very close.

Lang seemed unaware of her. He said, "He has come into France as Franz Staub."

The woman laid her hand upon his shoulder. Gently. There was no trace of surprise in him. Nor did he look up at her now. He simply lifted his own hand and placed it on hers.

It remained there as he said, "He is working for the German government. I am told he is a man who can do anything. Assassination. A bomb. He is very dangerous, a very grave threat."

"Do you know him personally?"

Lang drew a breath. Tilted his head a little. "Not personally," he said. "Before the war, for a brief time, he frequented the restaurant where I worked. I was told about him even then, that he was with the secret service."

Lang paused. He seemed to have nothing more to say.

I glanced from his face up to the woman's. They had the same focus, the same gravity. I figured I understood. I asked, "Does he know you are alert to him?"

Lang lifted his eyebrows. My implicit concern for him was a surprise. "Yes. I am afraid he does."

"Does he know where you are?"

"If he knew that, I would be dead already."

"I understand," I said. I looked up at the woman.

She was focused gravely on Lang.

"I'm sorry not to introduce her," he said. "This is Greta."

She lifted her face to me.

He did not elaborate.

I nodded. "Greta," I said.

She nodded in return.

"Please catch this man," Lang said. "But be warned. He will try to kill you. He does not hesitate a moment to do such a thing. You should not hesitate either."

I rose.

Lang did not. He and Greta remained where they were. He lowered his hand, but hers remained on his shoulder.

I went out.

As I crossed the *place*, I paused briefly beneath the nymphs. She had hardly been a nymph, but this threesome before me, in their diaphanous clothes, reminded me of Greta. Her late-morning dishabille, her hovering over him, her tender touch of his shoulder. And I thought of how naturally he requited her touch. For a couple their age, the thing between them seemed fresh. Recent. Now a German agent, who'd perhaps already killed in Paris, was her enemy. Had she known what she was getting into with her new man?

6

That night I took a fiacre to the New York Bar on Rue Daunou, near *l'Opéra de Paris*. No bistro tables and al fresco drinking here. This was a vintage American saloon behind a Paris storefront.

I stepped in.

Part of me twinged over a different bar tonight, that I should be there instead. In a cellar in the German Quarter. But I counterpunched that thought. The other men I was pursuing were here on Rue Daunou tonight, waiting for me. They had a story that needed telling.

The place was owned by a pretty fair American jockey named Tod Sloan, who had a reputation among the French turf gentry and railbirds. Sloan decided a few years ago that the Prohibition harpies in America would eventually succeed, so he dismantled a bar on New York's West Side and had it shipped to Paris and reassembled, mahogany walls and tables, zinc bar, brass spittoons, tooled leather ceiling and all.

The place was dense with tobacco smoke. It was packed with expatriates and with hyphenless Frenchmen who had a secret taste for things American. It also happened to be the favorite joint for American volunteer ambulance drivers, three of whom were supposed to be waiting for me.

I made my way through the smoke and conversations. No one was catching my eye or fitting the bill. I was running out of saloon and starting to worry I'd been jilted. Then I glanced to a far corner, and a face I recognized was looking at me. Supervising Nurse Louise Pickering, though she was in mufti—a shirtwaist and cardigan—and her hair was drawn up into a simple pompadour knot. She was sitting at the head of a table, presiding over three strapping boys in khakis and puttees, who, naturally enough, weren't looking at me at all. They were focused on her.

I had the feeling she'd been watching me for a while. There was no snap of recognition in her face now that our eyes met. After an odd moment of simple, placid staring, she merely gave a small nod of the head. Then her lips moved and the three young men turned around to look at me.

I drew near.

The driver who'd secured the place directly opposite Nurse Pickering—a broad-shouldered, flush-faced, auburn-headed lad—instantly gave way to me, moving his chair around to the longer side of the table, where his dark-haired compatriot slid his chair closer to Louise, with a couple of apologetic head bobs.

I pulled an unused chair from beside the next table and placed it at the alternate head of ours, glancing now to my left, to the third driver, who was straw-colored in complexion and hair and of a certain chesty broadness. He was of the same height and size as the young man who gave his place away to me. But across the table the latter was clearly solidly muscled while this guy gave off a sense of nascent corpulence.

I sat down and looked across to Louise, who was still watching me. I had not expected her to be here.

But she was showing me not even a hint of her thoughts.

Everyone at the table seemed of the same generation. Mine, technically. But the gap between my early thirties and their mid-twenties felt somehow like a big separation between us. Which made me think: *She's involved with one of these men.*

The most likely candidate, it seemed to me, was this guy to my left, who I now noticed had already placed himself a little nearer Louise than had the dark-haired deferential one. He had a square-jawed, cleft-chinned, Gibson-man sort of face. The kind certain women go for. Till he gets fat.

He smiled with more straight and glistening teeth than one usually expects in a smile, and he began the introductions with an offered hand, which I took and shook. A milksoppy shake.

"John Barrington Lacey," he said.

"Where from?"

"Boston," he said. Bahston. Beacon Street accent. A touch of hauteur.

Of course. This was her guy. From before Paris.

"Kit Cobb," I said, letting go of his hand.

"I'm here with the Harvard contingent," he said with what sounded like the intention of setting himself above the two rubes across the table. Or making a claim on Nurse Louise from Mass General. Or both.

As I turned to my right to meet the boys who were not from Harvard, I paused ever so slightly to observe Louise's demeanor. I expected her attention to have shifted to J. Barrington. But she was still looking at me. Still not showing a thing.

The reddish-tinted young man had a solid grip and shake, as I expected. "Cyrus Parsons," he said. "Princeton, Illinois. More or less. A farm out somewhere a little east of there."

"Got it," I said. A farmer's son. Therefore very likely a farmer himself through his boyhood and his young adulthood and most of his early manhood. Getting as far away from the farm as he could now.

The dark-haired young man was reaching across Parsons to shake my hand. "Jefferson Jones," he said. "From Richmond, Virginia."

A wiry guy. Pale. A little gaunt. I figured he'd been in France longer than the other two and was showing the rigors of ambulance work.

These three seemed like a good sampling for my story.

I turned once more to the Supervising Nurse in disguise. Her eyes were yet again upon me. This time she doled out a faint smile. "Louise Pickering," she said. "Gloucester, Massachusetts."

The boys all looked her way. J. Barrington chuckled, getting her little irony. The other two seemed merely to gawk. To me, even from the other end of the table in a noisy bar, even in spite of the feigned formal content of the words, her voice sounded downright mellifluous.

I said, "Do you haul 'em as well as heal 'em, Miss Pickering?"

She did not withdraw the little smile. "I'm just along for the ride tonight," she said.

So I took out my notebook and I talked to three young Americans, varied in many ways but not in age, ranging from twenty-one to twenty-five. Lacey and Parsons weren't even old enough to have voted for Woody Wilson three years before, but each of the three of them was a walking, talking, ambulance-driving rebuke to our gritless president.

I asked them why they were here. Jefferson Jones from Richmond, the oldest, had a postman father who would have been happy for his only child simply to be a postman too, but he'd named his boy after the guy he took to be the greatest rebel in history. Jones's middle name was even Davis, and he'd always wanted to be a soldier. No matter it turned out that the United States half a century later was still one nation indivisible. His boyhood military dreams were not of Bull Run or Seven Pines or Fredericksburg. They were of Cuba and the Philippines and Panama. He tried to enlist in the Marines when he was eighteen. They turned him down for flat feet. He tried again the next year and his feet were still flat. It was okay, he said. This was a more important war, and the U.S. Marines were nowhere in sight. His flat feet could push a Ford's clutch and brake and reverse sure enough.

Cyrus Parsons hesitated before answering why. He even glanced across the table at Harvard in a way that made me think Lacey'd been pushing him to answer the same question. I worried that my farm boy was going to be a washout of an interview. I needed at least three talkers for the story.

Finally he said, "I like being out there driving a wounded man. The wounded are everybody's brother. No matter who they are. That's very clear. Out there it's just you and the road and having to make time. Nobody to tell you nothing."

My worry was unfounded.

I made him pause a moment so I could get those words down exactly.

Part of Jones's answer was still stuck in my head and I was always looking for ways to stitch my talkers together. So I said to Parsons, "And your farmer father? Did he want you to stay on the farm?"

Parsons hesitated briefly. Then he said, "He comes from a big family. From Texas. But some of them moved to Illinois."

Cyrus seemed about to say more, but Harvard interrupted. "You need another beer there, Cy?"

Parsons looked at Lacey.

I did too.

He was starting to seem even more like an arrogant, privileged kid. He needed to keep his mouth shut while I was working.

He probably read my eyes. Lacey offered a lame explanation. "I'm about to call the waitress over."

"I'm okay," Parsons said.

"Just checking," Lacey said.

Parsons returned his attention to me and said, "The thing about my father is he used to be somebody else. But he got a few hundred acres to turn himself into a farmer, and ever since, he's happy clearing stumps and slopping hogs and laying in corn."

I wrote it down.

"How about you?" I said to Lacey, who had not yet called over the waitress.

"How about me?" he said, lifting his chin slightly, as if he required a formally rephrased question before he would answer a thing I'd already made perfectly clear I wanted from each of them.

I glanced at Louise. I was trying to decide if she was really connected to this guy. She was in the process of turning her own attention from Lacey to me. In the brief moment our eyes met, she flickered her eyebrows at me. Clearly she was not.

Growing up in the theater and cutting my reportorial teeth in Chicago politics, I knew how to keep my disdain for an interviewee well hidden. With a tone of unctuous respect I asked Lacey, "Why did you decide to drive an ambulance in the European War?"

He started elaborately constructing an answer from *Harvard Alumni Bulletin* boilerplate. When it was finished, it simply amounted to noblesse oblige.

To play against the answers of my two working-class boys, this was actually useful. I was, however, glad for the other thread in the interview so far, though I fully expected similar Brahmin bromides from him. I asked, "And what about *your* father? Does he approve of your work here?"

Lacey's hauteur vanished instantly. "His approval is irrelevant," he said, only a fist-clench short of full ferocity.

He fell silent with that. Parsons looked at him, but without surprise. He'd seen that before, I surmised. Louise's right hand turned back into a nurse's hand, moved out toward him, but did not touch.

The thought flashed through me: *Maybe it's just as well I don't even know who my old man is.*

The silence went on for another long moment and then Lacey himself shifted all of us away from whatever just happened. He turned on both spigots in himself at once, the one with his snootiness and the one with his sense of irony. He said, "Which of us do you think is the best driver?"

Parsons and Jones both groaned. Not this again.

"Really," Lacey said. "The one who handles his flivver the most adroitly. Harvard prevails."

The others leaped in.

Good stuff for the story and I encouraged it and the three competed for a time over driving honors, picturesquely, quotably, and then together they sang the praises of the hundred or so donated Ford Model T's converted into ambulances, their nimbleness on the crowded and shell-holed roads, their reliability, their ease of field repair. And the three drivers spoke of the physical grind they faced. Of how they were in duty rotation, a few weeks of peak stress, running between the front and the triage posts, then a few weeks between triage and the train depots or the field hospitals. There were four field sections for this duty. Then they rotated back to a few weeks in Paris, where they carried men between the converted freight station at La Chapelle and the city hospitals, including, of course, their own facility in Neuilly.

Through all this, Louise presided over us silently.

The four-way conversation wound down, and I let it. Enough for tonight. I would see more of the boys soon. I'd ride with them. In Paris, certainly. And, I hoped, to the front lines, though I was still waiting for permission from the Allies' wartime journalistic bureaucracy.

In the dark, in the street before the bar, the five of us paused. I shook the men's hands, after which they expected to accompany Louise back to Neuilly on the Metro. But she said to them, "I'll be along in a few moments, boys," and they clearly knew to hold their tongues with the tough Supervising Nurse, even though rude remarks flashed into their faces.

Parsons, particularly, looked at me, and then at her, and then back to me. No wink. No leer. But with a kind of worldly shrewdness in his look. He'd progressed well past clearing stumps and slopping hogs, I decided.

They gaggled off along Rue Daunou a little ways, and Louise turned to me.

Her face was lit softly by the spill of light from the bar.

She said, "I hope you didn't mind my joining you tonight, Mr. Cobb."

"Kit," I said. "No I didn't, Nurse Pickering."

She hesitated for a moment, fixing on me, but searchingly, shifting her gaze from one of my eyes to the other and back again. Then she decided; or she had decided earlier today—that was actually why she had come—and now she would make it official: "Louise," she said.

"Louise," I said, gently.

"I was just interested in what you'd bring out in them."

"Just that?"

A little too soon to press her. She looked away.

I added, "I hope you learned some things."

She returned to me. "I did," she said. "They're interesting, these boys."

But her tone was something else. It sounded offhand. *Un*interested. Up to this moment she'd always been in absolute control of her tone and demeanor. There was no reason to think that had changed. This was intentional. She was letting me know an interest in the boys was not the reason she was lingering on the sidewalk with me while the boys cooled their heels in the shadows and gossiped about us.

"Very interesting," I said, overplaying the words just enough, drawing them out just a little, to let her know I understood.

"Dedicated," she said. Just a bit too somberly.

"Dedicated," I said.

"I'm sure the story you write will be interesting," she said.

"I'll do my best," I said.

We stopped talking but she kept her eyes on mine.

I said, "We should have a drink together sometime, just you and me. I'd like to hear more of your story as well."

"Yes," she said.

"I'm sure it's interesting," I said.

"And yours," she said. "I'd like to hear."

"I could tell it to you."

"I'm sure it's very interesting," she said.

"You might find it so," I said.

We were starting to sound like a scene at the Moscow Art Theatre. But even as this struck me, Louise knew to ring down the curtain.

"Good night, Kit," she said.

"Good night, Louise."

She nodded and turned and moved off toward her three American drivers. I watched her for as long as I dared without following her and taking her by the arm and tipping my hat to the dedicated and interesting boys and whisking her away.

I turned my back on them.

And I realized that the air had gone chill. Winter was reconnoitering Paris once again. As I'd talked with Louise, I hadn't noticed.

I turned the collar up on my suit coat.

I pulled my Waltham from my watch pocket and angled it to the light from Tod Sloan's bar.

Not quite ten. The boys in the cellar bar would still be there. With maybe even a bomb maker among them.

7

But there was something I had to do first.

I caught a fiacre at the Opéra and paid the driver to wait for me before my hotel.

I went up and paused briefly, shirtless, my razor stropped and laid out on the basin, my shaving brush lathered up and poised in my hand, my face floating in the mirror, dappled in light and shadow from the incandescent bulb above me. I'd done this before, just a few months before, shaved my close-cropped beard to add a touch of credibility to my invented self. That was the first time. This would be the second. Beneath the beard, on my left cheek, was a scar. A long curve of a scar that a German eye would recognize as a sword wound and the eye of the sort of German whose acceptance I needed would further recognize as a *Schmiss*, the sword wound of a German university duelist, a badge of honor. The Americanized Joseph Hunter got his *Schmiss* when his American-immigrant father sent him as a young man back to the home country to matriculate at Heidelberg. Christopher Marlowe Cobb got his faux *Schmiss* last year in Mexico, in a sword fight that was a link in the chain of events that attached him to his country's secret service. For the men tonight at The Red and the Black and the White, the scar would do far more than a password to open the door to their company.

Still my hand paused.

Faux identification papers were stage props. This thing was part of me. Whenever I carried it openly I was this other guy. He was the scar. The scar was him. I couldn't step offstage each night and dip my fingers in cocoa butter and wipe him away.

But so it had to be.

I shaved.

I rinsed and dried my face.

I looked at my scar.

A German would assume he knew what this was. A Frenchman would assume it had been a tumble of shrapnel.

So be it.

I returned to my fiacre.

The air was cold now. I buttoned my overcoat.

And then I was walking along the Rue des Petites Écuries. I'd gotten out of the carriage a few short blocks away, not wanting to arrive at the bar with the attention-grabbing clatter of horse hooves and the ring of wheels. There, in the adjacent arrondissement, the street was called Rue Richer, where the Folies Bergère was filling its stage tonight with chanteuses and naked women behind a Zepp-darkened marquee.

But this stretch, as the Rue des Petites Écuries, was intended for commerce at the street level, with residences above. It was utterly silent and dark, inside and out. Had likely been so all evening. It was German, after all. The brasseries and shops—once the places for Wiener Schnitzel and Lederhosen, Pilsner and Taschen books, *Leberknödelsuppe* and Solingen kitchen knives—were all locked up behind iron shutters, their signs vanished. In the upper-floor residences, the shutters were also shut tight, with only occasional razor-blade cuts of light along the edges.

I had prepared for the unexpected. Inside my coat were my lock-picking tools. From another pocket now I retrieved my flashlight, a new one in the form of a fountain pen, with a brighter Mazda tungsten lamp, and I scanned the street facades till I found number nineteen.

Its entrance was an arched double door that yielded to a turn of the handle. Inside was a cobbled passage to an inner courtyard, but immediately to my right was a descending stone stairway, lit from below by a sconce with an incandescent lamp.

I went down. Tonight I was calm inside about going underground. It was a bar, after all. Its depth was shallow. I stood before a wide, wooden door with a sliding face-panel, presently shut. The handle did not yield. In the plate beneath was a simple ward lock. I pulled back a little.

But before I could lift my hand to knock, the panel opened.

A face appeared there, the lights behind it shadowing its features into invisibility. In German it asked me my name.

I responded in French: "*Et le Blanc.*"

The head in the sliding panel nodded and then waited.

I understood. After the password was given, the question remained. What was my name. I had not thought this out. Even in character, I had a choice of two. I decided the very complexity of the full answer would give it credence. I said, in my best German, "In the homeland I was Josef Wilhelm Jäger. As a resident now of the United States of America, I am called Joseph Hunter."

The head hesitated a moment. I was an unusual guest for this place. But the man nodded again and looked down and I heard the warded bolt being thrown. As with the last time I'd played this role, I was conscious of an irony: I felt temporarily thankful for Woody Wilson's spineless hesitation. A German from America was an instantly plausible sympathizer with the oppressed Germans in Paris. And Joseph Hunter, a reporter for a syndicate of American German-language newspapers, would even be a potentially useful one.

The door opened.

I stepped in.

The place was a little dank and had an underground chill impervious to the temperature aboveground. The drinking area was one low-ceilinged room, patchworked in electric light and cellar shadow, with a zinc bar and rows of bottles. At the far end, hugging the left-hand wall, was a passageway. It ran deep, and it implied other rooms at the back, to the right. Storage no doubt. An office perhaps.

All this I took in at a glance.

I paused for a slow breath.

At this late evening hour *Le Rouge et le Noir* seemed almost crowded, with maybe three dozen men, a row of them shoulder to shoulder at the bar and clusters of twos and threes at pedestal tables. Some of these denizens had turned their faces to me at the creak of the door. Only momentarily. Apparently it was enough for them that the gatekeeper had let me in.

He appeared at my side now, his face visible. It was middle-aged, fleshy, and blond-stubbled. As I turned to him, he squared around to confront me. He had a purposeful air and, indeed, seemed on the verge of speaking. But his eyes fixed on my *Schmiss* and his demeanor loosened. He looked me in the eyes and then looked again at the scar.

What he then asked had a casual tone that I'm sure would have been different if it weren't for what he saw on my face. "So who told you about us?"

"Dieter at the Café de la Paix."

"Of course," the man said. "Welcome."

He moved off.

My gaze followed him to the bar.

There was a spot at the rail, at the end.

I ignored it for now. I would use the search for a place to sit as an excuse to examine what faces I could.

I did a slow scan of the room.

Between those I could see and those who had given me a look when I came in, I'd checked out about half the men. None of them matched Staub's description. There were plenty left that I hadn't seen, but I didn't want to let on I was looking for somebody. I overtly directed my attention to the space at the bar. I headed for it, sidestepping between the burly backs of a couple of boys at adjacent tables. One of them looked up as I squeezed past.

I excused myself in German.

He nodded and returned to his conversation, which seemed, like every other conversation in the place, intense and *ernsthaft*. Very serious.

I arrived at the bar.

The fleshy face that let me into this joint appeared before me. He had a cloth in hand and began rubbing the counter space before me.

"Please tell me you still have an authentic beer," I said. He looked me steadily in the eyes. He knew what I meant. Which was good for Joe Hunter's credibility. Four centuries ago the *Reinheitsgebot*, the beer purity law of Bavaria, made it illegal to brew beer with anything but water, barley, and hops. A decade ago it was finally adopted in the unified Germany. If only that had been ambition enough for Kaiser Willie and he'd decided to conquer Europe with beer. A fine empire it would have been. Though among the boys surrounding me, I figured I'd better stay away from that last bit of editorializing. A German beer was simply a symbol of their innate superiority.

"You are from America?" the bartender asked.

"Lately."

"So is our German beer. What we get must go first to you and then come back to us. Though unofficially. This is the only way."

"So it's not what the room is drinking."

"We have not so much of it. And it is costly."

I glanced to the left, where the bar-rail boys were. The nearest three faces were turned to me, watching and listening openly.

I nodded at them.

They nodded in return, nearly in unison.

I looked back to the bartender.

I said, "Is it, however, a good one?"

"It has come a long way, but yes. It is a nice Bavarian from Kulmbach."

"Do you have enough for a round for the room?"

He gave me an *ach-so* lift of the brows and then an almost-smile like what a father gives a son who's done something very good but the father doesn't want to make a big thing out of it. "I think perhaps. Yes."

"Then I wish to buy," I said.

The American dollar in Paris had lately eclipsed even gold in value. You couldn't take gold out of the country. But you could cross any border with the gold-standard greenbacks. While going inside my coat for my wallet, I did some quick figuring in my head, marking up his Kulmbachers generously. Before he finished his count I put a five-dollar bill in the center of his freshly cleaned counter.

"Will that do?" I said.

He glanced at me and I inclined my head in the direction of Illinois Abe. His eyes followed.

He lifted his hand, but not to take the money. He offered it to me. I shook it. He had the grip of the bouncer he no doubt also was.

He prolonged the handshake. He did not need to give words to his gratitude, which was manifestly stronger than I'd expected. Then he withdrew his hand, saying, "I will get the beer now" in a cadence that made him sound apologetic for letting go of his grip on me.

"Good," I said.

"We will touch bottles, you and I, and you will tell me of your duel." He nodded at my *Schmiss*.

"Heidelberg," I said.

He spread his hands as if to say, *There you are. I could have guessed.*

"I am Hans," he said.

"I am Joe," I said.

"I understand," he said, giving me an untempered smile.

He faced the room and silenced all his customers' conversation with a cellar-filling voice he somehow made both genial and commanding. *Achtung.* Then, as they turned to him, his tone crispened, even as he spoke from the warmth I'd felt in his hand. "Gentlemen," he said. "We have a German guest who comes to us from America."

When I identified myself to him I had used the fully precise *Vereinigte Staaten von Amerika*, but he familiarized it, collegiated it by using the simple *Amerika*, speaking to these Germans' present hopefulness for a continued Wilsonian neutrality, which many of them even took to be covert sympathy.

He said, "He has bought each of you a Kulmbach *Schwarzbier*."

To a man, his *Herren* rose to their feet and lifted their bottles or their steins or their shot glasses to the American in their midst.

But before they could drink, Hans announced, "His name is Josef Wilhelm Jäger." Then he said in English, "Call him Joe."

In chorus they exclaimed, "*Heil* Joe!" And they drank to me.

While Hans went off to get the beer, some of them approached me at the bar, asking about America, where I was from over there and where I came from in Germany, what I did, what brought me to Paris. How and where I got my *Schmiss*.

The stage-role answers all came easily to my tongue: I grew up in St. Louis, but now I'm from Chicago. My father brought us from Berlin when I was a boy. I write stories for newspapers whose readers are the eight million Americans who have blood ties to the Fatherland. My stories give staunch support to an image of Germany that all you boys in this bar understand. I am in Paris to work on stories. The scar is from my college days, which were back in Germany, where I became a man.

But while I spoke, my mind slipped into a place that the actors I'd grown up around spoke of, especially during a long run, a place where they could hear their own performance, hear the words coming convincingly out of their mouths, while their real attention, for extended periods and in great detail, was on other matters, sometimes lofty, sometimes commonplace.

And so it was that I thought of Hans. And I thought of these men who were around me, not about their questions and my answers but about how it was that they were making me one of them. The Germans love putting words together to make new ones. In my actor's concurrent flow of disparate thought about these men, I even formed a word of my own, for this thing they were feeling: *Bindungsehnsucht*. A deep and complex longing for an emotional connection, for a bond. I was surprised to think of this. I was here as a spy. One of them—if he was not here at the moment, he could well have been—one of them that they would hide and even assist could be a killer of civilians in the name of war. The men in this room were the Huns. And the connection they were creating between us was built upon my lies.

But superficial lies. Lies that could easily have been replaced by equally superficial truths. So easily as to show how irrelevant lies or truth were to the making of this bond they sought. Because the biggest surprise of all was that I was feeling the *Bindungsehnsucht* in me as well. That they were Germans and I was an American or even that I was an American spy portraying an American German to help prosecute a war against them: all that seemed somehow irrelevant. In this moment we were simply men. In a bar. Finding things to bind us, to give us cause to shake hands, lift our glasses, drink in concert, prop each other up, get varying degrees of drunk together, come to a rapport. That the rapport could be achieved over trivial and interchangeable things only spoke to how deep was the longing itself and, therefore, paradoxically, how profound was the rapport.

Hans had returned. He was lining up bottles of beer on the zinc surface of the bar. A long, orderly row. When I would think of this later, with a reporter's reflex for glib metaphor, the bottles were disciplined and orderly like German troops marching into Belgium. In the moment, however, in a cellar in the German Quarter of Paris, it was all about how these men waited patiently for the bottles to be arranged, how they spoke to me even as they knew the beer was arriving and how they waited and queried and listened so they could learn about Joe, until all the bottles were arrayed.

Then they filed by and Hans opened the beers one by one.

And, yes, I watched each face, looking for the killer who had brought the war to the innocents of Paris, as the German U-boat commanders were doing in the North Atlantic, as the German troops did to Belgium to begin it all.

Franz Staub was not among them.

After the last man had filed past me with a nod and a smile and a cuff on the shoulder and a *danke*, after all these men had gone back to their places, they remained standing, without drinking, until Hans opened his own beer and mine.

Then we all lifted our bottles, and in the brief moment before someone spoke, I played my role with the complexity of the past few minutes driven into my head as deeply as for any actor at the Moscow Art Theatre. In a voice that filled the bar, I toasted, "*Deutschland über alles!*"

With those words, I was a German-American who had found his allies, and I was a guy named Joe among his new pals whose language I spoke and who shared their *Bindungsehnsucht*, and I was an American spy in the midst of the enemy. Every voice in the bar veritably sang the toast in response.

The beer was dark and malty and as cool as the cellar air. After I took my first sip I turned to Hans, who had just taken a sip of his. We touched bottles and nodded to each other.

And I noticed one unopened bottle sitting on the bar before him.

The simple explanation was that he'd miscounted. Easy enough to have done. But when my eyes fell to the bottle, Hans glanced at it too. He put his own bottle down and said, leaning to me, speaking loudly and giving the nearest drinker at the bar a little sideways smile, "I'm leaving my own beer for a moment. Keep an eye on these ruffians." *Unraffinierte Kerlen* was his phrase in German. A friendly wink of an insult. "Don't let them steal it," he said.

"You're safe," I said.

Hans picked up the unopened bottle and moved off. One bottle too many could easily have been set aside nearby. I watched Hans cross the room with it and disappear into the hallway at the far end.

The ruffian next to me caught my eye and nodded at Hans's bottle on the bar. "Do you intend to maintain your American neutrality about that beer?"

"I will defend that German beer as if it were my own."

The man lifted his own bottle and invited a clink of mine. I obliged.

"Good man," he said.

We drank.

He asked what story I was working on. I was doing okay without getting too far into a journalistic hoax. I was vague and he hadn't been all that interested anyway, as he immediately launched into a long diatribe about the British, and I simply was called on to nod and grunt. I needed only to shift my eyes a very little past his right ear to watch the door from the hallway.

Hans was gone for several minutes. Then he emerged without the beer and crossed to the bar.

There was a back room. Someone was in it. Someone not showing his face.

Hans arrived and we talked about Heidelberg and swordplay and the evolving weaponry of this war, and through all of it I was thinking about the man in the back room. Finally enough time had passed for me to excuse myself without arousing suspicion. In a brief lull in our conversation I leaned to Hans and asked for the toilet. There was only one place where it could be.

He motioned to the passageway across the room. "Last door."

I sauntered off. I stopped and shook an offered hand of a grateful beer drinker. I sauntered on. Nonchalant.

The corridor was empty and dim. A single electric bulb burned at the far end, beside what was apparently the door to the *toilette*. I walked lightly now. No noise. Along the right-hand wall were two doors. The first was dark at its bottom edge. The second showed a light.

I stopped there.

I held my breath.

I looked over my shoulder. No one in the bar had an angle to view this far down. I put my ear gently against the door.

Nothing.

Then a stirring inside. The rustle of a body. Brief. Then silence.

My options. Quickly now. What if I were to push into the room and find it was Staub? And find what else? The makings of a bomb? I would kill him. If it was Staub and around him were only a few personal things that a refugee would have? He might still be the man Fortier, by way of Lang, suspected he was. Suspected. Unproven in such a context. Yet even if the bomb making wasn't clear, he was still likely a German secret agent. But only by the say-so of an out-of-work maître d'.

I was thinking it out too much.

I was still wearing my overcoat, unbuttoned. I slipped my hand inside and beneath my suit coat and to the small of my back and drew my Mauser. I put it into the right-hand pocket of my overcoat and kept my hand on it.

Though there was a room full of German patriots between me and the way out, I had to know.

I put my left hand on the doorknob, took a breath, and I thought: *Gently now.* I tried to turn the nob.

It was locked. And it snicked at the attempt. Quite clearly.

The body rustled again inside.

And now a footfall.

I took a step back.

A slip bolt was thrown.

The door opened.

Wide.

The face was clean-shaven, gaunt. It had a scar angling down from hairline to left eyebrow. Staub. He was in his shirtsleeves. No tie. The door was fully open. On the wall behind him was a dresser and upon it, a shaving mug and an open travel case. Nothing else visible.

"I'm sorry," I said in my best German. "I thought this was the toilet."

He glanced to the end of the hall. To see if my mistake was plausible. There was no sign on the closed door. There was an indicative smell no doubt but that smell was also present where we were standing. A mistake was plausible.

He returned his gaze to me, seeming more weary than suspicious. "The door at the end," he said.

"I'm sorry," I said.

I did not immediately move away as he might have expected, nor did he. His eyes remained on mine, but impassively, as if I were a tree or a lamppost or a pattern in the wallpaper and he was simply lost in a thought.

"I didn't know you were back here," I said. "I just bought a round of Kulmbacher. I don't want to miss anyone."

"That was you?" Staub asked. His tone was flat.

"Yes."

"Thank you. Hans brought me one."

"Good," I said.

My hand was still in my pocket, on my pistol. At least for the present time, it seemed to me, small talk would be preferable to assassination. I had things to learn. There could be others actively working with him.

I withdrew my hand. Not too slow. Not too fast. He had a spy's nerves. My movement was within his field of vision, but he kept his eyes on mine and he did not blink.

"I am Josef Wilhelm Jäger." I offered my hand to him.

Germans love to shake. But Staub hesitated. I started to withdraw it but he quickly offered me his.

"Herr Jäger," he said. "I am Franz Staub."

"Herr Staub," I said.

He quickly let go. "I have only lately arrived in Paris," he said. "If you'll forgive me."

And he withdrew into his room and closed the door.

I needed to follow him.

I needed to search his room.

He bolted the door.

Not on this night.

8

The next morning the concierge of my hotel appeared at my table in the dining alcove off the lobby as I was finishing my coffee. He was a limping man with hair as off-white as the French ration bread, which he was once again apologizing for, though he could see I'd eaten it all.

"I am so sorry for it," he said. "It has been sabotaged by potatoes."

"Your wheat is off fighting the war," I said.

He bowed a little to me.

"This came for you," he said, producing a telegram.

I thanked him, and he vanished.

The telegram was from Clyde Fetter in Chicago, my editor in chief at the *Post-Express*, and I could hear his voice, with pauses for effect to draw on his cigar: *Kit old man.* He paused and puffed. *You got your wish, at least for ambulance angle. Frogs' War Ministry okayed you riding along in Paris and to front. Second-line trenches farthest.* He paused and examined the end of his cigar. *Need to wangle your way forward like a real reporter.* He puffed and blew. *Which you are.* The last two remarks were Clyde being Clyde. The needle and the pat on the back, in rapid succession. He was in on my doings with the government. He and the newspaper owner were the only ones in Chicago who knew. He was a patriot but he also was of the opinion that newspaper work was more valuable to the country than spy work. At this point in the cable I could see him lean forward and tap off his ash. *American hospital already informed. Off you go. Clyde.*

An hour later, the wartime superintendent of the American Hospital, an affable French bureaucrat named Pichon, examined the permission papers and grunted at the signatures, individually, with escalating intensity up the chain of command, from the *Section d'Information* to the *Mission de la Presse Anglo-Americain* to the *Cabinet du General-en-Chef* to the *Ministère de la Guerre*.

"Very well," he said.

I stepped from his office.

Louise was standing in the middle of the sunlit hallway, her hands crossed demurely before her, at her waist.

"Hello," I said.

"Hello," she said.

"Are you waiting for him or for me?"

She didn't answer. Her hands dropped. Her eyes had suddenly focused intently on my face. The left side of my face. Without shifting her gaze away, she took two steps toward me, coming within lilac-smelling distance, and I realized what it was.

My scar.

She kept her tungsten beam of a gaze on it for another few moments and then brought her eyes to mine. "Are there more of these?" she asked.

"Scars?"

"Yes."

"None to speak of."

There was a faint letting go in her, as if she were relieved.

I wondered if she knew enough about the enemy to recognize what the scar resembled.

I decided to intervene. "This one's from covering another war," I said, which was more or less true. "A shrapnel wound," I said, which was a lie.

She nodded.

I said, "I've been given permission to ride with your boys."

"I know," she said.

The superintendent had merely put on a little show, going through the motions of checking the signatures when he'd already passed on the word.

"That's why I'm here," Louise said. "You're in luck." And she turned and moved off at a near trot. She was all business now, content to keep me half a step behind her. She was, once again, Supervising Nurse Pickering, with no hint of last night, with even the recent comments about my scar seeming impersonal in retrospect, seeming like a professional interest from a professional nurse recognizing a battle wound and wondering what I'd been through.

Not looking my way, staying focused on her brisk lead, she said, "The engine of a train we expected last night from Compiègne broke down in the forest of Ermenonville. Sometime this morning they got running and we only just learned. It's due within the hour at La Chapelle. We have beds."

"Thanks for getting me," I said.

"You're welcome," she said, and after that she led on in silence until we emerged from the administrative wing into the cobbled courtyard.

Across the way and farther along, a dozen Model T ambulances sat closely side by side, some with hoods folded open, the drivers busying about, all of them khaki-clad with puttees and riding breeches. Louise stopped us abruptly. She laid a hand lightly on my forearm.

"I'll leave you to them."

"Thank you," I said.

But she tightened her hand on my arm to keep me from moving off. She had more to say, though she hesitated, dropped her face briefly, then lifted it firmly and looked me in the eyes. "You spoke of perhaps having a drink," she said. "I will be at the New York Bar tonight. I can arrange for the time to be private."

Something snagged in my chest and squirmed there briefly. How much better that prospect seemed than what faced me. Her hand was still on my arm. But there was the matter of Staub. It was bad enough I wasn't keeping an eye on the cellar bar right now, ready to follow him.

"I may be tied up tonight," I said. "I'm not sure."

"There's no obligation," she said.

"It's not about that," I said. "I want to. It's just that I'm working on other stories as well."

"I'll be there nonetheless," she said.

"I'll make every effort."

She nodded and slipped away.

I headed off across the courtyard, trying to put her out of my mind.

John Barrington Lacey's face made that more difficult. He was staring at me, even as he stood by the front fender of his ambulance. He'd been staring at the both of us before that, I would've wagered. Though I'd come to the conviction last night that there was nothing between him and Louise. Indeed, seeing him now, I figured what I'd picked up on at the bar were his longings for her that were going unrequited.

As I neared, he nodded. I nodded in return. At the next Ford down, his back toward me, a driver was rising from a headlong session inside his engine compartment. He closed the hood and turned. Cyrus Parsons.

I stopped a step or two past Harvard, splitting the distance between the two men.

"Good morning, gentlemen," I said.

John Lacey said, "Cobb."

Cyrus Parsons said, "Morning, Kit."

"I'm cleared to ride," I said.

"We're both off to La Chapelle," Lacey said.

"That's fine for me," I said.

We all three just stared at each other until I said, "So which one of you?"

Lacey turned his face to Parsons, who turned his face to Lacey, and they exchanged something more than a glance. I had the distinct feeling they'd already discussed this and the decision had not been a simple one.

"Why don't you go along with Cyrus," Lacey said.

Cyrus turned, and the smile he gave me bore the headline "Farm Boy Beats Harvard Varsity Debate Team."

And from the front gate a pea-whistle shrilled and all the drivers snapped to motley attention.

"I'll get the crank," I said to Cyrus.

He grunted assent and made for the driver's seat.

Then he was set and the battery began to chatter and I bent to the starting crank. He retarded the spark and advanced the gas and I gave the crank a firm tug.

The Ford started up and I was beside Cyrus in the front seat.

The dozen Fords pulled forward and turned, one at a time. Convoyed up, we rolled out of the hospital grounds and onto the Boulevard d'Inkermann.

I slipped my notebook and pencil discreetly from my pocket and kept them close, in the folds of my coat. I sensed it best with Cyrus Parsons to just let him speak as naturally as possible. I had a pretty good memory for the patterns and phrasing of news-source talk. I figured I'd rely on that as much as I could, to take the measure of this young man.

Led by a staff car to manhandle our way through intersections, we would make our cautious but steady way through mid-morning Paris, though our route would take us along the less busy northern edge of the city, eventually following the Right Bank belt railway.

Straight out of the front gates of the Lycée Pasteur, Cyrus said, "They don't go for this, the French powers that be. Us parading through the streets in broad daylight, showing what they've got going with their young men. They usually make sure the blown-up bodies arrive in Paris in the dark."

My note-taking hands twitched.

Cyrus somehow picked up on it. "Go ahead," he said. "I don't mind. You're a reporter. Report."

I'd simply been watching since he started in on the powers that be. He had good peripheral vision. Or he knew the impact of this statement and just assumed I wanted to write it down exactly. He must have glanced and caught me withdrawing the notebook and trying to keep it inconspicuous.

I flipped open the cover and lifted it a little to show him I was complying. I was happy to comply. But I didn't remark on it. I still wanted to recede from his active awareness, though that was my practiced instinct employed with the usual news sources and he already didn't seem usual.

He turned his face toward me. "If they don't like what I say, what are they going to do? Fire me?"

I smiled a soundless chuckle at him.

He looked ahead again. "Damn right they won't. They ain't paying me a dime in wages to do this. I'm the perfect workingman."

I'd talked to plenty of politicians who had one basic attribute in common with this farm boy: their strong opinions expected strong agreement. "Damn right," I declared.

I wrote down his words.

"And it's rough work," he said. "You're about to see."

"You were born and reared to hard work, weren't you?" I said. "Sure."

He let that sit for a moment, and another.

"Farmwork," I said. A lame prompt for more.

"Farmwork," he said. "Harder for my father. He took it on when the sweat got a farmer nowhere. Late eighties and through the nineties. I was born in the middle of that, when farmers wore the yoke of the railroad barons and the elevator owners and the bankers. The Grange got pretty strong, and the Populist Party had a few good years. By the time I was old enough to walk a plow and shovel grain and clear stumps, they'd made things better. Not that it'll last. To throw off one set of villains, we cozied up to another."

His words had gotten heated, and he stopped abruptly. Like a farmer taking a break from the plow and wiping his forehead.

He glanced at me and then back to his driving.

He let the silence run on. Like he'd said enough. Or like he had more to say and wasn't sure how I'd take it.

"I get it," I said.

He shot me one more look.

"Politicians," I said. The villains the farmers had cozied up to. It was easy to guess Cyrus Parsons' present enmity.

This time he was the one giving out the soundless chuckle, though he kept his eyes on the street ahead. He said, "They all put us into this war, didn't they?"

"So you think Wilson's right keeping us out?"

"It runs way deeper." With this, Cyrus went clench-jawed grim for a time and I let it rest.

We drove in silence as we passed through the Porte de Champerret and turned north onto Boulevard Berthier. Now the convoy began to run faster, just inside the last defensive wall of the capital, circling the city proper. The road would soon bend eastward, heading for La Chapelle.

I did not look at Cyrus, wanting him to relax back into his easy talk. But I did gaze across his field of vision at the earthwork embankment of the Thiers Wall, from 1844, as it ran with us along the northern edge of Paris.

Eventually Cyrus said, "Do you know what's on the other side?"

He'd watched me watching.

I could see an occasional rooftop or a distant smokestack, but not much else. "I know they call it The Zone." I knew more, but I waited to hear his take.

"Paris is two cities," he said. "The Paris of the wealthy and the powerful. They're on this side. Out there is the Paris of the poor, the beaten up. The gypsies and the carnival performers. The foreigners and the ragpickers. The laborers. The simple workingman. The forgotten and the thrown away."

"You've been out there?"

"I have."

"American Hospital work?"

"No. Not work. Just to answer the question."

"Of what's on the other side."

"That one."

I found myself rather liking Cyrus. I wanted to ask him his politics, but I figured I shouldn't use the word. Mention of the practitioners clenched his jaw the last time. But I found myself engaged by his intense talk about politics and power, about the rich and the poor, engaged, too, by his hands on the wheel of this ambulance and by whatever lay ahead of us at La Chapelle. I said, "You're a man in search of principles, it sounds like."

It wasn't good journalism. I needed to ask him a basic who-what-when-where-why, not give him the words I wanted to hear. But I was trying to think like him and I gave voice to that.

To my surprise he understood what I wanted. He said, "Shall I say that for your story?"

"I don't mean to put words into your mouth."

"Well, Mr. Cobb," he said, "you can quote me. I'm here in Paris driving to a railroad siding at La Chapelle because I'm searching for principles. I figure I might find some among all the blood and putrefaction coming in on these trains from the front."

He sounded sincere.

At least as I heard it.

He was keeping his eyes on the back of the ambulance in front of him. He wasn't looking for my reaction. Wasn't giving me a wink or a sneering smile. I'd seen those things with other sources in a moment like this and it was the tip-off they were just saying things I wanted to hear. Cyrus showed none of that.

Still, I pressed him on the matter. "Do you mean it?" I asked.

Now he glanced at me.

His mouth was set comfortably in a tiny, lopsided smile. He said, "Close enough."

What had I expected from a presumed rube fresh off a farm down a remote Illinois country road? Not what I'd been hearing.

Maybe I'd just been in cities too long. Or among other rubes in other wars who I never got to talk to in a situation like this.

So at least just to stir his pot, break up his self-assurance a little, get a rise, I said, "Are you really from a farm?" I asked it firmly, torquing the question to let him hear I would take no lie, no accommodation, no close-enough.

"I sure am. Exactly like I've said." He was sufficiently quick and matter-of-fact in his answer that I believed him.

But I still heard something. "The farm by way of what?"

"You never meet a smart farm boy before?"

"I probably have."

"You didn't grow up among them."

"No."

"Well you're right. They're a bunch of dumb shits. As tractable as cows to slaughter."

"Tractable," I said, stretching the word to let him know I was quoting it back to him. An example of why I asked the question to begin with.

"Books," he said.

"Books?"

"By way of books. My father wasn't always a farmer."

"What was he?"

"It was a long time ago."

Cyrus hesitated, as if with second thoughts about bringing it up.

"So what did your father do?"

He'd been watching his driving all this time, but he turned my way now to answer me.

"He was a newspaperman," he said.

It surprised me, of course.

Then I made the connection with his interview savvy. "Now I get it," I said. "Working out a quote for me."

"About that quote," he said. "You can keep it if it helps, but the truth is I *have* principles. I'm just figuring out where and how to live by them."

"I prefer *that* quote," I said.

He looked my way. "Do you?" he said.

"Yes."

He returned his attention to the road ahead.

My mind was still adjusting to Cyrus being both a farm boy and the son of a newsman. I went back to the night I met him. He'd said that his father was born in Texas but his family brought him north. That the man used to be someone else, then he became an Illinois farmer.

"Your father the newsman," I said. "Was that also Illinois?"

But as I asked this question we entered the shadow of a train-line overpass. Cyrus said, "We're almost there."

That tension I'd seen come upon him earlier returned now. Not just in jaw but in hands and back and in focused silence. Cyrus was suddenly, fully, an ambulance driver. I wanted to learn more about his father. Simply from personal curiosity. My own newsman self had a different focus now, so I didn't press this question.

The convoy slowed and crept as the vehicles made a sharp right turn, one after the other, into the Rue de la Chapelle and then almost immediately another right turn into an acreage of warehouses and train sidings, which pulled track from both north and east.

We drove a cobbled street toward the southern end of the warehouse park. Ahead was the last, vast warehouse, which had been turned into a receiving station. A canopied platform stretched along its trackside, leading to a row of stuccoed pavilions and then a separate cluster of cottages. But as we neared its northern end, we crossed the tracks and drove up a wooden incline and straight into the warehouse.

Entering the great main floor I expected dimness but was bedazzled by sunlight from a vaulted glass ceiling. The ambulances pulled in, noses to the side wall, and we got out to wait. Accustomed to it now as I'd become, the light was less dazzling and more diffuse, as the air was filled with dust climbing the morning sun toward the ceiling, as if the ashes-to-ashes and dust-to-dust of the battle-dead were mounting toward heaven in this train-yard terminus.

We waited for the delayed train from Compiègne, along with the French ambulances and drivers of other Paris hospitals. There was low talk and ropey French cigarettes and an undercurrent of nerve-gathering that felt like the pre-attack rituals of the soldiers I'd been with in the Balkans and in Nicaragua.

Cyrus kept his distance from me for a while. He fiddled under the hood of his ambulance—to no real mechanical point, by my covert observation—and then he walked off and had a cigarette down the way, speaking briefly to Lacey but mostly wandering and fidgeting on his own.

He strolled back to me on his third Gauloise, arriving with a minute nod of the head. He threw his cigarette to the floor with half a dozen good drags left in it, and he ground the butt with his foot.

When he was done, he looked at me and said, "We go into the train cars and take out the wounded. We work in twos."

"I'll work with you," I said.

He gave me a small, you-don't-know-what-you're-getting-into smile. "You sure?"

"I am."

"There are orderlies."

"I'll do it."

"Good," he said. "We take the men to the complex at the south end."

"I saw it coming in," I said.

He nodded and paused, as if to figure out how to put what was next. He decided on a tone of ironically measured matter-of-factness. "Not everybody gets to a hospital right away. There are always patients here. The holding pavilions are for the enlisted men, conscripted sons of the poor. Warehouse walls and pillars. The cottages are reserved for the officers. Their walls are painted buff and they have fucking potted plants."

He didn't seem to expect a response from me. I wouldn't have known what to say, exactly. He turned away and lit another cigarette. Before he could take a second puff, a pea-whistle trilled at the south end of the warehouse.

The train was coming in.

And we all worked a shift in hell. The cars were filled with air made stinkingly palpable by the flush of inner things from the bodies of wrecked men, their blood and their sweat and their piss and their ordure—things always with them but unmanageable now—and by things new to their bodies, things foul and ravaging and smelling even stronger. The sepsis, the gangrene. Smells those of us from the ambulances took into our own bodies through our lungs and through our skin.

And the men in their wreckage lay all around. One at a time we lifted them onto stretchers. Necessarily. But in doing so we enflamed their broken parts, aroused their pain, and though these men sometimes moaned, sometimes let out a stifled cry, sometimes spoke a beseeching *Mère de Dieu*, for the most part these men kept a rigorous, valorous silence until, as they were about to be carried away to the doctors, they whispered *Merci* to us, to us who had wracked them with pain.

Hours passed filled with these men.

I had enough for this part of my story long before I was brought back from that deep circle of hell and set free again in the passenger seat of Cyrus Parsons's ambulance. We went slow over the cobbles and through the turns and along the road to the hospital, twilight now, the defensive wall of Paris running along outside my window, a worthless thing in this twentieth century, in this modern war. We ran slowly and as softly as possible for the sake of the three shattered men on stretchers riding in the compartment behind us.

I knew not to speak to Cyrus. Entering this hell over and over was the life he'd chosen to lead. The men who populated this hell were legion. This part of the story I would write was as much about bravery as about suffering.

But Cyrus did say one thing to me on the way back from La Chapelle. He saw a rough patch of cobble ahead, seeing it in time to slow drastically but not abruptly, and as he drove over the uneven stones with astonishing little bounce to the men we bore, he said, "They're enlisted men for us tonight. At least that. No fucking officers."

9

It was dark when our three poilus were gently unloaded and taken inside the hospital. After the last of them had been carried away, Cyrus turned to me and said, "I have to put my Ford to bed. The day is over."

"Thanks for letting me ride with you," I said.

"Maybe I'll take you to the front," he said.

"I hope so," I said.

He went off into the dark.

I stood for a time in the courtyard. I looked up at the Renaissance facade of the Lycée Pasteur, a scattering of its mullioned windows ablaze with electric light. I thought of Louise somewhere inside there, bathing and treating the wounds of the men I'd dragged hurting from hell. My mind clung to the thought of her. She would be at the New York Bar tonight. I needed to see her at the end of this day.

But I stank. Stank of the Great War. It was in my clothes, in my pores. And the war for me, the fighting of it tonight in my own way, must be in a cellar bar in the German Quarter of Paris. I'd neglected Franz Staub long enough on this day.

I turned and walked across the courtyard and out the front gate and I caught a fiacre. I could not carry the smell of what I did today to a German cellar bar. I rolled my shoulders at the thought of my newswriter-cozy hotel. Maybe Trask was right. Spy work needed better accommodations. I was not going to get a proper bath tonight in my hotel room. Hot water was rare above street level in Paris. So I went to one of the establishments along the Seine and bathed till La Chapelle had vanished from my skin, and I returned to my hotel and changed into fresh clothes.

At *Le Rouge et le Noir*, a different face appeared in the door's sliding panel. But it recognized me at once. "Herr Joe," the face said brightly. He'd drunk my good German beer.

I went in to nods and greetings and lifted steins. I acknowledged the men as I moved to the bar and looked around openly, a privilege I'd bought last night. Staub was not here. This was several hours earlier than last night and the place presently had half the number of drinkers. Staub could well be in his room. But I feared he'd gone out, feared that Cobb the spy had lost him.

Hans was opening a bottle of beer on the lower counter down the way. He nodded at me. I nodded in return and put my back to the bar and leaned against it. The passageway to Staub was dim.

Then Hans spoke from directly behind me. "Hello, Joe," he said in English.

I turned to him. "Hello, Hans," I said shifting us to German.

He set a stein before me and beside it the bottle he'd opened. It was the nice Bavarian from Kulmbach we'd all drunk together. "I had one left," he said.

"Thank you, my friend," I said.

"In a stein or in the bottle?"

I picked up the bottle and toasted it at him.

While I took a long drink of the beer, I wondered how much trust I'd established with Hans. Or if not actual trust, at least how far I'd raised the threshold of his suspicion.

When I set the bottle down, he was lingering with me.

One thing I wanted to know could be gotten at indirectly. "You boys stay late last night?"

"We close down at midnight," he said. "We are careful about the police."

"That's smart," I said. Midnight.

He grunted assent and put the unused stein on the lower counter. "You are an early riser?" he asked. "Is that the way of a newspaperman?"

"Yes. The morning is good to do your work." I said. "The previous day's notes are easier to read, if you have a hurried hand."

Hans laughed a little. "I could not be a newspaperman. My hand is better to open bottles than dip a pen."

"You do what you do very well," I said, and through this little exchange my mind had been making the case: *If Hans is party to the bombing, Staub will already have mentioned my appearance at his door. If he is not, my bringing up Staub will not seem suspicious.*

So I said, "I meant to ask. Last night on the way to the toilet I accidentally encountered Mr. Staub. He seemed an interesting man."

I watched Hans carefully.

He shrugged. Convincingly. "He has said very little to me. Only recently arrived. He is a friend of the owner."

"I understand," I said. "A friend of your boss?"

"The owner. Yes."

It was enough for now to be taking an interest in Staub. I'd work on Hans later for information about the owner.

As for Staub, I would need to follow him. That was best if he could not easily identify me. But I'd already discarded that advantage in last night's exchange at his door. There was still the cloak of night, which for this day had already fallen upon us. And I could alter my appearance if I needed to follow him in daylight.

So I played the hand I had. I said, "Perhaps we should ask him to join us for a drink?"

Hans's second shrug convinced me he wasn't a threat. He was put off by Staub's aloofness.

I leaned to Hans. "Would you just as soon not have him out here?"

Hans grunted. He appreciated my picking up on his distaste for the man. But he said, "This is not a choice for me to make. We are a place of business."

It would have been easier for him to say the man was out. I hoped he wasn't simply guessing, as I was, that Staub was in his room.

"I'll be back shortly for that," I said, nodding at the bottle of Kulmbacher.

I crossed the bar and headed down the hallway, thinking: *If he's not here, I can search his room. For a few minutes, at least. Hans will think it's the boss's friend still being standoffish with the boys in the front but okay with the American journalist visiting in the back.*

I was at Staub's door and leaned into it briefly to listen. Nothing.

I knocked.

I listened.

There was a stirring inside the room.

He was here.

The tension I'd been carrying, that he was out preparing his next bomb, abruptly sprung loose in the center of my chest.

The door opened.

Staub was not wearing a coat, but the other two pieces of his three-piece blue cloth suit were mostly ready for him to go out. The waistcoat was fully buttoned. His tie was only slightly loosened at the stiff collar. He'd packed a pretty good suit in his refugee duffel bag.

"Herr Staub," I said. "I'm Josef Jäger. We met last night."

"Yes," he said, lifting his face ever so slightly, faintly flaring his nostrils. "When you tried my door."

I could see what Hans saw in him.

"I did indeed," I said. I twisted my head a little bit in the direction of the *toilette*, keeping my eyes on him. "I'd lost my way."

"I have no doubt," Staub said.

This did not seem to be going well.

I said, "I don't mean to intrude. I just thought to ask you to join me for a drink."

He cocked his head in what seemed like full-blown suspicion.

In the spirit of being in a man's-man bar, where you tend to think and even say things in an amplified way that you'd know enough not to actually act upon, I thought: *Just take out the pistol from the small of your back and shoot this son of a bitch in the center of his chest and get it over with.*

Staub uncocked his head and said, "I thank you for the beer you sent to my room last night. But I am afraid I have an engagement tonight."

"Of course," I said. "Perhaps another time."

"Perhaps so."

"Good evening," I said.

"Good evening," he said.

He closed his door.

I retreated.

I emerged from the hallway and approached the bar. There was an empty table against the street-side wall, out of the line of sight of most everyone.

Hans turned away from the couple of *Burschen* he was talking to and gave me an inquiring glance.

"Otherwise occupied," I said.

With a shrug he returned to his conversation.

I carried the Kulmbacher to the empty table to nurse the beer and wait, and it wasn't long before Staub passed through, looking at no one.

I followed.

As I hit the steps leading from the cellar, I could hear the upstairs outer door opening and closing.

I paused to consider the risk of going up at once. If he suspected me, it would be simple for him to pause just outside the doorway to let me tip my hand. But if he didn't and he walked briskly away, the dark would cloak him, and I didn't want to lose him.

I went up.

He wasn't waiting.

I stepped outside.

It was chilly and clear. There was no visible moon but the stars were bright in the strip of sky above the narrow streets of this quarter. I could see well enough to follow and yet fade into a doorway when necessary.

Staub was walking west on Rue des Petites Écuries. Briskly, but he was barely thirty yards away. He'd paused, too, before heading off.

I crossed the street and followed him from the other side, treading as quietly as I could.

We passed through an intersection. He kept up the quick pace and I tried to picture Trask's map, which I'd studied. The cross street was Rue d'Hauteville. The whole German Quarter was tightly circumscribed, with d'Hauteville its central north-south axis. The air smelled of coal fire and kraut.

In this empty street, in the dark, I was once again keenly aware of the pistol lying heavily against the base of my spine. I transferred it from its hiding place to my overcoat pocket. If he caught me following him and he was who he was, it might be necessary to reveal my identity and intentions and let the reflexes of war take their course.

For now, though, we crossed the Rue du Faubourg-Poissonnière and my attention shifted to what I knew was up ahead and I did not try to identify the end-stopping sidestreets we passed. I only began to wonder if our Paris bomber was heading for the chanteuses and naked women of the Folies Bergère a little farther along. I had trouble picturing Franz Staub's evening engagement being with a Folies girl. Though Lang had known Staub to be a German secret service agent. One of the girls could be a German spy. Or Staub was scouting the place as a target. It would be a prime one.

He was carrying nothing.

Certainly not a bomb.

Too bad, I thought. I could resolve this tonight.

But thinking of the bomb itself led to a consideration I'd been slow getting to. The bomb in Montparnasse had the sharp crack of sound peculiar to dynamite. Staub wasn't making his own explosives. The French feared that a sustained attack of civilian terror had begun. They were likely correct. And Staub couldn't carry that much dynamite hidden in a refugee's belongings.

Where was he getting it in Paris? Another path for me follow.

But for now Staub was slowing as we came to a near convergence of three small streets within a few dozen yards. The focal point was the Folies on the right side of Rue Richer, its neon switched off but a couple of liveried hawkers with flashlights were snagging passersby and directing ticket-holders to the entry doors. The facade was dim but unmistakable, two stories sectioned by faux Corinthian columns, round ones above, which framed panes of tinted glass, and rectangular ones below, which divided a front wall covered in posters, tonight announcing the sensation of Mistinguett's return to the stage, her blond tomboy face looking us in the eyes and laughing, as a high wind lifted her skirts.

Staub stopped before the theater, looked up at it. I expected him to cross the street and go in. But he simply gawked. Then he lowered his face and began to look around him. He was clearly unsure of his bearings.

This was suddenly risky. If you follow a man who doesn't know where he's going, you will quickly be found out. I was still on the opposite side of the street, the Folies side. I turned my body away from him, stepped to the nearest poster, ogled Mistinguett.

Staub was going somewhere unfamiliar to him. Which meant he wasn't going to the place I was most interested in, where he assembled or picked up his bombs.

After a moment I chanced moving my face slightly in his direction to catch him out of the corner of my eye. He was coming my way. I focused on the poster. His footsteps sounded near me and then receded along Richer, back the way we'd come.

I gave him a few yards and I followed.

But we didn't go far. He stopped at the nearby cross street, paused again, moved his hands out of sight, and then he shined a thin flashlight beam upward onto the edge of the building just across the intersection. He was looking for the street name.

The light vanished. Not the one he wanted. He strode on, still heading the way he'd come. The next street did not cross, went only north, to the left.

He shone his light.

He switched it off.

But this time he turned left and walked on. I approached the street, pulling out my own flashlight. I shone it up to the enamel marker one flight up.

With a little start I recognized the name, switched off my light, and followed Staub. We were heading north on Cité de Trévise. Bernard Lang's street. I hadn't recognized it because I'd previously approached from the Metro at the other end.

Lang expected Staub to come for him. Perhaps this was the night.

Perhaps.

Ahead, Staub stopped and shone his flashlight on a house number. He turned off his light. He was a good hundred yards from Lang's building. There were many buildings between here and there. And yet Staub continued slowly. Checking each building. Stepping back at a couple and looking up to examine the windows.

I stayed on the opposite side of the street and moved now from dark doorway to dark doorway.

Staub seemed not to have Lang's exact address.

We made our way house by house up the street.

He drew near number seven. Lang's building.

Staub shined his light on the number. Stepped back, studied the place. Just like the others.

And he moved on.

Now the street took its jog.

But Staub did not continue his examination of numbers. He hesitated a moment. Thoughtful. I pressed back into the shadows of the doorway at number eight.

I waited, trying to decide how long to give him to move on but not let him get too far out of sight, worrying, as well, that he might come back this way.

I removed my hat and let myself put an eye around the edge of the jamb.

I saw Staub just as he vanished into the little *place* at the jog.

I kept my hat off and stepped from the doorway, edged the twenty feet to the end of the building, looked carefully into the *place*, expecting him to be across it. The stars were bright enough and a solitary gas lamp was lit, casting its glow just far enough to reveal the nymphs at the fountain and Franz Staub standing before them, looking up at them, his back to me.

I would never have expected our diaphanous girls to work their charms on our stiff and cold Herr Staub. But they clearly did. And for a long while. Or so it felt. A minute or two certainly.

Finally he lowered his face, stood for a bit more, and then he moved on through the *place* and continued north on Cité de Trévise, with me following at a distance as he continued his examination of building numbers and fronts.

He was looking for Lang.

But he had only sketchy information.

At the far end of the street he turned east, headed back into the 10th arrondissement. He stopped at a tobacconist at the corner of Rue d'Hauteville and then went south, ending up at *Le Rouge et le Noir*.

He went in.

I lingered outside, thinking over the probabilities. Whether I left now or left at midnight or left at dawn, I'd still be leaving my surveillance of him on the basis of the same hunch. No. More than a hunch. A strong intuition backed up by pretty good reasoning. If this was a night for a bomb or for a visit to an accomplice, I couldn't quite get him waiting till nightfall to go out with vague information about a revenge killing that had to be pretty far down his to-do list and then buying a tin of pipe tobacco and returning to his back-corridor, cellar room.

At least that's how I figured it, and I figured I was owed the right to figure it that way. I could leave at dawn to prove my intuition correct or I could leave now. So I headed off to the New York Bar.

10

She sat in the same chair at the same table, wearing the same shirtwaist and cardigan, her hair knotted up in the same way. She was alone with a bottle of *vin ordinaire*. She gave me the supervising-nurse nod, but she added a small, considered smile to it.

As I approached, the sameness touched me. She had one shirtwaist, one cardigan, one simple way to fix her hair when she left her patients. I was touched too by the smile, offered to me from the place where she'd sat when we first met in this bar, and by her arranging to be alone, though she'd understood I might not be able to come to her. I was particularly touched that all these vulnerable, longing things resided inside the tough-as-a-poilu Supervising Nurse Louise Pickering.

The table was longer than it was wide and she was at the narrow end. I did not choose the facing chair but the one to her left side, drawing it still nearer to her in the process of sitting down.

She angled her face to me and let the smile widen ever so slightly, as if she recognized my intention of getting as close to her as possible and she approved.

A wisp of hair had come loose from her pompadour.

I wanted to reach to it and smooth it down.

I kept my hands to myself.

"You made it," she said.

"I did."

"I'm glad."

"I am too."

I nodded to her bottle of table wine. "I can do better than that for you."

She looked at the bottle.

It was still more than half full.

She returned her eyes to me. "I prefer it," she said.

I wondered if that was actually true. In the moment of my wondering, she intervened. "They don't water it down here," she said.

The grapes were probably too early. It had probably begun to turn. But I did not question her taste or her motives. I said, "Then I'll join you."

The waitress brought another glass.

I poured from Louise's bottle and she raised her glass and I touched it with mine.

The grapes were immature. There was an undeniable suggestion of vinegar. Of course the New York Bar did not water this wine down. Neither would they have this wine on the shelf at all if it weren't for the war.

She said, "You keep thinking about the wine."

"You can tell?"

"Is it too awful for you?"

"I'm here for the company."

She puffed a laugh, averting her face. When she came back to me, she said, "I wanted a clear head for that." She put her glass down and nudged it slightly away.

I took a slug of the wine. It would do.

She said, "How did it go with Cyrus today?"

I gave her an account, starting with our arrival at La Chapelle. She listened, with what seemed to be her professional detachment, through an account of the suffering of the men from the front. When I spoke of their bravery, she stepped backstage and fell out of character.

At least with her eyes, which widened and glowed and finally reflected the lights of the bar in nascent tears.

I hesitated at this.

She did not look away. We considered each other through the veil of her emotion for the men she saw every day as they suffered and died, or suffered and recovered, though often never fully.

"I can see why you came here," I said.

"Can you?"

"I can see it in your eyes," I said.

Even as I said it, I recognized my mixed motives. To acknowledge her tender feelings. Sure. But also to woo her. More that, perhaps. Not much to my credit. But even if my motives had been totally pure, the comment would probably have prompted the same reaction on her part: she snapped into awareness of her tears and she jerked her face to the side and lifted her hand to wipe them away.

I plunged my hand into a hip pocket for my handkerchief—brushing, as I did, the holster and the butt of the grip of my pistol—and I drew the cloth out. I was glad to notice that it was clean, which it easily might not have been, and I gave it to her. I was also glad that she took it readily. I was afraid she would be aggravated that I'd let her know I saw her tears. I liked strong women. I'd known a few pretty well. I knew their touchiness about this.

But she came back to me and handed me my handkerchief.

I felt another odd twist of tenderness at its dampness.

She said, "I'm glad you could see that for yourself," letting me off the hook for my observation.

"I admire it," I said.

She pulled her nudged glass of wine back toward her. She looked at it. It had barely two swallows left in it.

I lifted the bottle, began to pour the wine into her glass—ruing its cheapness anew—and she soon stopped me with a lift of her hand.

She took up the glass and sipped only a little and put it down again.

"Thank you," she said, staring at the glass.

I watched her.

Her eyes lifted to me. Then they shifted ever so slightly downward, remaining, however, on my face. "I can't see it from this angle," she said.

"What?" I said.

"Your scar," she said.

I understood. I was sitting to her left, at a right angle. We'd looked at each other to speak, but my left cheek had remained hidden.

My response was a small reflex that turned my face further away. Just a bit. Hide the thing from her even more.

"No," she said. "It's okay."

She brought her right hand forward, crossing the distance between us, and her fingertips touched my left cheek, just past the corner of my mouth. With a gentle pressure she turned my face, exposing my scar to her sight. Then her fingertips stiffened where they lay. I was not to undo this gesture.

She followed my scar with her eyes, slowly, from near her fingertips, up my cheek, to the point where a German's saber in the camp of a Mexican rebel had begun its slice.

"Are you sure you have no more of these?" she said.

"How can I convince you?" I said.

I didn't myself fully understand what I was suggesting until she gave me that complex look a woman can sometimes give, when you faintly shock and offend her, even as you compliment her and intrigue her, even as you move her to the possibility of the ultimate suffrage, a woman's right to elect to express love, or even simply desire, on her own terms.

Now I realized what I had asked. Of course I had.

And all through that look she gave me, she had not taken her fingertips from my cheek.

She removed them now, however.

She turned her gaze away, into the bar, which was growing crowded and noisy.

Then she leaned near to me, lowering her voice so that I could hear her through the gathering din but no one else could. She said, "I intend to marry."

I no doubt gave her that complex look a man can sometimes give. She smiled. "I'm not talking about you," she said.

I erased the look. Smiled. Shrugged. "But I *am* a catch," I said.

She ignored the banter.

Her smile was gone. Earnest, brow-furrowed focus had replaced it. "I say this so you understand the sort of woman I am, in spite of my independence."

"Of course," I said.

"Marriage is being spoiled for me," she said.

I didn't quite understand.

"I feel it so," she said. She pulled back a bit and hesitated. I could see a decision playing out inside her. Then she leaned to me again. "Men's bodies," she said. "I see them. Daily. Fully. I am a nurse, after all. But I am a woman seeing these men naked, who are not my husband. Our world's moral fastidiousness about these things is set aside for a nurse and the men she cares for."

She paused.

I let the silence sit between us and then thought this might be all there was. "Of course," I said. "Everyone understands."

She lifted her palm to me, but only slightly, as if intending to wave me off but not wanting to make the gesture a rebuke.

I nodded and kept quiet.

She took another moment to reconsider how to say what she'd moments ago paused to consider. Then she said, "And they are all wrecked. I am afraid these months and months of wrecked men, wrecked male bodies, the memory of them, the image of them, will forever spoil any intimacy having to do with a man's body, even a healthy one. Particularly the ultimate intimacy. Especially when I have known men's bodies only as I have."

She seemed to falter. She turned away, saying, "I did not anticipate this about my work."

But then at once she returned to me, her voice steeling itself as she spoke, "I need alternate memories. As a woman of this new century I will not be disenfranchised from my passion."

Somewhere along the way my hand had come up to the tabletop and had landed there in sympathy. Now, as the only sound between and around us was the boistering of an American-style bar in a city at war, she laid her hand gently on top of mine.

In the fiacre, Louise and I held hands. We said nothing. The carriage was enclosed and all we heard was the ring of the horse's shod hooves on the cobbles.

In my bed at the Hôtel de Seine, we said nothing, from our entering my room, to the locking of the door, to our disrobing, with her eyes avoiding my body from the beginning and through the slow touching and through the fullness of things and in the lying down beside each other afterwards, though the electric light at the bedside remained lit during all of this.

We held hands as we lay there afterwards. The sound of our breathing filled the room, and then it subsided, and we were quiet. Only then did she rise up and, with a lift of her hand, stop me from also rising.

She pulled back the sheet.

Now she used her fingertips and her eyes to trace my body, the unscarred, uninjured parts that she most often saw torn and broken and putrefying: my feet and my legs, my abdomen and my chest, my face. Every curve and plane of my face, all but my left cheek, which she assiduously avoided. Then at last she gently turned my head to the right and she traced my scar with the forefinger of her right hand. And she bent to it and kissed it, and she kissed me on the mouth once more.

With a soft exhalation of breath she then lay back beside me, and she let me lift the covers and pull them over us, for it was cold in the room and we had not noticed, but now she was beginning to quake. I tried to assume it was from the cold, but in fact I knew it was from feelings that were too complicated for her to name or speak of. So I covered us and put my arm around her and she drew near.

We lay like that for a time.

Gradually a question began to agitate in me. I felt I knew the answer, but I also knew I might have been self-absorbed and oblivious since we entered my room and was, therefore, wrong. So when enough stillness gathered between us, I asked, "Because of what you've seen, were we spoiled for you?"

She shifted against me, drew closer, her leg sliding up mine. "At the beginning," she said. "But you made me forget."

I'd been with women. More often than most men. I could not remember feeling anything like the impulse that now moved my arm to press her closely against me. Because of her words.

And we slept.

And I woke to the distant thump of a bomb.

11

There was light coming through the slightly lifted wooden slats of the outer casement shutters. The sound that had woken me was muted, and my mind thrashed now to replay it, to assess it, even as my eyes went to Louise and my hands moved toward her, vaguely, to take her up, to shield her. She'd slept through the sound. I stopped my hands. For a moment I watched her sleeping face in the gray glow from the window.

She was safe.

I had more important things to do now.

I took up my Waltham from the nightstand, angled it to the light. The time was a little past eight.

I rose, went to the window, opened the left-hand casement and its shutter.

Not that I expected to see anything. But I'd come to an impression that the sound was from the north, toward the river. I must already have been in the process of waking when it had gone off. The sound was starting to clarify in me. The sky beyond the roofline across the street was gray and empty. No blast-spewed plume of smoke. But from the bomb's seeming distance, I was not surprised.

"What is it?" Louise asked, her voice thick.

"I don't know," I said. "A sound."

This seemed to satisfy her. She said no more. She stirred as if turning to go back to sleep.

I stared at the empty sky.

The claw-scrabble of guilt began in my chest.

I should have found a doorway last night across from the cellar bar and watched for Staub.

"Kit," she said.

I turned to her.

She had not gone back to sleep. She was sitting up in the bed, clutching the sheet against her, covering her naked chest.

I'd left Staub for her.

If I'd simply remained the reporter that I'd long been, if I'd told Trask to beat it as we'd agreed upon, I could have been looking at her now with nothing but afterglow.

Instead, she caused the claws to dig deeper and faster. But I refused to regret what we'd done.

Her eyes slowly descended me now. I realized I was facing her naked.

Her gaze ended with a nod to the foot of the bed.

"Come sit," she said.

I closed the shutter and the window.

I sat.

We looked at each other.

I could feel her mind working, trying to shape words. She broke with my eyes, averted her face. "I despise the question I want to ask," she said.

I waited.

"Despise myself for even wanting to ask it," she said. "I already know how *I* feel about this. Which is fine."

I hated seeing her so uneasy with me. I said, "Then it's my answer that might be despicable. Not the question."

She turned her face back to me. "You've been swell. I wouldn't blame you."

"For what?"

"All right," she said, though it sounded as if that part was addressed to herself. "Do you think me a wanton? For what we did?"

"Certainly not," I said.

"I'm no free lover," she said. "No Emma Goldman."

The notion that I would in any way mistake Louise Pickering for Emma Goldman, the high priestess of anarchy and free love who had the face of a Bowery cop, struck me speechless for a split second. Unfortunately, the second was not split so fine as to prevent Louise from going stiff in the shoulders and looking at me with stricken eyes.

She'd needed an instant answer.

As soon as that fact registered, I said, "God no." Sharply. And I repeated it, gently this time. "God no."

The second invocation of God loosened her body.

But her eyes still cried out for convincing.

"There is nothing of Emma Goldman in you," I said.

To which she replied, "Not that a woman shouldn't be as free to express those feelings as a man."

I'd overcorrected my course. "I agree," I said, even as Staub's second bomb thumped again in my head, asking me to think about that instead of Louise.

But I managed, "Of course a woman is free."

"And I have freely rejected advances," she said. "Many of them."

"I'm sure," I said, thinking how my sleep or half-sleep, along with the distance, had muted the sound of the explosion.

"They were all just foolish boys," she said.

"Of course," I said, concluding that the thump of it could certainly have been dynamite like the first one.

But having concluded that, my mind luckily shifted to the *foolish boys* part of her declaration that I'd just endorsed.

I figured I knew enough women to understand I was getting into a different kind of trouble. I said, "A boy wouldn't have to be foolish to try to woo you."

"They just read too much," she said.

Her mind was drifting a little, it seemed.

I had work to do.

I needed to put her in a fiacre.

But her eyes had softened upon me now.

She let go of the sheet, which fell from her nakedness, and she reached her hand toward me.

I took her hand in mine.

For now I kept my eyes on hers.

"You were the first," she said.

I'd already assumed that.

I brought her hand to my lips and kissed it. I said, "Yesterday I lifted and carried the same bodies you've dealt with for months. I know how you earned whatever pleasure we had."

It seemed the right thing to say.

Twenty minutes later, I rose from the bed and dressed and left Louise. She intended to sleep a while longer. She had the late shift today and would take a fiacre back to the hospital. I told her I was working on other stories and we would see each other again as soon as possible.

Neither of us knew when that might be.

I went out.

The day Trask had taken me to Fortier's office, we'd first driven west along the Left Bank of the Seine as he persuaded me to cooperate, after which we'd crossed to the Right Bank and doubled back. In fact, the Pont Neuf was barely a five-minute walk northeast from my hotel.

I turned from the narrow Rue Guénégaud onto the Quai de Conti and saw the entrance to the Pont Neuf a short distance ahead. It was blocked by a hasty police barricade of gendarmes and saw-horses. No vehicles were allowed to cross the bridge.

I approached.

A gendarme broke off and confronted me as I tried to enter the sidewalk over the bridge. I presented the letter from Fortier signed by the gendarme's prefect. He waved me on. I walked the hundred yards to the Place Dauphine and turned in.

A couple more gendarmes flanked Fortier's door. They read the letter and rang the bell for me. Upstairs three of his boys were filing out of his office as I came in and the man himself was at the end of the room, standing beneath his Chassepot. He motioned me to approach.

"Have you heard?" he said, as he waved me to the chair before his desk.

We both sat.

"I heard the explosion," I said.

"Another satchel of dynamite. This one at the Pont Neuf Metro station."

Thus the closing of the bridge, and the gendarmes downstairs. The station was no more than two hundred yards from where we sat, on the Right Bank. "Close to home," I said.

"Very close to home," he said.

I began to relate my encounters with Staub.

Lang was right. The cellar bar was new information. It furrowed Fortier's brow.

When I got to Staub's behavior on Lang's street, Fortier said, "He knows something about our man but not yet enough."

"When I spoke with Lang, he clearly feared Staub. Perhaps he doesn't fully trust his own sources to keep his identity to themselves."

Fortier nodded.

I went on to the thing I didn't like to tell. There was no ducking it. I said, "From Lang's street Staub strolled back to his room in the cellar, stopping to buy tobacco along the way. I regret not watching for him through the night."

Though Fortier clearly had the rhetorical guile to let me sit with that in guilty silence for a time, he instantly said, "We did not expect him to be living there. We will find a window across the street from where you can watch."

"I was misled by one thing."

"Which allowed you to put him to bed?"

"Yes."

Fortier smiled. "Perhaps I know."

Be that as it may have been, I said it first. "That he went looking for Lang when he did."

Fortier finished the thought. "When he was but a few hours from placing a bomb."

We both paused.

Then he said, "Lang may be dirty."

That was possible. But it was also his preferred explanation. It would justify his previous hesitations about the man's information.

"That's possible," I said. "But if he is, why did he give this much away about Staub? He led me to the man's door."

Fortier shrugged a Gallic shrug, probably of the don't-look-to-me-for-an-explanation variety.

I would otherwise have questioned Staub's knowing Lang's street but not his address, but Fortier's shrug rendered that redundant. So I asked, "Do you grab Staub now?"

He shook his head no. "You felt it wise to follow him. I agree. Bernhard Lang aside, we don't know how many are involved. It may have been an accomplice this morning. Now that you've found Herr Staub, along with the window I will give you one of my men to relieve you. But I wish to keep it simple and expert. Which is why your Mr. Trask gave me you. Our procedures in this sort of work can be clumsy with larger numbers. I'm afraid of our wolf smelling us and vanishing into the woods."

Staub wasn't the only wolf in the forest: "I can handle it with minimal help," I said. "I won't misjudge him again."

Fortier waved this away. "Please. I have not doubted you."

I said, "I've heard both explosions. They sound like dynamite. If that's so, Staub couldn't bring in as much as he needs as a refugee. Where is he getting it in Paris?"

"He can't," Fortier said at once, emphatically. Then, less emphatically: "He shouldn't." Then: "I don't know."

"There are surely others involved."

"One thing we are good at is spying on ourselves. My people will return to every Parisian who dealt in commercial explosives in peacetime. They are now under strict controls. The building trade. We know them well."

"And I'll return to Staub."

We stood.

Fortier wagged his head sharply, and he circled back to how we began this morning, with the bomb just across the bridge. He waved a hand at the wall of his office. "Close to home, but not so close," he said. "He preys on the children on the village path, the livestock in the field. We can guard our own. I am safe. General Joffre is safe. President Poincaré is safe. But we cannot protect every bistro, every Metro platform."

12

I returned to my room at the hotel.

Louise was gone.

For the sake of what I had to do, I was glad for that.

But I did step to the bed. She'd made it. Crisp-cornered as a Boston hospital bed.

There was not a trace of either of us there.

As if she knew I was someone else now.

I packed my own satchel so that I could follow Franz Staub. I would not wait for Fortier's window.

I approached *Le Rouge et le Noir* on its side of the street. As I neared, I scanned the building fronts on the opposite side. The six-story building directly across from the bar was all French windows fronted by outer louvered shutters and waist-high iron balustrades. I noted, on this cloudy mid-morning, the floors and apartment positions where adjacent sets of both shutters and louvers remained closed. There were three of them. In this German Quarter these might have held tenants who fled or were evicted or arrested.

I went one floor up and knocked at the door of such an apartment. No one answered. The whole building had simple ward locks. Easy. I found the right skeleton key among my tools. I opened the door to a bare wooden floor stretching into darkness. Nothing was on the walls. I closed the door behind me. Softly, nevertheless. I lit my flashlight.

At the end of the hallway the front room was empty but for a couple of pieces of unsalvaged furniture.

I went to the windows, opened them, opened their shutters, closed the windows. From where I stood I could see the sidewalk in front of the bar. Whoever could have afforded this second-floor front could afford to escape Paris to a more remote place, away from the mob fervor against them in the capital.

I stepped back into the room and put my bag down. A few minutes later I was the image of a wounded vet with a cane and a limp and a bandage round my head and ready to go outside in a corduroy teamster's coat and a flat, wool cap.

Sitting randomly across the room was a dresser with a cracked mirror and a couple of drawers missing. I pulled it near the window and arranged its angle to let me sit upon it and watch the opposite sidewalk. I leaned forward and the Mauser tightened against the small of my back. I wondered if I'd have to use it today.

Then I waited.

And I told my mind—which wanted to dwell on the Pont Neuf Metro—to shut the hell up.

Not even an hour later, Staub emerged. I grabbed coat and cap and cane and dashed down the steps and into the street. I saw him heading in the same direction as yesterday, west toward Lang's street. He was walking briskly, seemingly unwary.

For a moment I hesitated, as I finished putting on my workman's coat. The bar was likely empty at this hour. A bomb had already gone off today, and this might be my best chance to search Staub's room and his belongings.

But I had to stay with him.

I lifted my stage prop of a cane and jogged after him to establish a comfortable following distance, and when that was accomplished, I slowed to match his pace, ready to touch down my cane and slow further to a limp at the first twitch of his shoulder or sideways movement of his head.

He gave a quick glance in Lang's direction, as he passed Cité de Trévise, but did not so much as break his stride.

He scudded by the Folies Bergère in full sail with no glance at all.

Less than fifteen minutes later we crossed Boulevard Haussmann, strode along the east side of the Paris Opera House, and emerged on the Place de l'Opéra.

On the west side of the *place* was a large Haussmann building built for a triangular plot with its flatiron-end clipped to make a fifty-yard facade. Along it ran the green-awninged *terrasse* of the Café de la Paix.

Staub skirted the front of the Opera in the direction of the café and stopped at the corner of Rue Auber to wait for a dray of beer barrels to enter the traffic of the square.

He waited patiently, his hands clasped behind his back. Then he crossed in the wagon's wake, stepping casually over fresh dray-horse apples, and he strolled before the café's *terrasse.* The morning was chill but the marble-topped tables and wicker-backed chairs had been set up for any hearty boulevardiers, of which there were a dozen or so. Staub passed them by and went inside.

I gave him a little time to get situated, and then I limped into the café on my cane.

The main room was all mirrors and gilt, with a high stucco ceiling. The lunch rush had not quite begun. A young woman was seating Staub at a table along the left-hand wall, which looked out onto the Boulevard des Capucines.

She approached me next, moving her eyes from the bandage around my head to the scar on my cheek to the cane in my hand, and she put her hand on my forearm to lead me to a table. I asked for one to my right, looking out on the *place*.

Seated, I held the menu before me and kept one eye on Staub across the way.

He too had raised the menu, though his eyes did not shift in my direction.

A waiter arrived at Staub's table in an evening coat and a white wraparound apron that extended from waist to shoe tops.

Staub put down the menu and lifted his face to the man, who bent slightly to him. They exchanged words for a time. It struck me from watching them that Staub was taking pains to get his order just right.

The waiter went away and Staub leaned back, took out a cigarette, lit it, pulled a drag, and blew it toward the window beside him. His gaze followed. He took off his hat and laid it on the chair next to him.

He seemed to be relaxing into a leisurely meal.

I put down my menu and rose and limped from the Café de la Paix.

I hurried across the *place* as fast as a plausible disabled poilu could. When I'd slipped out of eyeshot, heading toward Boulevard Haussmann, I lifted the cane and strode quickly east.

Ten minutes later I was standing at the cellar door of *Le Rouge et le Noir*.

It yielded to a skeleton key.

I entered, relocked the door.

I waited.

The place was very dim. No sounds.

I switched on my flashlight.

I crossed to the back hallway, entered its toilet-tainted air, stopped at Staub's door.

I picked the right skeleton key from my pouch and slipped it into the keyhole. I thought how appropriate it was: the simple thing getting past the complex defense. The protective wards inside the lock defended it only from an equally complex key. This stripped-down metal stem and bit slid through unimpeded, unnoticed, and turned the locking bolt.

Staub's door opened.

I stepped in and closed the door behind me.

My tungsten beam flashed first in the mirror over the dresser, fell to the dresser top, and then found the bed and the nightstand, which supported a small, electric table lamp. I went to the lamp and switched it on.

I looked around once more. Dresser first. The shaving mug and travel case were still sitting out. Beside them were a hairbrush and, stuck upright in its bristles, a comb.

Inside the case was a fine Solingen straight razor with an ivory handle. A badger-hair shaving brush. A pair of tweezers.

I began to go through the drawers.

In two side-by-side half drawers, I found merely toiletries. Toothbrush and paste. Toilet soap wrapped in a handkerchief. Witch hazel and talcum and a tin of brilliantine.

As commonplace as they were, these objects made me pause. I picked up the tin. Painted gold and green with embossed flowers. *Vinolia Brilliantine.* To slick Franz Staub's hair.

I put the tin back precisely where I'd found it.

I went through the full-width drawer one level down.

A union suit, separate sets of undershorts and undervests. Neatly rolled socks. A cotton nightshirt and a flannel bathrobe.

I lifted each item carefully. Felt through it.

In the bottom drawer were three carefully folded dress shirts, linen collars, two silk ties, one red, one blue.

I looked around the room again. On the floor at the foot of the narrow bed was a leather suitcase. I laid it on the bed and opened it. Folded inside was a three-piece sack suit of gray wool. I carefully lifted the suit out and placed it aside, and I went over the suitcase carefully, looking for hidden compartments.

There was nothing.

I refolded the suit and replaced the suitcase on the floor.

Staub was a cool customer.

Not that I had any doubts, but the man was no refugee. He'd packed like a gent on a business trip.

He had to have another base in Paris. The bombs had to be put together somewhere.

But I needed to search this room for every cleft and crevice where he might have put something that could yield a lead.

The obvious places first.

I lowered myself to my knee and shined the light beneath the bed. Nothing.

For ten minutes more I searched beneath and behind bed frame and nightstand and dresser. Behind and beneath each dresser drawer. Around and within a washstand in a corner. Along the walls.

Nothing.

I stood in the center of the room and focused my thoughts.

This place allowed Staub simply to sleep and dress. Not more than fifteen minutes had passed. I still could get back to the Café de la Paix before he had finished his leisurely lunch.

So be it.

I turned and stepped to extinguish the electric light on the nightstand. And I was struck by a thought: *This is a tiny room, under the ground, down a back hallway of a bar where German nationalists have gathered unmolested each night for sixteen months. If a German spy could feel safe anywhere in Paris, it would be here.*

As that thought blossomed in my head, my hand remained on the light switch without snapping it. I'd hesitated. I withdrew the hand.

I looked at the bed.

I'd searched behind it and beneath it.

I had not searched in a place where a German spy would never put something important. Unless, perhaps, he felt safe.

The bed was neatly made. Staub was as precise in this as a nurse. His blanket and sheet were folded back together in an even, layered flap. Centered on the exposed bottom sheet was his flat rock of a horsehair pillow.

I lifted the pillow.

Lying there was a five-by-seven manila envelope.

I put the pillow aside and I sat down on the bed.

I picked up the envelope.

It was well-handled and not sealed.

I looked inside.

There were two items.

I took out a sheet of pale blue bond. I unfolded it carefully, recognizing at once that it had been unfolded many times over many years. Its message was written in German in a florid hand rendered through a fine-point, flexible-nib fountain pen that narrowed and flared often. It was dated October 12, 1890. It read:

My darling Franz,

We parted only an hour ago. I still feel the touch of your hand on mine. I still see the brightness of your eyes under the linden trees. We must never part again, my treasure.

Forever your Greta

I slipped the other item out of the envelope. A cabinet card. I knew who would be pictured there.

A young Franz Staub, hair brilliantined, mustache twirled, sat in a chair in a Berlin photographer's studio. And behind him stood a young woman with her hand firmly on his shoulder, her hair rolled up, her collar high-standing. She was big-boned and wide-shouldered. A young Valkyrie. The Greta of the love note was the Greta who had seemed so freshly in love with Bernhard Lang.

That affair *was* fresh.

Franz Staub was no bomber. Probably no German agent. He was a wronged husband. He'd come to Paris to take back his wife from the man who had recently stolen her. And perhaps have his revenge.

And thinking of Lang, I heard him again warning me that this man was so dangerous that I needed to kill him without hesitation.

I was this wife-stealing German maître d's hired assassin.

To resist my rising rage, I folded Staub's love letter. Folded it carefully, for it was fragile after a quarter of a century and a hundred weepy readings in the past few months. I forced my hands to stay focused on a nonviolent task, though they were not happy about it. I put the letter upon the cabinet photograph, whose heavy card stock would protect it. I slid them both, together, into the envelope. I laid the envelope in the center of the upper end of the bed and placed the pillow over it.

I still was furious. But at least not actionably.

And then I thought of the matter of my password. The coached lie of how I obtained it. Dieter the waiter at the Café de la Paix.

I'd seen Dieter half an hour ago.

Staub had been lying or wangling or threatening or paying Dieter for Lang's exact address.

I rose from the bed.

Perhaps Staub would eat a thoughtful meal before doing what he had to do.

But perhaps he'd ordered only coffee.

Or nothing at all.

Perhaps he was heading straight for his wife and her lover.

When I stepped into the street before the bar, I was considering two courses of action. The easy one, the one that would satisfy my fury with Lang, though indirectly, would be to return to my hotel. Let Staub do what he felt he had to do. Let the three of them suffer whatever were the consequences.

But I'd still be responsible for whoever got killed, even if I wasn't calling the shots.

The second course of action would have me wade into the middle of a nasty love triangle. Which seemed like a very bad idea.

Nevertheless, I struck off west, heading for Lang's place. If I was lucky, I'd get there before Staub and all I'd need to do would be to warn the maître d', punch the son of a bitch in the face, and leave.

But climbing the stairs at number seven, Cité de Trévise, I knew something was wrong. The apartment door at the landing was half-way open and a woman was standing there staring up the staircase. As I appeared from the steps below, she looked me in the eyes as if I were a madman, stepped back, and shut the door quickly but quietly.

I paused at the foot of the steps to the third floor. Lang's floor.

I heard nothing.

I pulled the Mauser from the small of my back, released the safety, and climbed the stairs as softly as possible.

When my head was about to become visible on the floor above, I stopped. I listened again.

Nothing.

Lang's apartment was at the rear. My aural focus was in that direction.

But now from the other way, from the front of the building, an apartment door clicked open, then abruptly clicked shut again.

Silence once more.

If I was going to do this, I just had to do it.

I lifted my pistol and went up the rest of the steps, quickly, bringing the Mauser to bear down the hallway to the back.

Halfway along, Bernhard Lang's body lay facedown.

Beyond, the door to his apartment was shut.

I approached Lang.

His arms were sprawled outward. One leg was bent oddly akimbo. The bullet had gone into his spine between his shoulder blades.

I stepped around him and approached the door.

The door that seemed closed from a distance, wasn't. It had snugged up against the jamb just before the latch bolt caught.

I put my ear against the door to listen.

Nothing.

No.

Not nothing. Not quite. Heavy breathing. Gasping, for its sound to make it through the wood.

I stepped back, centered the Mauser waist-high over the threshold, lifted my foot, and kicked the door open.

Half a dozen paces down the hallway Greta stood facing me, absolutely still, wearing her flowered bathrobe with the tasseled cinch, her hair loosened and tumbled wildly over her shoulders, her arms dropped to her sides. She was gazing at the floor before her.

At her feet were Staub's feet. He was lying on his back. At my end was his brilliantined hair. Halfway in between, a kitchen carving knife was buried deep in the center of his chest.

Greta lifted her eyes to me.

She was finished with what she had to do. She was finished.

13

I found the wartime concierge, an old man, cowering in his ground-floor *loge*. He was happy to let me handle the telephone responsibilities for a couple of murders. I called Fortier first.

I returned to Lang's apartment. Greta was now sitting in her parlor, staring out the courtyard window, her hands folded in her lap. I sat quietly across the room.

Fortier arrived with the gendarmerie. He saw what he wanted to see, and he and I went out. At a bistro on Rue Richer, we sat inside, at a corner table in the rear, each of us with our back to an adjoining wall. All of this at his leading.

We'd been mostly silent on the walk here, and seated finally, I let him set the agenda for our conversation. He remained silent till we had our *cafés noirs* before us, as concentrated and bitter as Fortier's mood had been.

He finally said, "She did my work for me."

I had no reply for this.

After a clench and a release of his jaw, he added. "As did you, for which I ask your pardon."

"None of this was clear till I could frisk his room."

"I did not think the Germans capable of such sentimentality." He said this with surprising mildness, and a small shrug. It sounded almost like a grudging French compliment for this Boche *affaire de cœur*. Perhaps Fortier's gentleness, though, was for Fortier, forgiving himself for this possibility never entering his mind, even in his initial suspicion of Lang.

And even this American spy didn't figure it out till too late.

I was not so forgiving of myself. I'd been seeing the signs. *Poor Staub*, I thought. Not just all the queerness I'd discussed with Fortier about the man's initial visit to Lang's street, but how that visit ended. I watched Staub once more, in the depths of my *café noir*, stopping before the three gossamer-gowned, stone fountain nymphs in the *place* in the middle of Lang's street. He stood there a long while, imagining his Greta somewhere nearby, as wooingly undressed as these three, offering herself to her homewrecking maître d'.

But Fortier was right. I never expected murderously jealous revenge of him, not of the stiff and brilliantined Herr Staub, declining a drink with the boys in the next room. Things I'd missed continued to chatter back into my head. Lang's special anxiety about Staub coming for him; Lang urging me to kill this guy quick, which meant, of course, that Staub would have no chance to reveal his true motives to me.

I had both men pegged in certain ways, so these tip-offs simply hadn't registered on me.

"It has not been a total waste," Fortier said. "Your thought about the dynamite still pertains. That might lead us somewhere. And I'm happy to find out about the meeting place of the traitorous immigrants among us."

This last declaration thumped into my head.

I looked his way.

He took a sip of his *café*, watching me over the lifted cup.

"What's your plan for them?" I asked.

"Close the place down. Round them all up." He paused a moment and then lifted his cup at me. "Grind them and brew them."

This thumped again in me. Louder. Like artillery shells walking closer to your position.

Now that Staub had been properly understood, there was no evidence to suggest that Hans and the rest of the Germans in the cellar bar were anything but willing immigrants to France, with some original-home-team sympathies, who got together to drink and grumble. They did it secretly because they'd all found themselves, in Paris, France, guilty of treason by ethnicity.

I had not thought myself capable of such sentimentality. Especially not since I'd begun covertly to hunt and kill for my own country's felt enemies, who happened, indeed, to be mostly of this same ethnicity. What I myself had seen and done so far in this work was, it seemed to me, thankfully, justifiable.

Maybe Fortier was justified too.

There were a million Germans out there on the front ready to march into Paris and likely do unto the French what they'd already done, savagely, unto the Belgians.

Still. The country I was working for was pretty tolerant of folks grumbling. Immigrants or not. As a matter of principle. Hell. We were all immigrants.

I said, "You think maybe, instead, a couple of your boys should take over that window you were finding for me and keep an eye on the comings and goings? This particular crowd of Huns turned out not to be dirty over Staub. From what I saw firsthand, their wartime objective looked to be simply getting complainingly drunk. So watch for newcomers and shadow them. If the bad boys think *Le Rouge et le Noir* is safe, they may come."

Fortier snicked his mouth at this, like he was trying to remove something stuck in his teeth without touching it. But a couple of moments later he nodded. "Perhaps," he said.

That was as far as I was prepared to go for my erstwhile German drinking buddies. But I was glad to go that far. Fortier was all wrong anyway in the tactics he was professing. Anyone in that cellar who was the real foe wasn't going to grind very easily. The ones who were grindable would be as misleadingly worthless as Lang.

14

By that evening it had begun to snow.

I stood in the New York Bar, my foot on the bar rail, leaning on the zinc top, nursing a beer till our table at the back opened up and I took my seat on the side, leaving the narrow end open. Not that I'd gotten in touch with her. Given her agenda, I figured she might be done with me. I'd been missing clues lately. I was trying to fix that.

I thought of the crisply made bed.

And that was another thump inside my head on this very odd day.

But I was simply a reporter again. That felt right. And I was glad that was the only way she knew me.

I figured I had to touch base with Trask, but he'd find me soon enough. As far as I was concerned, I'd been unloaned to the French.

Paris did, however, still have its saboteur.

Maybe a bar was a dangerous place. Maybe it was the last place where I'd want Louise to show up. But surely this bar was okay. The Huns would only piss on their own shoes if they went after an American establishment. They wanted to unsettle the French, not rile up the Americans. There were far better targets for that.

So I sipped my beer and I waited.

And on my third beer she was there in the front doorway, in her shirtwaist and cardigan and with her hair in that pompadour knot, which I found myself suddenly liking with sweet intensity, since I now knew what her hair looked like unknotted and falling over her bare shoulders.

And here she was.

She saw me and she brightened—clearly so, all the way from the front to the back of this joint—and she came to me and took her place at the head of the table, the way we'd sat last night.

Last night felt like a long, long time ago. In between: a bomb, twice holding this woman as close as possible, a shadowing, two murders, an abrupt suspension of Cobb the spy.

She leaned a little bit toward me and said, softly, "I'd touch your hand…" Then she hesitated.

Did she not know how to finish the sentence or was it too hard for her to say?

I leaned toward her and said the thing that would be the most difficult for her, the thing that might have made her feel she had to declare it at once: "But it was only for the one night?"

"No." This came without hesitation but without conviction. At least to my ear. There were still conditions on what we were doing. Which was fine. I was merely helping out Louise Pickering's future husband, setting her mind right for him. He would need to be very modern about these matters. Maybe she even had the man in mind. Or I'd be a liberated woman's none-of-your-business secret past.

"Just not in public," she said.

Okay. Maybe that was the only limitation for now.

I said, "Are the Model T boys coming tonight?"

"I don't think so," she said. "Cyrus is being rotated forward day after tomorrow."

"Is this my chance to get to the front?"

"I took the liberty of speaking to Superintendent Pichot. He's got all he needs from the ministry. So that's between you and Cyrus."

"Thank you," I said. "Now it's my turn trying not to touch hands."

"Be careful," she said.

"Okay. No touching," I said.

"I mean at the front."

"I'm just along for the ride."

"Both of you."

"He's done this before, right?"

"Yes."

I said no more on that. We looked into each other's eyes for a long moment.

I could read them. She was tumbling deeper into worry.

Maybe last night and this morning weren't entirely about her future husband.

"When was the last time you lost an ambulance driver?" I said.

"A couple of months ago."

I'd thought it would be a reassuringly rhetorical question.

She read my surprise. And the tough girl in her turned mordant. "You've heard of German artillery, I presume?"

"I have."

She rolled her shoulders a little at making her point.

She looked away into the bar and then came back to me with another small smile. She said, "So it took that, did it?"

I didn't understand.

"My talking to the superintendent for you," she said.

I was still slow.

She removed the little smile and put on a pout. "To make you want to touch my hand."

"Be careful of the easy smiling and pouting," I said. "In public that's as telling as a touch."

She rolled her eyes and looked away.

An hour later we opened the outer shutters of my hotel room, and we lay deep in the bedclothes, watching the snow fall. And when we held each other closer still, we remained in the dark, beneath the covers. She no longer needed to look at my unwrecked body, though her last whispered words to me before we fell asleep were, "Be careful."

15

Louise and I sloshed through the ankle-deep Paris snow the next morning, the sun shining, the air warming, the quasi-smell of melting snow flaring coldly in our noses. Our arms clung tight around each other's waist and our hips rubbed together as we walked, recalling the night.

I hailed a fiacre on the Boulevard Saint-Germain. I was to come up to the hospital tomorrow morning, ready for the trip to the front.

The cab stopped. Louise and I embraced under the discreetly averted face of the driver and the over-the-shoulder gaze of the horse.

As we held each other, I felt a tremor in her. Of lingering fear, I figured. This was our last embrace for a while. She would work a night shift tonight, and we'd have no chance to kiss good-bye at the hospital tomorrow. So we kissed now. The public be damned. Besides, it was Paris, in the morning sun, in the snow.

When I returned to the hotel, Trask's Pierce-Arrow was sitting at the curb. His bodyguard driver had already spotted my approach and was waiting at the automobile's vestibule door. He opened it. I nodded to him as I drew near. He nodded to me as I stepped in.

Trask offered his hand when I sat down beside him.

I shook it.

He could be brusque even when he was pleased with you, so I took this to be an apology for loaning me out to a wild goose chase.

"No worse for the wear," he said.

"No worse," I said. "You talked to Fortier?"

"Tell me how you saw it."

I gave Trask the story.

When I'd finished, he wagged his head. Shrugged. Said, "Hell, look at how this war started. A punk kid anarchist trying to be an assassin who misses his chance in the Archduke's big parade. So an hour later he's standing in front of a delicatessen, his pistol still in his pocket, and the duke's driver takes a wrong turn and stops right in front of him."

Trask shook his head again and looked out the window.

True enough, what he'd said. Ironic enough. But it felt a little fuzzy to be coming from the mind of James Polk Trask.

I waited.

He looked back to me. He snorted to herald his explanation. "The prime ministers and the presidents and the emperors think it's all about the big things, always. But in our business, in this day and age, we sometimes have to pay attention to what some little punk might do. And some other punk might be the only guy who knows the plan."

"A punk like an unemployed maître d'," I said, seeing his drift, drawing his still-shaky comparison on his behalf, perfectly willing to let Trask and Fortier both off the hook.

"On any given day," he said.

It was time to move on. I said, "I've got a chance to go to the front."

He nodded with clench-jawed solemnity. "Go work on your cover identity," he said, like sending a penitent off to do fifty Hail Marys.

Ten minutes later Trask kindly dropped me at the nearest approved Press Bureau telegraph, in the central office of the *Postes et Télégraphes* on Rue de Grenelle.

The censor sat in his separate office, the tunic of his unranked military uniform sprinkled with cigarette ash on the chest and dandruff on the shoulders. I wrote out the telegraph form at a small desk across from his. This message would clear with no problem. Addressed to Mr. Clyde Fetter, editor in chief, the *Chicago Post-Express*, Chicago, Illinois, USA.

Going forward tomorrow. Will get back to Paris to do story as soon as I have what I want.

That was all Clyde really needed to know at this point. But I thought of my previous ride with Cyrus, to La Chapelle, and of the follow-up question I'd not gotten a chance to ask. It felt marginal to my story, but I was still curious. So I wrote to Clyde:

You ever know an Illinois newspaperman by the name of Parsons? Turned into a farmer downstate a couple decades ago.

I went back to my room and packed my kit bag and I lay alone in the dark. Before I slept I did my Traskian Hail Marys. Instead of dwelling on my mistakes with Lang and Staub, I determined to wake up restored to my newsman's frame of mind. I thought: *The guy beneath my byline wouldn't have made those mistakes. You let a source talk freely and you listen closely till he shows you what he really is. You set your preconceptions aside.*

But was that so? Us gentlemen of the inkpot are only too happy to figure out our subjects ahead of time—at best, by whatever we already think we know to be true; at worst, by whatever the public would eat up—and then we only hear what fits the thing we intend to write.

Usually without fatal consequences, however.

I didn't sleep all that well.

But the morning was bright and the snow had melted mostly away and I suddenly felt pretty good. Whatever other newsmen generally were apt to do, I had mostly done journalism my own way, and somewhere in the night I'd convinced myself I was pretty smart, pretty rigorous about trying to write an authentic story.

I rushed through my breakfast and was striding to the front door of the Hôtel de Seine, clad in my war correspondent puttees and carrying my kit, when the concierge saw me and circled from behind the front desk with his hand raised.

I stopped.

"Monsieur Cobb," he said. "You are returning when?"

"Hard to say," I said. "A couple of days. A couple of weeks."

"We have you booked here for two weeks."

"I'm leaving things in the room."

"Of course."

"I'm off to the front. If it looks like I'll stay longer, my newspaper will wire you more money."

Something dawned in the old man's face. He lifted a forefinger to keep me where I was, and he went back to the desk.

He returned with a *Postes et Télégraphes* envelope. I glanced through its glassine window. A cable from Clyde. A cheery go-get-'em, I assumed.

But I was running late. So I simply stuck the envelope in my pocket, thanked the old man, and strode on.

In Neuilly, I went straight to the courtyard.

There were only three ambulances, waiting side by side. The other two drivers were talking together at the far Ford. Jefferson Davis Jones was one; the second was an older man, middle-aged and paunchy, who I did not know.

Cyrus was lounging against his front fender. He looked my way as I crossed to him, and he straightened. He shot me a mock salute.

"Watch out," I said. "I know what you think of officers."

He barked a laugh.

I said, "We're just a couple of boys who like books, you and I."

"Sure," he said.

He turned and shut his hood.

"They've moved us up an hour," he said. "Won't be long."

I nodded toward the other drivers. "Just the three?"

"This time. From here we're joining a larger city convoy. We all go to Compiègne together, where we get dispersed to a sector along the Front."

"Our man Lacey?"

"On a different rotation."

I circled the Ford and put my bag behind the front passenger seat. Then Cyrus and I stood away from the auto a few feet and smoked together.

He was almost chatty for a time, playing his role of driver. He rattled on about tires and spark plugs and lubrication points. Then he fell silent.

I didn't initiate further conversation. We had plenty of time before us. A journalist's luxury. If your source has a chance to feel comfortable being silent with you, he'll be even more comfortable in talking later on.

We just smoked.

Then the pea-whistle chirped from the direction of the gate. I looked. A guy in a suit.

"Let's go," Cyrus said.

I stepped to the crank, caught it from beneath with my left hand, pushed it in, engaged its ratchet with the shaft, waited for Cyrus to advance the spark, and then I gave the crank a sharp lift.

Our Ford started up its phlegmy muttering, and we were ready.

The older driver led us out. Cyrus followed Jones.

We fell into a brisk pace. For now the only thing Cyrus said was in explanation of this: "We're playing catch-up."

And then no more words, as we pushed through intersections with our horns rather than our brakes.

Beginning an undercurrent of thought that I expected to be commonplace on this trip, words started bumping into each other in my head, grabbing partners, reeling along, improvising little tentative segments for the story I would write. In this case, the words were about our initial rush through the streets of Paris.

The coalescing story made me think of the message I'd received from Clyde.

I dipped into my pocket, pulled out the envelope, removed the telegram, and unfolded it.

Clyde wrote: *Good luck at front. As for your question I feel old realizing you are too young to recall Albert Parsons. 1884 he created, edited weekly Chicago newspaper, The Alarm. Younger brother Thomas his managing editor. Albert hanged 1887 for part in bombing at Haymarket Square labor riot. Thomas not implicated at Haymarket but paper was suppressed. He took off. Could be downstate. The two brothers were the newspaper voice of the anarchists.*

16

I'd been wrong once in this whole affair. About a German cuckold come to France to murder his wife's lover. I didn't need Trask to tell me I sure as hell better not be wrong about an American farm boy come to France to drive an ambulance in the war. But the smell of dynamite in public places was as much the smell of anarchy as it was of German terror.

As we blared our way across the *place* at the Porte de Champerret —prime bomb bait, certainly—I very casually folded the telegram, put it in my inner coat pocket and turned my face to the anarchist's son at the wheel.

He didn't look my way. But almost instantly he said, "Am I scaring you?"

I don't spook. Still. My farm boy surprised me.

His not looking my way didn't mean anything. I was in his peripheral vision. But you have to be thinking about the far edge of what you see in order to see it, and he was driving fast at the same time. Which meant he was watching me with intent.

Not that I took him for a mind reader.

It was his driving he was talking about.

I didn't reply.

He let the question sit between us for a few more moments.

Then he said, "We figure we own the streets of Paris when we're on the job."

Sure. It was about his driving.

He had no reason to suspect my suspicion.

I said, "A boy who can plow a straight furrow for his Pa can drive a flivver fast."

Let him hear me thinking about his father.

He barked a little laugh, though he mostly covered it with a simultaneous punch of the hand-horn at something before us.

He said, "What makes you think I ever mastered a straight furrow?"

"Farm boy to bookworm to ambulance driver. Princeton Illinois to Paris France to the front lines of the Great War. I bet you can do anything you put your mind to."

"Well, I'll be dogged," he said. But the words came after just long enough a hesitation—no more than a few ticks but long enough—to belie their intended impression of spontaneity.

I'd been around enough actors to hear them playing.

But I also heard myself. The way my mind was going. I'd mistakenly assembled Staub just like this. Finding little things. Thinking them out, seeing emotional logic in them. Believing they fit together in a pattern I was already expecting to find.

I looked away from Cyrus Parsons.

Just let him drive.

For now.

We were dashing freely along a stretch of great, peak-roofed, brick warehouses grouted with train tracks.

"You're right," he said. "I can do anything."

Anything? Was he baiting me?

I didn't turn to him.

There was time. We'd be a few hours on the road.

"This is the way to La Chapelle," I said. Small talk for now.

"That's our rendezvous point with the rest of the convoy," he said. "We head out through the city gate there."

He said this with his eyes forward. I looked forward too.

So we rushed on into the 18th arrondissement and arrived at the La Chapelle railway station and fell in behind a dozen other ambulances waiting for us there, Cyrus and I at the very rear. Then we moved off and out the city gate at La Villette, where the guard didn't even glance at our offered papers but cleared us by reaching out and patting the red cross on the side of our ambulance.

And through it all, what little Cyrus and I had said to each other were mere isolated exchanges, like the way through the warehouse park or the eventual fate of an oblivious pedestrian. No subtext. No complexity.

This arrangement had sprung up silently between us as surely as if we'd openly negotiated a cease-fire.

So too did the arrangement spontaneously end.

The convoy finally had sloughed off Paris, and all about us was the flat countryside of Route Nationale 2. We entered a long run of the road edged with poplars, and I was watching the dappled flash of tree trunks when Cyrus said, "So what's your assignment in France exactly?"

I looked at him.

He kept his eyes on the road.

Jefferson Davis Jones's flivver was a few dozen yards up ahead.

I wasn't answering instantly. Not as a rhetorical strategy. I was hesitating in order to stop myself from plunging forward at once as if he were guilty and he knew that I knew it. My strategy was still in the works, but at least for now I figured that would not be it.

Still. It was easy for me to catch an edge in the ambiguity of his words, even if I had to remind myself that it might just be me hearing what I expected to hear. Once again.

After a moment he clarified the question. "You interested in American ambulances or the action in the trenches?"

I said, "So you see through me, do you?"

That wasn't the way to go either, feeding the ambiguity back to him. It would do no good to stir up a suspicion in him.

"Do I?" He looked my way.

But I had to get to the bottom of this guy.

"The politicians," I said.

He furrowed his brow briefly before bringing his eyes back to the road.

I leaned a little his way. "You said yourself they got us into this war. Well, to keep us in it they don't trust us boys of the press to get too close to the action. Tending to the wounded is okay to report. The carnage and the despair in the first trench is another matter."

Cyrus nodded a faint smile. "So the ambulance stuff is just your ruse."

"Not entirely. I expect to do that story too."

"Both of them for the folks back home?"

"Primarily."

"You expect they'll help push America into the war?"

"My stories?"

"Yes."

I wasn't exactly sure what the anarchists would think about that. Would the intervention of still one more government authority be worse than a quicker end to an imperialist war started by other government authorities?

I said, "If you didn't have a father who was a journalist I'd just shrug my shoulders in reply."

"Act like the stories were of no consequence?"

"Just between us."

"If I wasn't afraid of running up Jeff's tailpipe, I'd turn around and watch that."

A quick calculation: I was good at playing roles. I'd play dumb. He himself had brought up his father's previous profession, after all. So I said, "Didn't your old man ever make a difference with a news story?"

"You ain't driving. Watch me shrug."

I looked at him.

He glanced at me and away. He shrugged.

Not to ask the next question would be more suspicious than asking it. I said, "What was his newspaper?"

"He made a difference for pigs and chickens."

He said nothing more.

I backed off.

I looked out the window.

We ran clear of the poplars.

Across a field of winter wheat was a tree line.

I thought of Cyrus's anarchist father turning himself into a farmer. And how Cyrus might have picked up the man's abandoned principles with a vengeance.

Then Cyrus asked, "What does *your* father do?"

For my country, over the past year and a half, I'd faced a dueling saber, various pistols and rifles, and a U-boat torpedo while standing on the deck of the *Lusitania*.

This felt like that.

I had no idea what my father does. Or did. Other than spawn me. Or even who he was. I could not remember ever being asked that question, the denizens of the backstages where I grew up understanding situations like this implicitly, particularly as part of the mystique of a great actress. I'm not sure I ever asked the question myself more than once. Not aloud. In my head, I still fought it off now and then.

I kept my eyes on the French farmers' fields.

For too long.

I didn't want the silence to suggest more to Cyrus than it already had.

I turned to him. Still not answering.

He flipped me a look, just to see what was going on.

The question still hung between us. What did my father do?

"Pigs and chickens," I replied.

Cyrus raised his eyebrows and said nothing.

Once more I put my eyes on the fields out the window.

But my mind was roiling around. Trying to yield up a strategy. I could fake a vague memory now. One connected to Cyrus. I could give him a *Wait a minute.* A meditative *Parsons, Parsons, Parsons.* A suddenly enlightened *Wasn't that the name of a newsman who got himself hanged in Chicago for inciting the anarchists' Haymarket Riot?*

What could that possibly get me? His admission of a connection I already knew. A connection that was a long way from making this American ambulance volunteer an anarchist bomber in Paris.

It could all be coincidence. An anarchist's act started the war. But why would an American anarchist want to blow up French civilians in a country at war with a German madman wearing a *Pickelhaube?*

More likely was a German saboteur in Paris. He just wasn't Franz Staub.

Whisking by were rows and rows of crop, the stubbled green crowns of winter wheat.

The front of my head muttered away: *This was enough for now. No more talk. I'll wait. Let him lead.*

Something else, however, deeper inside me, was beginning to assemble itself.

The great flat space of a crop field.

The trees at the edge.

Did the farmer own the abutting trees?

The echo of Cyrus's talk. Here in the ambulance. Rippling on back to the New York Bar. The disappointing father.

The field vanished now, hacked off in my sight by a stream.

And then another wheat field.

Out in the middle was a single, vast oak tree.

Cyrus spent his boyhood farming beside his father.

The field rushed past but the tree remained in my head. Winterleafless but full-branched. For a moment it struck me as odd. The farmer surely considered removing it, an impediment to plowing. But then I realized the tree was a place to pause and sit in the shade while doing his work.

All this clutter in my head, from the man driving the ambulance, from the passing landscape where I'd retreated.

And then it began to fall together: the stand of trees, the farmer's option to cut down that oak, clear it away, clear its stump. Clear the distant trees, too, if need be. And Cyrus coming as a young man to sneer at his once-anarchist father, a cause abandoned, a man become a farmer now. A man, in Cyrus's own words, happy slopping hogs and laying in corn. And clearing stumps.

My breath caught in my chest.

Farmers cleared and maintained their cropland with dynamite.

Cyrus the farm boy knew his dynamite.

And France needed its food. France needed all its arable land at full efficiency. Fortier and his boys had a tight grip on the dynamite in Paris. But did they harass the farmers over it as they tried to feed the troops?

I drew myself from the landscape. Slowly. As if with an empty head.

I faced forward in my seat.

I was conscious of Cyrus, though I did not look his way. He was driving his ambulance through this French farmland. Part of a convoy now but soon to be a free agent, solo with his ambulance, with duties at battlefield dressing stations and evacuation hospitals and railheads but with time alone on the road and time off as well. In a vehicle that checkpoint guards, without question, patted affectionately on the side and sent on their way. And every farm we passed had a storage shed with dynamite.

17

I had to think through what was next. Opportunity does not prove guilt. Even in coming to actionable conclusions while operating outside the law, as Trask and I and all our secret service cohorts and enemies were readily doing.

The momentum of the caution induced by the Staub mess persisted in me. All this could be more illusion. Or coincidence.

But the coincidence cut both ways. That I should have been sent on a wild-goose chase for the bomber of Paris and end up sitting next to him in an ambulance bound for the front line; or that this innocent man sitting beside me should have all these indicators of terrorist guilt.

But hell. Life is full of coincidence. Especially in war. Every battle I have covered was heaped with dead bodies rendered that way by coincidence. You coincidentally take a step this way instead of that and you're dead.

For now, though, I tried to convince myself that I didn't have to jump to any final conclusions on this venture to the battlefront. If the worst was true of Cyrus Parsons, he wasn't going to throw a bomb at the front line of the Great War. No one would notice. He was playing his other role now. Ambulance driver. As was I. Reporter. I could do all that I needed to do back in Paris by following the man in his off-hours.

So I considered accepting this caution, in full, as a present plan.

But that made me instantly, actively uneasy. To shadow a suspect is often an uncertain art. And ahead of us, for Cyrus and me, there were hours together on the road. For a man with a reporter's soul, this was a chance to dig. I had this guy sitting next to me who was redolent of dynamite.

But if I dug too much, pushed too hard, how deep would his suspicion run? Surely I would still only be a newsman to him. As long as my seeming foreknowledge, my lines of questioning, were no more than might come to a newsman, then there would be nothing to make him realize I am what I am. I suspected his two selves. He had no reason to suspect mine.

The point was to stop the killing of civilians.

Which meant I had to know if it might become necessary for me to kill him.

And with that thought I stopped thinking.

I listened to the agitated mutter and slap of the Ford engine, its pistons and its belts, felt the rush of the air around us.

I had no choice but to see what I could learn.

I'd go a little easy with the questions at first, but not from excessive caution. From the instincts of a reporter on a loose deadline dealing with a source potentially full of secrets he dare not divulge. Easy as if, for all that he would know, I was simply gathering information for the ambulance story.

The convoy began to slow and shift as far left on the highway as possible, into the oncoming lane. We passed a group of older men, too old for the trenches, wearing the blue tunics and red trousers of the last century. They were Territorials, breaking rocks and filling holes in the highway.

Beyond them we came up to speed again.

I squared around a little to Cyrus and said, "Can I get back to my job now?"

"Sure." He said it quick. As if he knew of only one job that I might mean. If he had doubts at this point, I'd fed him the perfect cue line to once again play it with ambiguity. *Which job is that?*

But he didn't.

Good.

I hesitated a moment. So I could start with easy questions but with my own agenda hidden in them like a roll of dynamite in a canvas bag in a corner of an ambulance.

I said, "That shrug I gave you earlier. I still have to write for those Americans, the ones who won't be swayed one way or the other about the war. The ones reading about you over their toast and eggs. Can you tolerate them for a few minutes?"

"We've got a long drive ahead of us."

"They want to know what daily life is like for an American ambulance driver in Paris. Where have the hospital people put you? Where do you sleep?"

"They've got a wing for us at Pasteur. Bunked up like patients."

Not a great setup to commence a shadow.

"How many around you?"

"Just me and Jack Lacey."

"Not bad."

"So you'd think." Meaning, in his tone, that I'd be wrong.

I figured I knew where he was going. The two men had seemed reasonably tolerant of each other at the New York Bar. But if Cyrus was a full-fledged anarchist, a guy like Lacey—from Harvard and, no doubt, from plentiful money made through demon capitalism—would be a constant irritation or worse. Cyrus had referred to him as "Jack." Not what Lacey insisted on, I bet.

I twisted my head slightly with a hint of a knowing smile. I'd think wrong if I thought he was fine with his roommate.

Cyrus saw it.

He smiled too. And he said, "He snores like a Brahman bull."

Cyrus surprised me enough to make me laugh out loud, given my assumption about his attitude and his multilevel wordplay from caste to class to Boston money, all caught in the breed of his animal metaphor.

He took my laughter without expression, but with a play in his eyes as if his blank mug was deliberate and he knew its effect and he was enjoying it with me. He did all this with the panache of a vaudeville comic. And I had a moment like the moment on our way to La Chapelle, when he spoke with feeling about the other Paris in The Zone beyond the Thiers Wall. I found myself liking this guy. The previous twinge was about his seriousness. This was about a light touch I hadn't expected. Objectively I realized the remark wasn't all that much, middling clever at best, but when somebody surprises you with a side to them you don't expect, especially a bad guy, it's easy to overvalue it.

I let that sequence of thought slip through me very quickly. To vent it off. To avoid losing my necessary ruthlessness, if and when it was called for.

So I played my upended expectation back at him. I said, "See, that surprises me," and I paused.

"What does?"

"Your humanizing him over his snoring, even if it's with a punch line. Especially when it's about a guy like John Barrington Lacey. You've made your feelings about authorities clear to me, from banks to politicians to military officers, even if they're wounded. I ask this not for the story. Just between us. Isn't a guy like Lacey a big problem for you?"

I was looking at Cyrus when I said this. He was looking at the road in front of him. He immediately shrugged. Just a little. Without playing to an audience. A goddamn sincere little shrug like he was giving a guy who was the very embodiment of one of Anarchism's enemies a free pass.

Cyrus glanced my way.

And he said, "He's all right," the words another mitigating shrug.

Why did all this piss me off?

Because I wanted Cyrus pure. If he was the bomber, I wanted what needed to be done to be easy. I was trying to put these little markers of humanity together with a guy who can bomb bistros and Metro stations, and I was having some trouble with that. Which made me understand what I was really wanting. For Cyrus Parsons to be the bomber, so Paris—and I—could have done with it.

I said, "Does our man from Harvard have depths?"

Cyrus looked over at me. Sized me up for a moment. Said, "Nah. I just stick cotton wool in my ears."

I let that stand.

I realized I should be happy if my own countryman turned out *not* to be the anarchist bomber of Paris.

We fell silent as the convoy squeezed right and we whisked past a farmer convoy of two horse carts, full of shipping tubs of milk.

Closer in to Paris, some of the farmers went all the way to Les Halles in their carts. Loaded up with food, a secretly munitioned farmer would get his own affectionate pat from the checkpoint guards.

Selective humanity does not prove innocence.

I had to go about this differently.

I pressed. "Aren't you letting him off the hook?"

Nothing from Cyrus for a moment. And then he said, "Do you care?"

I squared around to watch him now as we talked. "More than you realize," I said.

Cyrus glanced my way, noted my move, turned his face forward, rolled his shoulders as if he'd just settled into a pose he intended on keeping.

I said, "Not about him. About the folks beyond the wall."

"He's insignificant," Cyrus said. Sharply.

I thought: *That's more like the man I suspect.*

I said, "You've been honest with me from the jump. I appreciate that. I know a lot about where you stand. Let me be honest with you. You've got a sympathetic ear sitting next to you."

I paused for a moment to let that sink in. He was neither embracing or disputing the assertion.

I said, "That shrug again. I think we were both being a little too glibly cynical. I don't know anything about your dad's newspaper work. I'll take your word about the pigs and chickens. And it's true I get fed up with my own paper's boneheads whose two cents' worth every morning is to cluck and turn the page. But putting the word out has always changed minds. From Moses to Jean-Paul Marat to Thomas Paine."

I hesitated very briefly as I almost added Cyrus's Uncle Albert Parsons and made this all above board. But I'd just played dumb about his father. So I left it with Paine and added, "Hell. There were three revolutions that got a big boost from newspapers, a satchel full of pamphlets, and a stone slab."

This drew a glance from Cyrus. He was listening.

I said, "Those boys are in some whole other league. But I know how to get the attention of more than a few readers."

At best I expected another glance from him. But I got words, instant ones. "Like you said, I've been honest with you from the jump."

Thatta boy. I knew my way forward with him. I said, "So you and I agree this is a war about big business, big capital, big governments trying to grab all the wealth and power and then letting their competitive greed wreak even greater suffering on all the regular Joes of the world. The folks on the other side of the wall."

I paused again. To let him absorb this.

To let me absorb it.

I'd started playing a role inside a role. The reporter I can become—the reporter I *am*—was himself playing a role, one that I'd played with many a Chicago politician or policeman or gangster. You become the other guy. He hears a pal talking who understands him. So he can talk freely in return. What makes that succeed is playing your role right. Which means for as long as you stay in character, you actually see things the way you're saying them. The other guy hears it. He trusts you. So while I was feeding Cyrus what I knew he believed—what any full-fledged anarchist would also believe—for as long as I sat there saying it, giving it my best words, I believed it too. And maybe at least some of it I believed for real. Which was starting to muddy all this up again.

"So," I said. "What do you think I should tell my readers about this war? What do you think we all should do about it?"

Cyrus looked at me. He said nothing for a time. For a long time. For too long a time to be driving an ambulance in a convoy while looking hard into my eyes. Then he turned back to the highway before us, and he said, "You used the word yourself. Carnage. Rub their faces in the carnage. It's the only language people understand if they need to put their minds right. All carnage is equal, so just make the carnage real, make the carnage talk directly to them and they'll change whatever needs to be changed."

The place where I sat was cold. The open sides of our driving compartment were sucking the late autumn chill into our space at thirty miles an hour. But a singular dead cold suddenly surged up inside me that made the rest seem balmy. There were still questions about Cyrus Parsons. Questions that needed answers. But I was convinced now—in the visceral way reporters and spies needed to trust—that this was a dangerous man sitting beside me.

He turned his face to me briefly once more and said, "Can you do that?"

At first I thought he was talking to me. *Are you a good enough writer to do that?*

But then he said, "Can you do that with words?"

And I understood he meant it as a rhetorical question. A question for which he already knew the answer. *No. No you can't. Words aren't enough to make the carnage real.*

I decided to play dumb. I said, "I'll do the best I can."

He shrugged once more. To make up for my limitations, he was going to do the best he could, as well.

18

Something between us had shifted.

I didn't quite know what that meant for the trip ahead. I doubted that he did either.

If I was right about him, my real work would begin when we returned to Paris.

But for now it was clear enough to both of us that we had little more to say to each other.

Route Nationale 2 forked east toward Soissons, and we turned north and west to skirt the dense Forêt de Compiègne, the birch and beech hunting ground of French monarchs. Before the end of the afternoon we expected to be in Compiègne, where tomorrow we would be given our sector assignment.

We crossed the Oise and on its opposite bank joined the road that led east to Compiègne from Le Havre. But we'd barely made the turn along the river before a gray-and-blue Renault staff car overtook us, its Klaxon blaring, and it vanished from our sight up ahead. Soon the convoy slowed and then each of us in turn, by the example of the driver just before us, pulled off the road. We shut down our engines.

Our Fords sat end to end along the highway and we got out and a single word was passed along to us. "Troops."

We could already hear music, faintly cacophonous, and the low, massive thump of marching men. Cyrus and I sat down, side by side, on our Ford's running board. He bounced his pack of Gauloises at me. I waved it off and pulled out one of my Fatimas.

We lit up.

And soon they drew near. The tramping became the rock-grinding crunch of hobnail boots. The music at the head of them clarified into bugles and drums maintaining a familiar military marching cadence but laid over with the exotic nasal wanderings of hautboys.

These were not the men we expected. They were black men. Tall, powerful, beautifully precise, inspection-ready in their dark mustard uniforms. Chests with medals. The silver wreaths of the *Médaille Militaire* and the bronze, flare-footed crosses of the *Croix de Guerre.* These were veteran, tough, volunteer fighters from the French colonies. The *Tirailleurs Sénégalais.* Come from Senegal and French West Africa.

They marched past endlessly now, a yellow flag with crescent and star carried before most of the companies—the Senegalese were all Mohammedans—and a band played before each regiment. The company captains always seemed to be the largest of the men, towering well above any of us who sat with our ambulances watching.

And in their uniforms and bearing, these captains were sublimely strict in their adherence to regulations. Except in one detail. Always they wore their flat-topped kepis subtly askew, angled slightly toward one ear or the other, or pushed back a little from the brow, or tipped a bit forward.

The effect of all these distinctive, professional fighters flowing past was to mask with awe the silence between Cyrus and me. We smoked. We took an occasional pull on our water canteens. As the parade went on and on I daresay Cyrus had the same thought I did about the arrogance of the French commander who ran us off the road for his colonials just to assert his authority over us, when he could easily have let us make our faster way ahead of him and his troops. But we did not voice that between us.

Only once did Cyrus speak. Somewhere in the second hour, after we'd eaten hardtack and cheese from the provisions locker, Cyrus lit a cigarette and lifted his chin at the passing Africans. "This is not their war. They were once free men, freer than any of us have ever been. But the things the Allies rightly despise about the Germans in this war, they are guilty of themselves. France and the Brits and the Belgians—all of them—they marched into Africa and subjugated these black men and their tribes. No one had the right to do that."

A couple of hours before I'd stopped feeling the need to actively play my role of Cyrus's philosophical sympathizer. But I myself had seen enough of the world for this fragment of anarchist screed to make sense to me.

And somehow, ironically enough, his comment finally allowed me to put Cyrus's small touches of humanity together with his suspected capacity to plant bombs in bistros. Words weren't enough. Bombs and civilian blood were necessary to save the oppressed and compliant peoples of the world. Nothing else had ever worked. So make the carnage real.

Then at last they were gone. A division's worth.

Their hobnails still rang in our ears.

The late-autumn early dusk was upon us.

We cranked our engines and reassembled our convoy for the final dozen miles to Compiègne. It was quite dark now and our electric headlights lit only the red cross on the back of Jones's ambulance up ahead. We set off at a marching pace, as the division was still ahead of us. But that didn't last. We began to accelerate, and as we did, I looked at the passing dark. The *Tirailleurs Sénégalai* had left the road and somewhere out there they were bivouacking.

Half an hour later, on the edge of Compiègne, we turned off the highway and into a graveled field on the bank of the Oise. Other ambulances were already there. We parked in an orderly row and pulled our kits from our Fords and crossed the field, heading toward an adjacent barracks, our raggedly arrayed group and gravel-shuffling feet put to shame by the lingering image in our heads of the marching men from Africa.

I was the only initiate in the group, and I gathered quickly that we would drop our kits and reconvene in double time to head down the

highway to a tavern at the nearby inn. I followed Cyrus up the barracks
stairs to the second-floor common room, dim with gas lamps turned
low and full of metal bunks. I picked an empty bed and laid my kit in
its center. Though we'd spoken little, Cyrus stepped to the next bunk
and claimed it, setting his bag on the floor at its head, on the far side.

He turned and looked at me.

We held each other's eyes for a beat. Then he nodded, and he
said, low, "Sleep long tonight. Tomorrow I'll get you to the front line."

At the tavern he drifted away from me. The air was thick with
French cigarette smoke, smelling as if the timbers of the room
were invisibly on fire. I sat with other drivers—two French and one
Canadian—and played the part of an American newspaperman doing
a story about volunteer ambulance drivers in France. If Cyrus got me
to the front in the morning, the first thing I had to know was when he
rotated back to Paris. That would become my return date too.

The wine was *St. Pinard*, the poilus' wine in the trenches, rationed
half a liter per day. It was made for courage not taste, a poor red with
a hint of gasoline in the nose. My heart wasn't in the ambulance story,
for which I had enough information anyway. But the Frenchmen were
charming and each had been involved in early battles, one at the Marne,
one at the Aisne, and they had good war stories, the latter's directly
relating to the battlefield where I was headed. So I prepared myself
for the trenches for about an hour and then excused myself from my
drinking companions.

I squeezed my way around the room, once, looking for Cyrus,
but I did not find him. He was right. I should get some rest. If I was
going to spend a night awake, it should be tomorrow, as close to the
first trench as he could get me.

I went out into the night and walked the half mile back to the
barracks.

At the doorway a sound made me pause and turn to face northeast.

Distant thunder. At the night's invisible horizon.

But of course it wasn't thunder. It was the sound of the German
150s saying good night to the boys in the trenches.

I went up the stairs.

The gas lights were turned even lower. Men were snoring down the way.

I approached my bunk.

Just beyond was Cyrus, sitting on the side of his bed, his back to me.

I stopped.

He was absolutely still.

I hesitated. But then I stepped past my bunk and stood before him. He looked up.

In the dim light, his face darkened even more by my shadow over him, I could not make out his expression. I said, "What's on your mind?"

He did not answer.

The silence went on long enough that I thought to simply move away.

Just before the thought turned to action, Cyrus said, "My uncle was also a newsman. They hanged him for it."

Was he ready to talk anarchism?

I said, "So somebody thought words mattered."

As quietly as if talking to himself, Cyrus said, "I never even knew him."

I waited for more.

But instead, he swung his feet up and lay back on his bed.

The theater has helped me. As a reporter. As a spy. But sometimes it makes me stupid. Standing there over Cyrus Parsons it felt to me as if the curtain had simply gone down on the act and intermission had begun.

But when I woke at the first swelling of predawn light, Cyrus was gone.

19

It took a little while to figure out how gone he was.

His bag was still there, though eventually it would yield only a few pieces of clothing.

The bed was unmade. But he had seemed deeply weary when he'd lain back. It would not have been surprising to find that he'd fallen asleep at once and had arisen only a few minutes before I was now arising.

Eventually I was standing in the center of the parking field and recognizing the empty space where his Ford had been parked. And realizing that it was the only one missing from the cluster of our convoy's ambulances.

Still my mind was slow.

I thought perhaps now was when Cyrus was meeting with a local farmer, a collaborator, who was supplying him with dynamite. And perhaps indeed he was—or had been some hours ago, in the middle of the night—but for the moment I could not bring myself to fully let go of the possibility that he would return. Perhaps Christopher Cobb the newsman was trying to play dumb, trying to think he still had the upper hand in me, still could get himself to the front lines and do his story.

I went to the French lieutenant who was the commanding officer of the assignment station. He agreed to take over the search, saying, in English, "The men they are very full with stress. I know from some different time one man who just runs away for the stress. They only volunteer, you know."

He made a sympathetic shrug.

His shrug clarified things for me.

How inadequate it was.

I knew without a doubt that Cyrus was not returning. Cyrus was abandoning his cover identity. Cyrus was returning to Paris to fully devote himself to the carnage.

I asked the lieutenant to arrange passage for me back to Paris as soon as possible.

Compiègne was a railhead, and by mid-morning I was in a sideways wooden chair at the end of a car in an ambulance train. Heading for La Chapelle. An officer car. With a nurse in constant attendance and single bunks along its length instead of three-high stretcher racks. I was conscious, of course, of the irony, chasing Cyrus while surrounded by the privilege of the ruling class. Amongst his "fucking officers." They suffered, however, with the same muted moanings and muttered thank-yous in the same matrix of stoic silence as did the working class.

And I was very conscious of how complicated this work had become. The Mexican revolutionaries and the German secret agents and the Turk pashas were simple. Germans in love were another matter. And there was nothing more complicated for me than the enemy likely being one of our own. An American. With the vestiges of an American conscience.

All of which was on my mind when I telephoned Trask at the embassy from the French commander's office at La Chapelle. I'd alerted him by telegraph from Compiègne, saying only that I was returning at once from the front and urgently needed to see him at my hotel and that I'd call him from the terminus as soon as I got in.

He wasn't in his office.

He was sitting on my doorstep in his Pierce-Arrow when I arrived.

His man opened the door to the vestibule.

Trask moved a stack of newspapers from the seat to the floor in front of him.

I sat down in their place.

"I called," I said.

"I had to read the dailies anyway," he said. "For you to give up the front has captured my interest."

I told him the story of Cyrus Parsons.

Through it all he did not ask a question, did not say a word. I was used to the man, used to his opaquely black eyes never wavering when I spoke, used to his persona of command, which involved seeming always rational. But when I quoted to him, with a reporter's precision, Cyrus's tribute to carnage, his own spy instincts would not be suppressed. His eyes moved sharply away from mine, pulling his face with them. He listened to the rest of my story while staring out the side window.

The vision he pondered in his distant stare became clear as soon as I was done. He turned back to me, his eyes fixing me once more, and he said, "We can't let this be an American."

For diplomatic appearances, his basic thought was rational. What I'd expected. His eyes were rational again. But his phrasing was still emotional.

He nodded slightly downward, at the stack of newspapers, without moving his eyes from mine, and said, "Especially with the Brits and the French about to put their heads together."

I looked.

The paper on top of the stack was the *Excelsior*. It gave me a deep thump of regret over getting caught up in the spy stuff to the detriment of my war correspondence. I was tempted to jump out of Trask's car and beat it back to the front and write the real news. The photo-infatuated *Excelsior* was published daily for the Parisians who'd happily given up reading books to go to the movies. Virtually its entire front page was a photograph. A front page that had never shown a dead French soldier. Instead it gave us the image of a very recently built luxury hotel, the first on the Left Bank, the massive Hôtel Lutetia, with a ripple of balconies across its massive facade, each wreathed in Art Nouveau stone vinery. This was war news straight from the French

government's rah-rah storybook, the Lutetia being the location of the
big meeting, day after tomorrow, between General Joffre and General
Murray, chief of the British general staff. The French and Brits would
work out a winning strategy for the Great War in a timbered suite in
a luxury hotel over a glass of Château-Lafite or a pot of tea.

For one odd moment, from the very same prompt, I simultaneously understood and sympathized with both Cyrus Parsons and
James Polk Trask.

The Parsons half of this, which had lent some power to the thump
of regret, faded quickly. His desire to make the truth of the trenches
known and his sympathy with the working masses of humanity were
just features on a mask to disguise an all-too-human face. Lying and
killing was the father of all of us and it showed. And Cyrus was eager
to embrace it for his own ends.

My basic quarrel with Woodrow Wilson was his hesitation to go
to war. To my surprise I even understood and sympathized with Woody
as well. It was a grisly nuance to tell one bullet from another, even if
the nuance was true and right and the whole goddamn point. Woody
needed a backbone to come in and help end this thing as quickly as
possible. But he needed moral authority to effectively do that. I knew
what Trask was getting at. These boys over here, fighting to protect or
enlarge their empires, would just go on and on if they stayed in charge.
America needed to run the show. If Wilson's best play for America
was for us to stand on the moral high ground, we couldn't have weeds
growing at our feet up there.

Trask said, "Have you been to Neuilly?"

"I came straight here. Neuilly's next."

"He won't be there."

"I'll look for leads," I said.

"How?"

"As his friend, with the people who worked with him. My assumption will be theirs. He cracked. He's in emotional trouble. I can
help him."

Trask paused for a few moments.

Only with his words. His gaze intensified in a physical way I could not identify. Nothing to do with his eyes. But it was somehow clear. He was powering up his focus on this problem and I felt it just as I'd felt Cyrus's guilt.

Then he said, "You have to work this alone."

"I understand."

"Keep Fortier out of it."

That kept America out of it. I understood. But finding Cyrus wasn't going to be easy. And it could quickly get harder. I didn't like the chances of his having left any discernible clues to his on-the-lam plan with the do-gooders at the hospital.

I said, "I understand about Fortier. There are important nation-to-nation issues involved. But those same issues are at play if I fail to catch this American, and catch him quick, because the police, or even Fortier's boys themselves, might get lucky at some point and collar him themselves. Especially if Cyrus steps up his game."

"So what are you saying?"

I knew I had to say it firm and fast and without pause and not give Trask time to pick at me without the whole argument in his head. I said, "We could use some eyes and ears. Looking for the ambulance, for instance. Cyrus will likely abandon it pretty quickly, but we'd like to get to it and the area it's in as soon as possible. Fortier owes us. Owes *me* after the Staub affair. Tell him I'm back building my cover story. Being a reporter. Covering the ambulance boys. He can at least alert his people to the missing ambulance and let us know if they spot it. Hell, you're at the embassy. He owes you too. Tell him the ambassador himself is worried about our saintly American volunteer. Can he help us out? There is no way he'd guess that the missing driver is connected to the terror. He's still thinking the Huns are behind the bombs."

I rested my case.

Trask hadn't tried to interrupt, though his eyes never left me. He even allowed the following silence to have its own brief, distinct moment.

Then he gave me a thoughtful humph.

He said, "I'm ready to buy part of what you're saying. But what if, for now, the ambulance was stolen by a party unknown. A German saboteur potentially. An American ambulance can get into places a man with a satchel of dynamite over his shoulder couldn't. If that's the threat they think they're helping with, you'll get the same lead from its discovery without our having to show our hand. And with a keener motivation for them."

Trask laid all this out as if he was conferring with me. I knew he'd already made his decision. But he was right.

"You're right," I said.

He nodded once, with a slight of-course-I-am head twist to it. "I'll talk to him. You should keep in periodic touch with me by telephone. At the embassy. Or my room at the Hôtel Montaigne. Be careful, of course. These instruments are technically not secure. But the risk of a German spy infiltrating a French telephone exchange is very low. The odds of being overheard are even lower. The vast amount of irrelevance and the randomness of things for a given operator make it unfeasible for them. Let's just be mindful of what we say."

The beat that followed made that sound like the end of it. But before I could reply, Trask surprised the hell out of me. He added, "I trust you, Kit. You know what's involved. Not just telephones. In all of it."

If pushed on the matter, I'd have assumed as much. But this sentimentality wasn't like him. I almost asked him if he was feeling okay. Alternatively, I almost thanked him. I did neither.

I gave him a tiny, Traskian nod.

He shifted in his seat as if to slough off whatever it was that had come upon him. He said, "In some ways it's peculiar. If Parsons was going to break cover, why did he bother to drive you to the front?"

Not so peculiar. An answer to that had been gnawing at me off and on through the train ride back to Paris. One that I'd assiduously not examined. I accepted it now. Too bad it would undercut the recent bona fide compliment from this man. I said, "That was me. My questions got too close."

"You the reporter." His tone was matter-of-fact. Almost exculpatory.

"Me the reporter."

"That you is even better working for his country," he said, though this too was free from rebuke. It sounded almost like an addendum to his compliment.

"I left that guy in Compiègne," I said, firmly. "Except as disguise."

"Good. But it's also true if Parsons had picked up on the real Cobb, if he'd thought you identified him as the bomber, you'd have been found dead in your bunk this morning."

True enough.

It was my turn to look out the side window to examine my own thoughts.

"So who is this Cyrus Parsons guy?" He didn't ask this rhetorically. It sounded like a sincere, shared puzzlement. "What flushed him?"

I found answers out in the cobbled street. Several of them. They all worked together, I figured.

"His father. His uncle. The Africans," I said, bringing my face back to Trask to enjoy the flicker of puzzlement in his eyes.

I said, "From the start I got him talking about things that were working in him. It finally all added up. The father he criticizes was an anarchist who ran from the game. The uncle he reveres was an anarchist who played out his beliefs in public and went to the gallows for them. And on our last day, Cyrus and I watched ten thousand African volunteers march by to fight an unholy war for the country that had conquered and subjugated them. Cyrus was already executing a plan to upset a world like that. He decided to do it full-time."

Trask puffed a soundless little laugh. "Hell. What's a parade for?"

I said, "There was that moment when I heard him for what he was. You heard it too, when I told you. I bet he heard it about himself. Yeah, he's an American. A regular entrepreneur. He's got a better brand of carnage. He's out on the road to promote his product."

"Well then," Trask said. "Go find him and quietly kill him."

20

I entered the hospital at the Lycée Pasteur an hour later. It had now been nine hours since they knew in Compiègne that Cyrus was gone. I struck off down the hallway of the administrative wing, heading for the superintendent's office, and the ease with which I'd approached the building and entered it dropped a satchel of dynamite into the center of my thoughts. If Cyrus had come back to Paris to resume his bombing with singular commitment, what would he see as the most effective settings for his tableaux of carnage? I feared I was walking in one. The officers' ward no doubt. And anyone in its vicinity. This thought came to me even as I entered the dim blur of afternoon sunlight from the window before which Louise had asked about the scar on my cheek. *Are there more of these?* No there aren't. And she chose me so as to forget the carnage.

I forced all this from my mind.

Not that I could kid myself. Louise was in danger.

Which presented me with a serious dilemma when, shortly thereafter, Pichon burst from his office at the sound of my voice to his aide. He grabbed my hand and shook it and let it go and with a bowing, urgent sweep of his arms ushered me into his office and into the chair in front of his desk.

Clearly word had arrived that one of his drivers had vanished. He sat down.

But my dilemma was a moral one whose only resolution concerned how to suffer the biting of my own tongue without letting on. With this man, my course of action was already decided. He and his hospital and everyone in it had to come to this place without knowing the danger.

But so would thousands of other people in a hundred other settings in Paris.

I said to myself: *For my mission, for my country and, potentially, for its eventual role in this war I had no choice.* There was only one way for me to protect these people. Including Louise.

"I come to you as Cyrus's friend," I said to Pichon, speaking careful French.

"He has not returned with you?" Pichon said.

"No."

"We have had only a brief telegram from the authorities," he said. "Only that our driver and his ambulance were missing. We were to tell them if Monsieur Parsons were to appear. No mention was made of you. Our hope was that you were somehow called back to Paris and he consented to bring you."

"No. Of course not."

"Ah yes," Pichon said. *Mais oui.* "Of course not. It was simply our hope. But when the authorities suggested you might appear here, that hope seemed justified. Our *fear*, however, was that he took you onward to the trenches as you wished and you were both lost to the German guns. I am very happy to see you. We all will be."

I heard in that a reference to Louise. She was worried. That brought an upswell in me. A tender thing. And a fearful thing, as well.

Pichon went on. "Of course there is one other reason we might expect him at our door. We have had other men leave their duties abruptly. The work can become too much."

It was time to play a new part. "That's my fear," I said. "Please understand that I have returned to Paris and come to you not as a reporter but as a friend to Cyrus."

"I appreciate that, Monsieur Cobb."

"He is my countryman. On the road to Compiègne he found in me a person ready to listen to his feelings. He suffered greatly with the wounded. You are right. It became too much for him. But I am in good position to help him. I criticize myself for failing to make that clear. You and I both care about him, Monsieur Pichon. May we share information as we find it?"

"Of course. We will do everything we can for him. He is a true friend of the people of France."

"It's urgent to find him," I said.

"I agree."

"Do you have any idea where he might go if he has returned to Paris?"

Pichon knitted his brow, angled his face downward. "I am trying to think if he ever said… The drivers frequent an American bar. Somewhere near the Place Vendôme, I believe. But I did not socialize with Monsieur Parsons. I could not say for certain."

Cyrus was not assembling his bombs at the Lycée Pasteur. I approached the crucial question. "He lived at the hospital facility?"

"Ah yes. We provide a place to live."

"But he would live with another driver?"

"They live in twos or fours. All the Americans are in Lycée recitation rooms, so yes, he would have one roommate."

"Do your volunteers ever take a separate room somewhere in the city? Perhaps for occasional privacy?"

"It is permitted. They are not strictly bound by military rule. At least not in their free time. Some days they must be available here. Most days. But not all."

"Do you know if he took a room away from the hospital?"

"I do not. Some of them tell us so. But there is no requirement. No way for us to check. Monsieur Parsons never spoke of such a thing."

I thanked Pichon and we rose and shook hands. "I think you may be right," he said. "It is urgent. It is sometimes difficult to predict just how fragile someone might be."

"I will do my best to help," I said. "Can you tell me how to find two people at this hour? Supervising Nurse Pickering for one."

"Ah yes. She will be glad to see that you are safe. She is likely with the wounded officers."

I worked hard not to show the special concern this stirred. "And John Lacey."

"Monsieur Lacey? Ah yes. Now that you say his name…This of course is why you ask."

"Yes. His roommate."

"I am not sure of the drivers. But when they are working in Paris, they often take care of their ambulances."

I had one other destination in mind. I was happy to have a way to ask for it without risking any scruples Pichon might have about me going through Cyrus's things. I said, "If Monsieur Lacey isn't working on his vehicle, perhaps I could catch him in his room. Can you direct me there as well?"

"Yes," he said. "Realize that none of the drivers yet know about Monsieur Parsons. It is time to amend that. But you may find Monsieur Lacey first."

A few minutes later I was at a closed door in a presently deserted wing. I listened. There were no sounds inside. I knocked lightly and spoke Lacey's name. No answer. I tried the handle. It was unlocked.

I went in.

The place was comfortable for two people. Flanking the set of mullioned windows were single bunks. At the foot of each was a canvas trunk. Against the opposite wall sat an oversized wardrobe.

Both beds were made neatly.

Both trunks held nothing but the foldable components of the standard-issue driver's uniforms and generic men's underthings and casual civilian clothes. One had more of these items and also a leather bag for toiletries. This was Lacey's trunk, I presumed, Cyrus's equivalents being in the valise he had with him on the trip to Compiègne.

Beside the wardrobe sat Lacey's leather Gladstone bag, which was empty. Within the wardrobe, one side held the hangable components of the standard-issue driver's uniforms and an assortment of civilian clothes. The other side, clearly Cyrus's, held only a couple of short-sleeved shirts. On the floor, a pair of shoes and a pair of boots, each of which I shook, finding nothing inside.

The double drawers at the bottom of the wardrobe distinguished the two men. One had letter-writing materials but no saved correspondence; its three books were Joseph C. Lincoln Cape Cod novels. Lacey, a Harvard man with plebian tastes in literature.

In the other drawer was a layer of everyday items. Woolen socks. Pocket handkerchiefs. A union suit. But beneath these, Cyrus began to show himself. An Abercrombie sheath knife with a six-inch blade and an ebony handle, which I pulled from its leather holder. Knowing it was his, I held it up before me and considered its fine steel blade. Had he ever killed a man in a personal way? Face to face? With this? I doubted it.

I returned the knife to its sheath.

The last item, lying facedown in the bottom of the drawer, was a book. Its boards were red cloth. I picked it up, turned it over. In fancy letters on a fancy gilt banner, the title was simple: *Anarchism*. Beneath it: *By Albert R. Parsons*. Uncle Albert. Four parallel black lines partitioned the upper couple of inches of the cover and provided the horizon for a rising gilt sun, beside which were the golden words:

Though dead,

He yet speaketh.

I opened the book and it yielded a place readily, a quarter of the way in. Readily because the page was marked by a photolithograph of a mustachioed man, printed on heavy tobacco-card paper. I removed the card but before I turned my attention to it, my eyes fell to the middle of the page.

A passage there had been marked by a thin pencil line in the margin. "We have said to the toilers that science had penetrated the mystery of nature—that Jove's head once more has sprung a Minerva—dynamite!"

Now I looked at the man on the card.

He startled me.

I thought for a very brief moment that it was a picture of Cyrus. It was a young face. And though the man had a wide-winged pointed mustache and Cyrus was clean-shaven, these eyes instantly evoked him, in shape and demeanor. They were prominent, engaged, but narrow set. The shape of this face spoke of Cyrus too, the quick narrowing of the jaw from ear to chin. The bloodlines were unmistakable. I did not need to read the name beneath the image to know who it was. *Albert Parsons.* And beneath his name, three words: *Sentenced to Death.* These cards were sold as souvenirs at the hanging.

I put it in my pocket.

I closed the drawer.

And I made my way to the officers' ward.

I moved along the hallway, pausing at each room. In one a nurse had her back to me. The uniform alone stopped me, but the shape within it was wrong and instantly I moved on. I paused at the next doorway, and just as I was turning my head to look inside, I saw a movement up ahead.

Louise emerging from a room two doors up.

She saw me and squared to me, her face opening. She came to me, swiftly, as if she were going to throw herself into my arms and I took a step toward her, hoping for that indeed.

But she slowed abruptly, her face not changing in its joy but nodding a little as we wordlessly shared the reason she hesitated, to keep our private acts unsuspected, and then she was near me and nearer still, less than an arm's length, but we both knew we should not embrace here.

It was late afternoon and the lilacs had utterly vanished from her. She smelled of carbolic and of lime liniment, which did not fully mask the smells of wrecked bodies beneath.

I realized these smells were also a reason she held back.

Because I realized that, I said to her, very low, "You are very beautiful right now. Doing what you do."

At this, her hand came to me and I took it and we held tight and she said, "I was so very worried for you."

"I know."

"I'm glad it was this."

I squeezed her hand gently.

"If it had to be something," she said. "I'm glad that it didn't catch you up in it."

"I understand," I said.

"Can you come to me tonight?" she said.

"Where?"

"I live away from the hospital," she said, and she gave me her address, not far from the hospital, toward the river along the Rue Perronet. "I'll be finished here and presentable to you by nine."

"I'll be there," I said.

"Poor Cyrus," she said.

"I'm trying to find him."

"Yes," she said. "I've thought for some time there is something going on in him. He should not be alone with whatever it is."

"I agree."

"Be a friend to him," she said.

For my country, to do my job, I have played roles with a number of people, deceived them, lied to them. This present lie was easy to conceive and absolutely necessary to live by, but it stuck in my throat and I had to will it into words. "I will," I said, and the egregiousness of it was because I told it to Louise. Because I lied about something she wanted of me, prompted by the gentle, nurturing nature in her.

But lie I did. And once it was done, I now had to repeat it to make sure it remained a lie, did not become true, even for her sake, because of how this all had to end. So I said, "I will be his friend."

"If there's anything I can do to help," she said.

"We'll talk tonight," I said.

We let go of our hands. And I ached to take her in my arms now and kiss her, and I knew for certain she felt the same way.

But we did not kiss.

Having let go of our hands, at the very same moment we nodded to each other.

And I turned and walked away.

21

I found Lacey with his Ford, along with a few other ambulances and their fiddling or lolling drivers, at the maintenance shed near the porte cochere of the hospital's cobbled frontage. His front axle was up on jacks and he was on one knee working at the driver-side wheel bearings with a wrench. He heard my footsteps on the cobble and glanced up as I drew near. He reared back, stood up. Not from deference to me personally. I'd read him sufficiently at the New York Bar to know that much. He knew where I was supposed to be and was surprised I wasn't there. Was he inferring trouble concerning his roommate?

"John," I said, and I offered my hand.

He looked away, took up a rag draped over the wheel and wiped the grease from his right hand. He then shook mine.

"They teach you this at Harvard?" I said, nodding at his wheel.

"I've always been handy," he said. And then, "Aren't you supposed to be at the front?"

"Yes," I said. I let that stand for a brief moment. I found myself instinctively approaching Lacey as if he had a story I needed to finesse from him. How an anarchist crypto-bomber and a Boston Brahmin figured out a way to get along was an interesting enough question that my reporter's guile had kicked in. I'd give him at least an initial chance to guide the conversation according to his relationship with Cyrus.

"Is there anything wrong?" Lacey said.

Once I was standing before him, shaking his hand and making small talk, the only thing *wrong* one could infer about this would concern my driver, not me. So yes. Lacey had a reason to infer trouble around his roommate.

"I'm afraid so," I said. "Cyrus and his ambulance took off sometime late last night or early this morning."

I watched Lacey closely.

He went absolutely dead still for one beat. Two. Then it sunk in. Or he let it sink in. Or he decided no reaction at all was unseemly, that he was revealing too much, such as he despised this guy he lived with. In theory, he would despise him. He compressed his brow and eyes and swung his face away. "Good Lord," he said.

I let him have the gesture in peace for a few moments and then asked, "Does this surprise you?" I twisted the end of the question to suggest I doubted it.

He turned his face full upon me again. The deadness was gone. But so was the compression. He seemed to be assessing me. I said, "I think I saw concern in you as you rose a few moments ago. Before I said a thing."

He rolled his shoulders a bit. "I forget you're trained in this, trying to read people. For your work, I presume."

"I don't mean to sound critical. And I don't presume to read you. I'm not doing my work now. This isn't for the newspaper. I genuinely like Cyrus. He seems to care about how the world runs, that it should be fair to all, and I can respect that."

I expected Lacey to do a Beacon Hill tut tut at this, but he did not. He looked at me steadily for a moment, as if reassessing me. Then he said, "Took off?"

"Yes. Your man Pichon says it happens sometimes. The stress."

"He's not my man."

"The superintendent."

"I have no doubt it does."

"Did you see the signs in Cyrus?"

"I don't read people."

This clearly wasn't the way to work this guy. So I said, "Look, I'm sorry I got us off on the wrong foot. It's just that I spent some extended time with Cyrus and I liked him. His honesty, for one thing. He's pretty open about his politics. Even with me, a prying newspaper man. I want to help him. I liked him. His . . ."

For the second time in the past half hour I had trouble saying the lie I knew I had to say, though for an opposite reason. I got it out: "His *humanity* I'd call it. That had to be a big part of why you're all here. He had it strongly. Now he's vanished and I have no doubt it's for that. He just couldn't be around the suffering from this war."

I paused. Whatever I didn't like about John Barrington Lacey, he was indeed here in Paris, driving an ambulance.

But my revised approach didn't seem like it was doing much good. Lacey was listening to me but he'd gone blank again.

I said, "I just want to help the guy if I can. He's out there somewhere alone and maybe breaking down. From the time you've spent with him, can you remember anything that could lead us to where he might go?"

Lacey didn't answer for a long moment, never altering his face, his gaze. He could have been trying to remember something that could help. He could have been cursing at me from a high and superior perch.

Then he lingered on my own transitional word from a minute ago. "Look," he said. From a high and superior perch. "I got thrown in randomly with this hayseed autodidact Cyrus Parsons from Illinois, and I have made the best of it. I heard the same talk you did. But I don't know a thing about him. I doubt you do either. If he's chosen to go somewhere away from all of us, then I'd suggest we all just let him be."

The silence that followed was a that's-all-I-have-to-say silence and I gave him some of his own blankness. I would let him break this off.

He did so with a flourish of Ford Baroque. "My vehicle has a loose front wheel. I have examined the spindle in the front axle and found it to be tight, so I have, as well, carefully examined the spindle cones, along with the balls and races in the wheel. And now I am adjusting the wheel bearings. All of which will allow me to safely transport the wounded of this war. Would you mind if I return to my work?"

I did not allow my sigh to vocalize itself. I said, "You are indeed one handy Harvard man."

"I am indeed," he said.

"If you didn't snore you'd be perfect," I said.

22

For personal reasons I didn't want to see anyone else on this day but Louise, but at this point she was also the next best hope for an immediate lead. A quarter past eight, I stepped out of my hotel, but before I sought a fiacre, I walked down to the Boulevard Saint-Germain and passed under the blue night-light of a post office and into the lobby and into an oaken *cabine téléphonique*. I called Trask at his hotel. He answered.

"Are they helping?" I asked.

He said, "The gendarmes will keep an eye out for the ambulance. I think I caught Fortier after a bottle of red. He grew sentimental over our American volunteers and their touching love for *la belle France*."

"A reminder of why I better work fast."

"My very next words to you."

"How urgently will he tell you if they find the ambulance?"

"Urgently. I portrayed our man as a potential suicide."

"Even in the night?"

"It's possible. I would send my driver for you at once."

I had to make a tough, quick decision.

I said, "I am about to see the Supervising Nurse. She is the best and perhaps the last chance from the hospital for a line on Cyrus. I'm meeting her at her rooms."

I let that sit in him a moment.

"Do you understand?" I said.

"You know your work," he said. "Is there a telephone?"

"Not with her. Perhaps in the building. I doubt it."

There was a moment of silence.

Usually this was a very odd thing, with a telephone. An unsettling invention, really. A person is with you, very much so, inside your ear, inside your head. And then he seems to utterly vanish. Like a kind of death.

But in this instance, Trask and I continued to communicate somehow. He did not have to ask. I said, "105 Rue Perronet. Second floor rear."

"Call me when you are elsewhere," he said. "Whenever that might be."

"I will," I said, and we rang off.

To his credit, his tone had been flat in his last remark. Not a wisp of a leer. *You know your work*, he was saying. Having to draw Louise into this conversation like that was necessary for my task. But I felt bad. In a complicated way. Shooting an enemy to death was quite a lot simpler.

I arrived before Louise's *maison* in a dark stretch of the street. The concierge was asleep on a wooden chair in his *loge*, and I went up the staircase to the second floor and knocked at her apartment.

Almost at once the door swung open and Louise was before me in a kimono negligee, brightly beflowered. Her feet were bare. She smelled of lilacs once more. She took my hand, drew me in, and closed the door.

I took her into my arms.

We kissed.

And then she took up my hand once more and we continued to say nothing as she led me to her bedroom. She closed the door behind us and extinguished the electric light immediately, while we were still clothed. She did not need to view my body on this night. I was no longer a matter of therapy. I was glad for that.

As soon as the room was dark, I heard the rustle and tumble of crepe de chine.

And I was glad for the dark, as well, so that I could wrap my Mauser inside my shed clothes, unseen.

For a long while thereafter, in the bed, we touched and touched, and still not a single word was uttered.

Then we folded ourselves together, the darkness around us mitigated only very slightly by the seep of starlight at the edges of the shutter louvers. I could see the shape of her as she pressed against me, but when she lifted her face for a coda of a kiss, I could not see her eyes.

Then we lay still, as if to sleep, though neither of us did.

I began to think of what I needed from her, of what I needed to withhold from her. How to balance these things. How to do this while we still lay naked together.

But it was Louise herself, after a sudden sigh and a rippling adjustment of her body against mine, who brought up Cyrus. "Are you any closer to finding him?"

"Not yet," I said.

"Will you be able to apply your skills?"

I angled my face toward her, stalled very briefly by my mind hearing reference to the killing set of skills presently animating me. But of course she meant the skills of the only Kit Cobb she knew. She sensed my hesitation and she giggled us back to what we had just done together. "Skills as a *reporter*," she said.

I said, "Your lilac water has gone to your head, Supervising Nurse Pickering."

She slapped me lightly on the cheek.

I grabbed the hand and kissed it.

She turned her palm against mine and we interlaced our fingers and we held on for a time, even after our outburst of playfulness had dissipated.

I was surprised to find that I felt content.

Then once more it was she who drew us back to business. "I've been thinking what you might ask me to understand Cyrus's story. To help you find him."

"And?"

"He didn't confide in me particularly. The things I know of him he readily showed. He was angry. And he was passionate for the wounded. But very angry. On their behalf."

"He made that clear to me."

"But we all are, those of us so close to the personal consequences of this war. I'm angry too."

Louise was smart. The world was alert to anarchy. If Cyrus's anger came across to her as focused wholly on the suffering of the battlefield, he must have carefully modulated the expression of his fuller beliefs with people like her. Some of the things he said to me, the scraps of anarchist screed, seemed simply to slip out, but I was beginning to realize that nothing he told me was inadvertent. Maybe this was the answer to Trask's puzzlement over why Cyrus took me to the front before vanishing. He'd planned his disappearance from the start. He took me to engage the press in its coverage of the carnage. And to use his empty Ford truck on his return to restock his dynamite for the long siege to come.

Louise said, "But that much doesn't help."

"It does," I said. "It helps me to know how he spoke to you."

"I had that answer ready for you, from my thinking what you might ask. But it came out wrong just now. Not wrong. Imbalanced. The anger was in him. But he cared intensely for the wounded. Almost tenderly at times."

I knew what was probably hidden from her. Cyrus's hierarchy of care. "Was he evenhanded in his tenderness?"

"What do you mean?"

"From what he said to me, it was evident that he despised the officer class."

"Really?"

"Passionately."

She did not speak for a moment.

I suddenly recognized what had just been a pulse of jealousy in me, that she should be drawn admiringly in these ways to another man. Which was a clue that Kit Cobb the spy might read in the Kit Cobb lying in this bed to understand his growing feelings for Supervising Nurse Pickering.

She said, "I was at the receiving door once and he was helping transfer a wounded officer. An elegant man, a major, who spoke excellent English. As Cyrus handed off the litter, the officer looked up at him and said, 'You are our brother.' And Cyrus said, 'Brother to your gypsies and ragpickers.' I think at the time I was struck only by his care for the poor. But it was a harsh thing to say to the major."

I thought to go on, to explain away, once and for all, whatever warm feelings she had for Cyrus Parsons. But I let the other me take over now: "Who was he close to?"

"At the hospital? Which is all I know about. I thought about that question too. Only John Lacey."

"Who he lives with."

"Yes."

"I talked with him. No help."

Louise humphed.

I said, "Do you know if Cyrus might have had lodgings separate from the hospital? I understand some do. You do."

"I do, but they put me here."

"The bossy Supervising Nurse."

She reached up and slapped me again on the cheek. Only a tiny bit less softly. "You liked that nurse bossing you in the dark."

"I liked her well enough," I said.

At this, she stirred again against me, not putting any distance between us but going briefly restless in her legs and letting the one that was draped over me undrape. If, knowing my job, I could communicate over a silent telephone with Trask, I could read Louise in the bed next to me. This moment had stopped being playful. I connected the withdrawal of her leg with a clue from our first time together.

So I said, "No, I do not think you a wanton."

The leg returned at once and she lifted up and laid her chest on mine and brought her face very near.

Now I could make out her eyes.

"Who are you, Kit Cobb?" she said.

Not what I expected from her.

In this city, in the dark, at this moment, this was not a question for which I could find a simple answer.

She did not demand one. Instead she kissed me. And I returned her kiss just as ardently. Perhaps, for now, as a sufficient answer to her question.

Then she laid her head on my chest and said, "He never mentioned another place."

I had no more questions for her. Not that I could ask. The one that suddenly sliced its way into my head was: *Does he know where you live?* The knife edge of it was that he could be a danger to her. But I could not tell her why I asked. That he was a dangerous anarchist bomber and it was my duty to find him without the authorities being involved because I was an American spy. And if I could not tell her why I asked, it would sound as if I were suspecting her of wantonness.

I had to apply my reportorial skills.

I said, "It sounds as if he wasn't close to anyone. But if he has second thoughts or realizes he needs help, can you think of anyone he'd possibly reach out to? Did anyone at all give him a sympathetic ear?"

She considered this. Then: "I can't say yes, really. If not John."

I was on the verge of gently suggesting *her* when she said, "Perhaps me. I did listen."

"And you admired his tenderness. Did he realize that?"

"I didn't express it to him with that term, of course. But yes. I let him know I was sympathetic with his feelings. Shared them even."

"So he might reach out to you."

"He might. I hope he does. Perhaps I can persuade him to come back. To find counsel for his feelings."

I was a damn fool. I was putting dangerous ideas in her head. But I remembered his knowing look at me and at her as we all parted after the New York Bar. When it became clear that I was a threat to him, he might try to get at me through Louise. I said, "If he wants help, he might not want to return to the hospital. Is there any other way for him to find you?"

I found it hard to draw a breath in the silence that followed. Then she said, "I don't think so. Outside of the hospital... That night we all met at the New York Bar was only the fourth or fifth time I'd gone. But a couple of times he was there too. Should I go? He might show up?"

"No," I said with perhaps too much force.

She lifted up from me at the chest.

"Sorry about the vehemence," I said.

It was highly unlikely he'd return there. But I had to discourage her from any contact with Cyrus.

She was still hovering over me.

I said, "But I've seen sides to him you haven't. He might be in a difficult mood. A man's mood. I will find him, I assure you. Please leave it to me."

"I will."

She settled down upon me once more.

I wanted to make her promise, but I knew that was going too far.

She said, softly, not unsympathetically, "Men have their moods."

"We do."

She moved her head to the hollow of my shoulder and sighed an off-to-sleep sigh. My brain was rattling with so many scraps and shards from this day that I could focus on no one of them, and so I soon followed Louise to sleep.

Till the banging on the door thrashed us both upright in the dark.

23

Rapidly came a dream-thought that it was a bomb and then it was Cyrus at the door, even as Louise threw her arms around me and I slipped one of mine tightly around her waist.

Banging still.

Then I thought of Trask, the yielding to him of this address.

The banging paused.

And I realized from the pull and press of her that Louise had her arms around me to protect me, not to be protected. My tough girl.

Then three more fist-bangs. Measured now.

Fortier's people had found the ambulance.

I disentangled from Louise.

"I think I know who it is," I said.

"Cyrus?"

"Not him."

A voice now from outside the door. "Mr. Cobb."

I rose quickly, groped into the dark.

"I'm Mr. Trask's man," the voice said.

I found my pants, pulled them on. My back to the bed, I wrapped the rest of the clothes together, the Mauser secreted at the center of them.

"What is it, Kit?" Louise said.

"I'll tell you in a moment," I said.

Though I was far from sure I'd figure out how.

"Stay here," I said.

I stepped from the bedroom and closed the door behind me. I laid the clothes down.

Two more bangs.

"I'm on my way," I said.

A muffled "Sorry" on the other side.

I turned the knob bolt and opened the apartment door.

The light was dim in the hallway, but there was enough of it to recognize the wide-shouldered bulk of him and his young man's tightly cropped beard. It was the muscleman who'd been driving the Pierce-Arrow.

"Sorry," he said again. "He sent me to you. We located the ambulance."

"Right," I said. "I need to dress."

Now the man offered a hand. "Sam Mandeville," he said.

"Kit," I said. We shook.

"I'll wait downstairs."

I closed the door.

I put my clothes on, thinking hard, trying to phrase an effective lie of omission.

I strapped the Mauser into the small of my back.

I knocked lightly at the bedroom door. "Louise?"

She opened it.

She was wearing her kimono.

"Who was it?" she said. "What's happening?"

"I have a friend at the American Embassy," I said. "I asked him to alert the French police and let me know as soon as the ambulance was found. This was a man who works for him. They found it."

"Where?"

"I don't know yet. I need to go now. Cyrus might still be nearby. He might have been seen. We have to catch his trail if we can."

She stepped to me, embraced me. "Will you return tonight?"

"I'll try," I said.

"I'm on the same shift the rest of the week. Come as soon as you can."

"I will."

And a few minutes later I emerged into Rue Perronet. The Pierce-Arrow sat at the curb. Mandeville stood in his accustomed place beside the vestibule door. He straightened at the sight of me and reached for the handle.

I approached. "I'll sit in the front with you," I said.

He nodded, clicked the door back shut, slipped over to the driver compartment door and opened it.

As I was stepping in, he said, "Mr. Trask has put me on call for you. Till your mission is complete, he said."

"Good," I said.

"Mr. Trask briefed me fully last night."

"Fully?"

"Yessir. About Cyrus Parsons."

"Then my first instruction is that you stop opening doors for me."

"Thank you," he said.

A courteous young man, but not afraid to let me know, in his tone, that he wasn't crazy about opening doors in the first place.

The Pierce-Arrow had a self-starter and we took off down Perronet.

"Where is it?" I said.

"The hospital facilities at La Chapelle," he said.

"La Chapelle?" A rhetorical question. Expressing my surprise.

"Yes sir."

"Parsons wasn't there with it?"

"No sir, he wasn't."

The question had been rhetorical. Louise would have assumed, would have hoped him to be. But that was a possibility only if I'd been wrong about him.

I wasn't.

So what was this move of his, abandoning his ambulance at La Chapelle? I tried to picture him. Tried to crawl inside his head. He made his break in Compiègne, secured his dynamite, arrived in Paris. He unloaded the dynamite at his hiding place. He had to get rid of the ambulance and he had choices. He could have driven it anywhere away from his living place. Left it on a street in Paris, walked to a Metro station, vanished. He didn't have to hide his true purpose anymore. He'd already let me figure him out. That was the point of his telling me as much as he did. I was to report on the carnage. I'd explain how an anarchist looks at that. That it was all homeopathy. Administer doses of carnage to those in power or in safety to initiate their natural antidotes. The press would help deliver the antidotes into the general bloodstream. So since I already knew who he was, why the ambulance at La Chapelle? As if he cared about the hospital operation and its equipment. Was he trying to look to the rest of the world like an innocent man? He was leaving hospital service, but he was scrupulous about returning their goddamn ambulance? That didn't fit.

I went cold.

I turned to Mandeville. "When did we learn about this?"

"Within the hour."

"How?"

"A call to the embassy."

"From who?"

"I didn't take the call. A man who didn't identify himself. We assumed one of Mr. Fortier's informants."

"So he was French-speaking?"

"Yes."

"What did he say?"

"Only a few words. Just that the missing ambulance was in La Chapelle."

"Did you inform Mr. Trask?"

"They were putting in a call when I left. He'd said to come to you instantly."

Something didn't seem right about this, Fortier having eyes on La Chapelle in the middle of the night.

That the caller came off as French gave me pause. But my instincts told me there was only one answer. Cyrus had tipped them off.

And if he'd tipped them off, I understood something else. Cyrus didn't unload quite all of his dynamite. He left a bundle and a time-fuse.

I would be happy to be wrong, but I couldn't assume it. I said, "No talk now, Sam. Get us there fast. As fast as you possibly can. Lives are at stake."

"Yes sir."

Sam opened the throttle and the streets were clear in this late hour and soon we were racing fast along the city's periphery road, just inside the Thiers Wall. Our six cylinders pounded us through the dark and every moment was crucial, but I myself had no choice but to sit there, impotent to shave even a single second from our arrival.

I sat back. I closed my eyes. Forced into passivity. I thought of that earthen wall whisking by in the dark. Seven decades old. Keeping people out. And beyond it, in this modern age, the ones excluded. Cyrus's precious gypsies and ragpickers.

And it struck me: *He was there.* I still feared what he'd left for us inside the ambulance. The fuse might be sparking into the powder even as these thoughts passed through my head. But there might have been another reason as well for the placement of the first bomb of his siege. He could park his ambulance and walk across the road and into the other Paris, the Paris of the poor and the beaten up, the outsiders and the forgotten and the thrown away. The people in Paris he felt to be his brothers. He could vanish in there.

And we whisked past the Porte de Clignancourt, swerving a little and crying our Klaxon's *ah-oo-gah* at a ragpicker's cart emerging from beyond the wall, and I knew La Chapelle was near, a fraction of a mile. I looked ahead, guessing its place in the dark, and the sky was quiet, no smoke, no aftermath, and I thought *We might be on time, I might act swiftly enough, or I was wrong* and even as these words rushed through me they vaporized with a sharp slam of sound and in a slice of dark above La Chapelle a roiling flame leaped up, shaping into a fireball, bulbous and bright.

"Holy Jesus," Sam said.

"Cyrus Parsons," I said.

The great orb of fire rose and loosened its smoking tendrils and rose and dimmed and vanished into the night sky, leaving a thrashing thicket of flame below, the burning wreckage of whatever building Cyrus had chosen.

Sam had instinctively let up on the gas. We'd slowed.

"Keep on," I said.

He throttled up.

I thought about Cyrus arranging this. I could read the explosion. The sound of a stick or two of dynamite had been instantly dissolved into the sound of gasoline exploding. He'd probably taken pains to fill the Ford's tank. I figured I knew where he parked.

And soon we approached the train yard. I said to Sam, "Pull over outside, near the entrance. Keep things clear for fire and rescue wagons."

Sam slowed and slid over and parked just off the road. When we were stopped I said, "I'll walk in. Wait here."

There was no one at the entrance. The security hadn't been severe even in the morning I'd come here. They never dreamed the place would be a target, and they knew who was coming out. In the early morning, if there was anyone here he'd be heading for the fire, which was deep into the grounds.

If I wanted to talk to them, I'd have to return tomorrow. But it would be a waste of search time. At best I'd confirm, by their description of a man walking away, what I already knew. That it was him. Maybe I'd learn in which direction he turned. But I'd still be left with hunches. And I had a good one already.

I walked on. Quickly. Down the cobbled street toward the southern end of the warehouse park, toward the bright burning center of the dim shapes ahead.

As I drew near the working buildings, I could see first the massive warehouse receiving station. Unscathed. The fire was beyond. I began to jog. I realized I was thinking too much. Casting myself in the role of utter outsider. Instead, I might be of some use.

The warehouse loomed and then I was passing along its canopied platform. And now the flames surprised me. I thought I knew what Cyrus's target would be. The cluster of cottages where the wounded officers lay. But I was wrong. They were farther along. These flames were closer. Much closer.

Ahead was shouting, was the rushed movement of a dozen men, paths crossing, buckets in hands, pointing, flashing out of sight toward the fire. Behind me, in the distance, the hooting whine of fire trucks and city ambulances. Civilian ambulances coming for the wrecked bodies of men already wrecked and ambulanced from elsewhere.

I emerged from the loom of the warehouse.

Cyrus had bombed the nearest of the large, stuccoed treatment pavilions. It was always nearly filled with those waiting for transfer to a hospital. The pavilions. Parsons had gone after not the officers he despised but the poor poilus he was supposed to feel such compassion for. But of course. The officer cottages were smaller. Less populated to start with. And the officers had received their ruling class privilege for priority transportation to a hospital bed. The carnage was Parsons' goal. Seeing the masses suffer. It was all a dramatic tableau. The poilus were better theater.

The pavilion was awash in flame now from end to end and side to side. And downstage center, in the midst of the fire, was a dark specter, the skeletal metal frame of the ambulance. The ambient heat was searing and I backed off a ways. Half a dozen smoldering bodies lay on the cobbles. Some of the night staff were crouched over them. Other staff stood watching. Simply watching now. Some had buckets in hand but they knew how useless they were. The inferno ruled.

The carnage was sufficiently clear.

24

And Cyrus had declared himself. To all of us. Or so he intended. But Trask had this covered. The way he'd played it, the bomb only made the speculative thief in our lie a confirmed truth to the French. We were up against one or more clever German saboteurs. And so it would fall once more on me to find the bomber. The lead this time would be our own. A stolen American ambulance. The French had no idea how well I already knew the bomber.

But I had to know him better still. I had to think like him. Another role I had to play, at least in my head. I still had nothing else to go on.

I walked back out of La Chapelle.

As I emerged from the gateway of the freight station onto the boulevard, I heard the starting sputter and then the roar of an automobile engine. I turned to face the Pierce-Arrow, and its headlights flared up from the tops of its fenders.

The driver door was opening.

And it struck me, hard, that it was Cyrus.

His plan was inside my head: *Plant the bomb. Wait in the shadows for Cobb to arrive. Confront him. Kill him as the final touch on the evening. Only then walk into The Zone and disappear.*

I stepped toward the car, my hand moving to the small of my back, the Mauser there.

With the motor still running and the lights illuminating him, Sam crossed the bright beam and stood waiting for me, framed by the headlights.

Not Cyrus. Sam.

Cyrus was capable of what I'd envisioned, but if he'd wanted to kill me at this point, it would have been in Compiègne. He did not know I was an agent. He did not know I was actively pursuing him. He did not yet know I had absolutely no intention of writing a single word in a newspaper about his anarchist sophistry.

I approached Sam.

"You okay?" he said.

"Yes."

"Is it bad?"

"It's bad."

Without another word we broke off, moved to the car. He revved the engine, made a half-circle turn, and we headed back west on the peripheral road.

"Where to?" he said.

I didn't have an answer.

I wanted to complete the night in Louise's arms. More than ever. But I was in deep now. I had the same hesitation in going to her as a spy that she had in coming to me smelling of gangrene and blood and body fluids. On this night there was nothing to wash me clean.

La Chapelle was a crucial operation and would soldier on without pause. And though I strongly suspected the event would be kept from the newspapers, one of the Neuilly boys would soon be there. If any of the La Chapelle staff saw the ambulance come in or even saw it sitting there before the blast, there would be a tale to tell. It was hard to say how it would get pieced together. But at least the basic facts were going to find their way to Supervising Nurse Pickering. Soon. And I'd already given her the crucial piece to the puzzle. She would figure this was where I'd run to in the night. She knew it was about Cyrus.

The news must come from me first.

"Back to Rue Perronet," I said.

"Yes sir," he said.

"One more instruction from me," I said.

"Yes sir?"

"Call me Kit. Never *sir*. I'm not a fucking officer."

He barked a sharp laugh.

"Got it," he said.

And I got it. I heard myself. Fucking officer indeed. That was from inside Cyrus's head.

I tried to stay there. Tried to sense him beyond the passing wall. It occurred to me I should go out into The Zone first thing in the morning. Try to find him. I had a picture of his uncle who might look enough like him for somebody to recognize him. But the place was vast. If he was out there in a settled way, as a vocal sympathizer, the gypsies and ragpickers and the rest of the oppressed were not going to give him up. On the other hand, I couldn't see him establishing a secure bomb-making space for himself among the huts and hovels and gypsy caravans. The hardscrabble life for his neighbors would draw thieves or informants to him.

But I circled back again to my earlier thought: *I have nothing else to go on.*

There was also nothing to do about it tonight.

And I had a tricky task immediately ahead of me. How to tell Louise. How *much* to tell her. It was getting increasingly difficult to talk with her.

Ten minutes later, we stopped before her building.

Sam said, "Is there a message for Mr. Trask?"

"Tell him now we know why the Germans stole the ambulance."

Sam exhaled a chuckle. His briefing had covered our lie, as well. Then I sensed something shift in him. He said, "Should I let him know you figured out the bomb? That we rushed as fast as we could?"

I shrugged and said, "Sure. Let him know. Not that it did any good."

"Sorry," he said.

I heard a little catch in his voice. He looked out the front window, into the night. I realized what the shift had been and how my last, offhand comment sounded.

"Sam," I said. "You did everything you could."

"It's been in my head ever since," he said. "If I'd just gone faster."

"If we go faster we hit that ragpicker's cart at Clignancourt and we never get there at all. It worked out the way it had to."

He brought his face back to me.

I said, "Stop thinking about it. Instruction number three."

He nodded.

I said, "If you can't, then get out of the service. The job is going to eat you alive."

He rolled his shoulders. "I can."

"Good."

"Thank you," he said. "Kit."

"Tell him I want to follow a hunch first thing in the morning. You and I will go into The Zone."

"Got it."

"I'll see you at this curb at seven-thirty," I said.

"Seven-thirty."

I opened the door and stepped out of the Pierce-Arrow. I shut the door. It thunked solidly. A beautiful car. The car of the wealthy class. It would only be a provocation and a target on the other side of the wall, and a liability for anything else I might get up to thereafter.

I leaned back into the driver's compartment. "One other thing, Sam. Does the embassy have another vehicle? Made in France? A little less obtrusive? Maybe even modest?"

"They do."

"Make it ours."

He nodded and drove off.

The concierge was gone.

Of course. It was nearly 2 a.m. Still. It stopped me. I turned. I stepped back outside. Sam was gone. I strode out to the sidewalk, looked up and down the street. It was impossible for Cyrus to have followed me. But I worried for Louise being drawn in to all this. He might know more about where she lived than she realized. He could have followed her here any evening.

I shook myself by the lapels: *He doesn't care about her. He doesn't know my connection to her.*

Still. I found myself worrying.

I went up the stairs.

For the last flight and across the landing and with my approach to her apartment, I trod lightly.

Part of me still wanted to turn, to go, to make my way back to my hotel. But not the strongest part.

I laid an ear against her door.

And through the door I heard her voice. "Are you listening there?"

"Yes," I said. "I thought I'd crept here quietly."

"Not quietly enough."

"It's me."

"I've already figured that out. I'm awake."

"I've already figured that out."

Then I heard a stirring inside and the knob bolt being turned. The door opened.

Her hair was down, her kimono gaped almost entirely open. She grabbed my hand and drew me quickly in and the door was closed and the bolt thrown and we embraced.

After we kissed and kissed again, and I felt a faint trembling in her, felt it, then felt it subside, I said to her, "Were you afraid?"

"Yes."

"How did you know to be?"

She drew back.

Her great, dark eyes riveted me in the room-glow of electric light.

I said, "Why were you fearful?"

"A banging on the door? Ripped from sleep? The American embassy sends a man in the middle of the night? I couldn't help it."

She was smart. She was probably picking up on even more that she wouldn't know how to put into words. I wished again that I hadn't come back to her on this night. And I was relieved that I had.

"Can we talk in bed?" I said.

"Such a fine idea," she said.

She repeated those words a few minutes later, the next words either of us spoke. *Such a fine idea* that we were in each other's arms, beneath the covers, naked even just to speak and to sleep, with the lights on but only because we wanted to see each other's eyes as we talked.

And having reprised her approval, she let more than a moment pass, let that sentiment thoroughly sink in, before adding, "What's happening, my darling? I must know the truth."

I'd come here to deliver a straight, factual news story that she needed to know. But I snagged on *darling*. The word, the fact of it, made things harder. I found—somewhat to my surprise—that I didn't want to jeopardize that.

She was waiting.

I said, "There's been an explosion at La Chapelle."

She let go of me, sat up.

"What? When was this?"

"An hour ago."

"How did you hear?"

"I was there."

"Is that why they came and got you?"

"No."

"I don't understand. You go off and come back and this is the message? But it's not why they came in the night to get you? You said that was about Cyrus's ambulance."

She was smart, this woman whose darling I was. She was instinctively asking the tough, sensible questions. I saw two choices. Tell her that for reasons I could not reveal, I could say nothing more about what happened tonight or about anything that I would be doing for the days ahead. Tell her only that, but realize this choice number one immediately ran more deeply. I could never tell her about who I really am or about anything I have done and will do as that man. Which meant we would soon be done for.

Or. My second choice. Tell her more or less everything. To sensibly consider this choice I factored *out* the effect of her sitting before me in the lamplight we'd left on for the conversation, which meant I was seeing, in an ongoing way, far more of my naked darling than her eyes. And I factored *in* the circumstantial impossibility that Supervising Volunteer Nurse Louise Pickering from Gloucester, Massachusetts, was a covert secret service operative for a foreign power.

I didn't have to decide at once. As if from a city editor's mandate to a cub reporter covering a train crash, I'd just give the facts.

I spared none of those. Including the pavilion for enlisted men engulfed in flames. The few bodies drawn out, smoldering and dead. Through this part she drew up, she stiffened. But with toughness and self-possession, in her persona as head nurse in a hospital serving the Great War.

I arrived at the ambulance. I painted the reportorial picture. That it sat at the center of things, consumed in the fire. As I spoke of this, her professional reserve turned to restrained agitation in her shoulders, in her hands, which drew up the sheet to cover her chest. And in her eyes, in her focus, I saw the unanswered questions forming in her head. Questions that would force me to make a tough decision.

When I finished the narrative, she let go of my eyes. She lay back on the bed.

I lay down next to her, my head propped on my angled arm, watching her.

Then she turned on her side to face me.

She said, "Is he dead?"

It was impossible to tell her he was not and then find any plausible lies for her follow-up questions. *Are you certain? How can you be? So was it the ambulance itself that exploded? How could it do that?* If I knew he was not dead, it meant there was a much bigger situation here. I could shut this all down, letting her know that I understood the bigger situation but could not, would not tell her.

But I realized there was one more possible lie.

The only lie I could get away with was my own complete ignorance. *I don't know if he's dead. I have no idea why the ambulance exploded. I'm just a newspaper writer trying to find a missing acquaintance.* This was a simplified choice number one. When I first imagined this path, I instinctively wanted at least to be honest about the reason I was withholding things. This simple way forward didn't occur to me till now. I knew why. Because this woman deserved more, deserved better. And I didn't want to lose her. This simplified choice had an inevitable ending. I'd do my secret work in Paris and perhaps be with her a few more times and when the mission was over, my lies and I would walk out her door and never return. She'd marry some Massachusetts physician and she'd go to her grave with, at best, a few weeks of memories from a fleeting darling in Paris. And I would go to my grave with Louise Pickering a line item in a ledger full of regrets.

And I thought: *Maybe, in spite of some useful skills, I am profoundly wrong for this fucking job.*

I am just a writer.

Maybe a romantic lead.

I thought, *Does James Polk Trask have a longtime darling? How about a wife even? Do any of his boys have a wife? Is it possible for the wives never to know what their husbands do? How do husbands and wives live a life like that?*

Louise waited for an answer.

Though rendered here fully as thoughts and questions and conclusions, all of this actually thrashed through me more as feelings than thoughts, emotional logic as spontaneous and rapid as the flames of La Chapelle.

I sat up.

She sat up and faced me.

I said to Louise, "No. He's not dead. But before you ask anything more I need to tell you that I have two jobs. I work for a newspaper, as you know. I also work for our country. I'm sure, my darling, you have no one to reveal that fact to and no interest to reveal it. It's very important that you don't. But if we are to be darlings, you and I, and indeed if I am to keep you safe in the days or weeks ahead, you need to know this about me."

I paused in my tale to give her a chance to answer her own first few follow-up questions in light of what I'd just told her. I felt her mind working.

But what came next was the lifting of her hand.

She touched my cheek.

The scar. She spread her hand over it, covered it, pressed her palm gently against it, keeping her eyes fixed wide and unblinkingly on mine.

I wondered if she too had snagged on *darling*. Wondered if she'd even heard the rest of what I said.

As if I'd asked that very thing, she said, as soft as the press of her hand, "Nothing we ever say or do, you and I, is anyone else's business."

I reached up and put my hand over hers, kept it there a moment, carried her hand to my lips and kissed its palm.

I let it go.

She lowered her hand to her lap.

And she asked, "Did he deliberately do this?"

"Yes."

She took a sharp, deep breath. She let it out. Composed herself.

"Are you sure?" she said.

"Yes."

"And he just walked away."

"Yes."

"Why?"

"So he can do it again. And again."

She shuddered across her shoulders and through her chest. The visible tremble there, in the center of her nakedness, spoke to me of her vulnerability, told me I was doing the right thing. I was about to fail Cyrus in his expectations of me as a newsman, and when I did, he might try to make the carnage strike close to me. Louise needed to know everything, even if only for her own good. To be on guard.

She said, "I meant why did he set off a bomb?"

"You only know part of what he believes. What he's passionate about. Those things have led him to anarchism."

And I told her about Cyrus. About his full beliefs. That he was determined to vividly demonstrate the carnage of war to the people of Paris. I told her about the bomb at the Montparnasse café. And I told her about the bomb at the Pont Neuf Metro station, the one that woke me the morning after our first night together.

"I remember," she said. "You said it was just a sound. Did you realize?"

"I suspected."

"We were close enough to hear."

"Yes."

"So he'll do it again," she said.

"If I don't find him and stop him."

"Is the hospital in danger?"

I gave that a moment of serious thought. I would talk to Trask about a guard for the place. My fear for Louise was more personal. I would have to stay away from her, I realized. Until this was over. Cyrus would have no reason to go after her except on account of me. For the moment he still thought I was useful. So I was truthful in saying, "No. I think the hospital is safe. He's already sent a message to us at La Chapelle. From this point on, it's the French he's trying to provoke. As with the first two bombs."

"You have to find him."

"I know."

"Do you have a way?"

"Not yet."

"It's about where he might go."

"Yes. A place where he's already established. He did not make those bombs at the hospital."

She paused, shook her head slowly from side to side. "I can't think," she said.

"One thing," I said. "Does Cyrus speak any French?"

"At least some. He seemed to be picking it up. The few times I was at the New York Bar it was always with the drivers. I once heard him say something in French to the waitress."

The La Chapelle informant only spoke a few words on the telephone. Likely he spoke to an American. No dialogue. Cyrus could very well have managed that.

As I took a moment to think this through, Louise turned her face, lowered it a bit. The mind there that I was coming to respect was also working at something.

Then she came back to me. "You said you talked to John Lacey."

"Yes."

"And he was of no help."

"None."

"It's hard to think that John wouldn't have some clue about Cyrus."

I said, "Men can be like that. They can easily live in a room together for months and never open up to each other."

"I have no doubt," she said. "But I'm pretty sure these two go back further than Paris. First of all, they came to the hospital together."

"Together?"

"At the same time."

"Is that unusual?" I asked.

"Not necessarily. But there's more. At the bar. They always sat near each other at our table, the two of them."

"That can be men too," I said, though a moment flashed through me from the road to Compiègne: Cyrus's initial resistance to fully attack Lacey. *He's all right.* The mitigating shrug. That can be men too. Sure it can. These two don't agree on politics, but while drinking in a bar and talking about their flivvers and their tough job, they can be all right with each other. So I'd jumped to that interpretation.

Jumped.

Nevertheless, I stuck with my opening line. I said, "Men make superficial connections at bars that can look like friendship." This rang hollow now. So I spoke the reason I was still half a step behind the truth I saw up in front of me: "From what I could see of the two of them, and from talking to Lacey, they didn't appear to be close at all."

"But I picked up on something," Louise said. She lifted her forefinger, touched the air between us. "Give me a few moments. Let me recover the details." Then she curled her knuckle against her lips.

And while she did, I recovered a detail of my own. Cyrus calling Lacey *Jack*. I'd heard a sarcastic dig at a Brahmin. But that's what I was listening for. *Jack* could have been the fellow fighter for the oppressed, a refugee convert from the ruling class. Maybe a bankroll for bombs and a place apart in the city.

I'd failed to learn my lesson with Staub.

"Okay," Louise said. "Here's how it went. It was that waitress at the New York Bar. I was sitting just to John's right. Cyrus was on his other side. A conversation was going on across the table that I'd been following. But the waitress came up with our drinks. I looked at her as she arrived. Out of the corner of my eye I saw them both turn her way. She served us and went off and the conversation on the other side of the table resumed. But I heard Cyrus say to John, 'Chicago.' He said it low, just for John, but I heard him. And John said, 'Southside Delicatessen.' And Cyrus said, 'The waitress. What was her name? Spitting image.'"

Louise paused, started thinking again.

She'd given me enough already.

Lacey said he was thrown in with Parsons randomly. That he didn't know a thing about him. He lied.

"Florence."

My attention returned to Louise. "Her name," she said.

"The waitress in Chicago?"

"Her name's irrelevant, I know." she said. "I just wanted to finish the story in my head."

"Kit Cobb the newspaper reporter admires your digging for the detail."

"And Kit Cobb the worker for our government? By the way, is that a euphemism for a spy?"

"You've just been a big help to that guy. For which he admires the hell out of you."

"I'm so glad," she said.

"Yes it is," I said.

She flickered at this.

"A euphemism for a spy," I said.

She smiled. "The word will never pass my lips."

I said, "Something else very important, my darling. You must treat John Lacey as if nothing has happened. You know nothing. You've said nothing."

"Of course. I don't often see him. But if I do, it'll be business as usual."

"One more thing you must keep hidden. Tales will come from La Chapelle. It's unlikely but possible that people will speculate close to the truth. That it was Cyrus's ambulance. That he was the one who put it there. Perhaps even that it was the source of the explosion. It's important that you don't encourage that story. You simply don't know anything about it. All right?"

"Of course."

"You must leave all the rest to me," I said.

"I worry for you," she said. "Is that all right?"

I hesitated only a moment. It was. "Yes," I said.

"If you need me. For anything. Or want me. I will be here tonight. Again at nine o'clock. Tomorrow is my day of rest. I will be here all day and night. You must come to me if I can help you in any way."

What I needed was for her to be safe. I was afraid I made her less so until all of this was resolved. So I made no promises.

I simply kissed her.

She asked for no more than that.

Then the light was out and we were settled in, entwined beneath the covers. Almost at once her breathing slowed and deepened and she was asleep.

It took me a while, as my head filled with little things I'd noticed but either not recognized or had misinterpreted. A word, a glance between these two mugs at our meeting in the New York Bar. Lacey's barely contained fury at his father, the guy in the family who was the active member of the ruling class. This was also about men. Fathers and sons. Parsons was taking up where he felt his father lost his nerve and failed; he got to beat the old man at his own game. Lacey was tearing his old man down. Utterly. Tearing him down.

That thought started to gyre and then dissolve and I was in the dark and any move I made bumped a barrier, I tried to stretch my leg, tried to throw my arm to the side, tried to press my hand upward, but everything was blocked and the air was tight and my chest clamped shut and I struggled to breathe and I knew what had happened, I'd gone into the trunk backstage, hiding from some man in my mother's life, another phony father, an actor, and he didn't know I was hiding and my plan was vague, to leap out at him, but rehearsal was over and everyone was gone, and I pushed both hands hard above me, tried to lift the lid but it would not yield, it was sealed shut and now the lid and walls and the very stage floor were closing inward, squeezing the air out of the trunk, out of me, and I screamed and I screamed, I had to get out but the air was gone and there was no sound and I fisted my hands and pounded above me, pounded and pounded as if I were buried dead alive and the lid was my coffin and above was only six feet of earth. And then the lid flew open and I jumped up gasping and now all around me were flames. The Lyceum Theatre was on fire. The curtains and the flats and the auditorium before me, all the seats, everything was on fire, and then the flames overwhelmed it all, made it all vanish, and for a moment I saw nothing but the flames and I could only wait to vanish within them forever, but something began to take shape around me in the inferno, a skeletal form, and I could make out doors, and then a roof, a front window frame, a dashboard, and just as I understood where I was, the flames vanished and I was sitting in the passenger seat of a Ford ambulance and all around was darkness except for the headlights thrown before me, showing nothing, but I was moving. No. I was being driven. And I knew who it was sitting beside me, behind the wheel. I turned. And he was not there. No one was there.

25

When I stepped out of the door just before seven-thirty, a Renault Torpedo was approaching on Perronet from the east, a strikingly recognizable marque, its radiator set behind the motor, which allowed for its distinctive low-swooping coal-shuttle hood. But at least it was not an American limousine. The Renault's black canvas top was raised. It would do just fine for what lay ahead. Which did not include what I'd thought it would when Sam dropped me off a few hours ago.

The car was right-hand drive, so he was prominent before me as he negotiated the curb. I began to move toward the street.

A short time ago a bleary-eyed Louise and I parted sweetly, briefly. And informatively: I now had a pretty good idea of the ambulance drivers' typical daily schedule. Lacey would have opportunities to slip out. If Cyrus had accelerated his bombing plan impromptu or if he'd consciously orchestrated it to include our trip to Compiègne— either way—this was a good day for him and a coconspirator to meet up. And if not today, then soon. The best thing I could do now, with the few circumstantial clues I had, was follow Lacey.

The sun had not yet risen on this late-autumn morning. At the hospital, the drivers were heading for the dining hall in the basement.

As I arrived on the sidewalk, Sam engaged his hand brake and idled for me. I circled the car to the passenger side and slid in.

"Good morning," he said. "Mr. Trask wants to see you first thing."

"At the embassy?"

"Yes."

I wasn't surprised.

I had news for him anyway.

But we could lose Lacey.

"Is he in his office right now?" I asked.

"Yes."

"There's a post office near the Place Parmentier. Stop there first. I want to telephone him."

Sam hesitated for only the briefest moment. His order from Trask had no doubt been to bring me to him first thing, no delay. I was countermanding it.

"Right," he said and he throttled up.

"I've got a new lead," I said. "A good one but immediate. No longer the Zone."

"You're the guy who tells me what to do," Sam said. No explanation being necessary.

He had good instincts. From what I'd seen of wars, the authority in the field should always take precedence over the authority in the office.

We pulled away, the engine's four cylinders as full of pattering notes as a ragtime drummer.

I said, "You were obviously up early."

"Is this one okay?"

I was starting to like Sam. Good field instincts and he was quick. I'd have to lecture him at some point about hearing only what you're listening for when there might be an alternative. But in this case he was right. The Renault.

"It's swell," I said and said no more for now. We were shortly turning into the Avenue du Roule, just above the *place*. Ahead, in the dark, the post office's blue light was still on, for the dark hours of the morning.

In front of the building, a stacked and stuffed horse cart was just pulling away from the curb, the post office probably its last stop of the day. The Cyrus lately occupying my head had me notice him. This guy was a ragpicker. There were thirty thousand of them, though most only had gunnysacks on their backs. Every one of them was at work every day in Paris. And they were all citizens of Cyrus's oppressed masses, their labor made a crucial part of the city's trash management for no wages at all.

The man on the cart prompted me to briefly second-guess myself. Even if Cyrus's bomb-making was elsewhere, he might well have friends, associates, certainly sympathizers in The Zone. He could even have a hideout where somebody teaches him waitress French. He could be there right now.

But Lacey was the hand to play. If Cyrus was indeed in The Zone, that's where Lacey would lead us.

I closed the door to the telephone booth, dropped my coins, and found Trask in his office.

His immediate words to me: "This about your morning intention?"

Sam had dutifully delivered my message.

"It's changed in the past couple of hours," I said. "As a lead, dramatically for the better. As a development in our larger concerns, dramatically for the worse."

"Being mindful then, we do need to talk in person," Trask said.

"But on-site," I said.

"Where?"

"The Lycée."

"You'll be watching?"

"Yes."

"I'll find you."

And we rang off.

I came back out to Sam and the Renault.

I worked the crank for us and got in.

"Is it okay?" Sam said.

"He'll meet us there."

"And where's the new there?"

"The Lycée Pasteur."

"The American Hospital."

"The American hospital."

On our way, I told Sam the story of J. B. Lacey.

We parked on a right-angled side street, Rue Alfred de Musset, lined with plane trees and commencing directly across the Boulevard d'Inkermann from the Lycée's main gate. There were several other automobiles along the street, on both sides. Facing forward, beneath the trees, with other cars keeping us from standing out, our trilbies pulled low, we were in good position.

The sun was still down. The air was chill. Sam and I settled in. Fifteen minutes later the Pierce-Arrow turned onto our street from d'Inkermann and parked directly across from us, facing in the other direction.

I stepped from the Renault.

Trask emerged from behind the Pierce-Arrow's steering wheel. Before dawn, with his man assigned to me, Trask drove himself.

We met in the middle of the street.

We simultaneously offered our hands and shook, while our breath plumed before us and vanished, plumed and vanished.

Trask said, "Sam tells me you figured it out on the way."

"It struck me Parsons was probably the anonymous caller."

"That occurred to me as well."

"I've since confirmed he speaks some French. Enough to leave a terse tip."

"If only we got to him in time." This came out of Trask not brittle with criticism but muted with sadness. Not quite what I'd expected of him. He was starting to surprise me with some regularity.

I said, "Nothing was going to tell us where he'd leave the vehicle."

"I know," Trask said. "I know. And he played that trump card with a time-fuse."

I said, "I got nothing I could recognize as a lead in my first pass at the hospital. But I've got something now."

"It's the dramatically worse thing that I've been waiting for."

"Another American is involved."

"Judas priest." The oath was spontaneous, but spoken low, as if in deep disappointment.

I had to make it even worse for him. "Another driver at the hospital."

He turned his face sharply away. His breath wasn't pluming. Not for a long moment. He'd sucked it in with the news and wasn't letting it out.

Then at last he exhaled.

I said, "I think he can lead us to Cyrus."

Trask looked back to me. "What's his name?"

"John Barrington Lacey. A Harvard man no less."

"The world has gone mad." This was growled.

I wondered if it took an anarchist Harvard boy, the spawn of the ruling class, to finally bring James Polk Trask to that conclusion.

"We'll keep watch," I said. "If Cyrus has gone rogue, Lacey might follow. If they want to raise the ante on the carnage, why keep one of them under cover?"

"This is good work," Trask said. "But I'm going to need to pull you away for a couple of hours a little later in the morning."

"Fortier? About last night?"

"Yes."

"Surely that can be rescheduled," I said. "Tracking Lacey is our one lead and this could be our only chance. We don't want two needles in the haystack."

Trask was staring down the street toward the gate of the Lycée.

I knew I'd said all I could say.

I waited for him.

He looked at me and said, "Washington has already taken an intense interest in this, as I expected. Even over a goddamn farm boy. But two Americans now. *These* two, for Christ's sake. Their diversity compounds our jeopardy and undermines the president. Undermines the country. Fortier is a very important man. He sits close to both Poincaré and Joffre. He's impressed with you. With his reach to the highest levels, an hour with him at this juncture is crucial. The meeting needs us both."

"We can't lose Lacey," I said.

"Sam Mandeville. Don't be deceived. He drove me around but that's because I'm hand-grooming him. He's got moxie. He can take care of the surveillance for a couple of hours. This man Lacey might see and identify you anyway. He won't know Sam."

He stopped. He waited for my assent.

I didn't like the whole plan. In operational ways. In ways that were new to me and I was yet to figure out. But he also made some sense. Especially about both our targets being able to recognize me. On the way back to the surveillance I could alter my looks. This morning the operation had to be impromptu, and some of its flaws were unavoidable. Maybe even including a rookie working on his own for a while.

I still didn't like the larger thing.

Trask didn't like my hesitating to assent. He said, "I'll come get you in a couple of hours."

"I may be somewhere else," I said.

"Right," he said. "We hope so. Be at Fortier's office at eleven o'clock."

I had no choice. "I'll be there," I said.

"Good," he said. "And since we won't have a chance to speak again till we're with him, this is how it needs to go. I'll talk first and lay out our story."

"About the German ambulance thief?"

"About the Germans. You can then add any plausible details you want. Like writing your newspaper stories."

Trask was sounding like Trask again. I let his disdain for newspaper news pass. What troubled me more were the lies he was having us weave. Official, covertly arranged, high-governmental lies. Trask knew best what was at stake between Washington and Paris and what needed to be done about that. I couldn't argue with strategy. But the tactics still seemed off.

"This new complication," I said. "Doesn't that change things out here in the field? We kill one guy with no lies preceding, you give them the body and Americans took care of one rogue American. I see how it goes no further. We assassinate two Americans, one a Harvard boy, that we claimed ahead of time were Germans, and what's your story?"

James Polk Trask actually put a hand on my shoulder. "This is why you're free for a few hours and why we won't move on these two till you and your skills are in place. We just need to find out where Lacey ends up. Once we have the hideout, we just watch until you're back in place and we're sure both of them are present. Then you take them out in your own special way in their own private place. You let me know when it's done. Then you leave the rest to me."

The hand that was on my shoulder had shaken me gently a couple of times for emphasis. Now it withdrew.

And he said, "There were only American heroes involved."

26

I slipped into the passenger seat of the Renault.

Moments later the Pierce-Arrow engine snare-drummed into life. A drumroll to herald a worry that I'd made a stupid call in switching automobiles. The Pierce-Arrow was probably the only vehicle at the embassy with a self-starter. True enough it would also be a neon-lit windmill parked down the street from a hideout. But having to crank, we were stuck with a delay in beginning a pursuit. Sam by himself would be delayed even longer. And alone, he'd be physically vulnerable in the process, having to put his back to the action.

But it's what we had to work with.

I made sure to caution Sam about that latter worry as I finished recounting my conversation with Trask. To which Sam instantly replied, "I can handle myself, Kit."

I figured he could. I liked him for his spirit. But if he'd been acting as a chauffeur while being hand-groomed by the office boss, he still had a lot to learn from field experience. Untempered reliance on that spirit could be dangerous. That wasn't, however, something I could reason him out of. I said no more.

We set up a surveillance protocol together.

Then Sam produced a small pair of Huet binoculars from a bag in the floor of the backseat.

We settled in to wait.

The sky was only beginning to fade a bit into gray.

One thing from my conversation with Trask, which I had not mentioned, I now gave to Sam.

I said, "You've impressed the boss."

"You think so?" Nonchalant.

"It's clear," I said.

"I'm ready," he said.

"Just be careful," I said. "There's much to learn out here that Trask doesn't know to tell you. Nobody does, until things happen."

In reply, he lifted the binoculars. "You or me first?"

I was maybe ten years older than Sam Mandeville. It felt suddenly like much more.

"You," I said.

Shortly after sunlight began to make its entrance in our little scene, I took the binoculars.

Not five minutes later, Lacey appeared.

He emerged into the cobbled frontage of the hospital with Jones and another of the drivers. I quickly passed the binoculars to Sam, drawing his attention to our man.

I was relieved. Sam needed to have a clear look at Lacey in the flesh before we needed to act.

That necessity came within the hour. I'd slipped behind a forward plane tree and discreetly watched from there, getting a good angle on the south end of the frontage. The third man checked his tires and a thing or two under the hood and left a few minutes later. Jones and Lacey kept their hoods open.

But I could tell Lacey had something going on. While Jones ran through what appeared to be a routine check of lubricating tank, grease boxes, crank chamber, and gearbox, Lacey fiddled around. He kept an eye on Jones, doing nothing much when the man was absorbed, returning to fiddling when Jones pulled back and seemed about to glance his way.

Finally Jones closed his hood.

The two men exchanged a few words.

I felt certain I knew Lacey's next move. By the schedule, the drivers needed to assemble now and remain on call. But as soon as Jones disappeared into the porte cochere, Lacey strode around to the back of his ambulance, leaned in, and pulled out his Gladstone bag, which was stashed there, no doubt during the night.

Lacey was about to bolt.

I beat it back to the car.

I pointed at the crank as I approached and Sam nodded. He gassed the carburetor and I bent to the crank, and as we went through the drill to fire up the engine, I tried to interpret what I'd just seen. Lacey went for his bag without even taking time to close his hood. He knew he wouldn't be back. No appearances to preserve. And he wasn't going to take the Ford.

The Renault sputtered itself alive and I circled toward the driver's seat, not looking back, not showing my face. Even if Lacey glanced this way, I was just a man from behind, starting a car. "He's on foot," I said to Sam.

Sam adjusted the throttle for me, watching through the front window. "There he is," he said, starting to slide from under the wheel, toward the passenger door.

I paused to keep my back to the hospital for a moment.

Then Sam said, "Clear. Turned right on d'Inkermann." He got out of the car. The plan was for him to follow on foot till Lacey took to a conveyance.

I slipped up behind the wheel.

By the time I was situated to drive, Sam, at a jog, was almost to the corner. Lacey was out of my line of sight. Sam slowed abruptly before he came into view of the receding Lacey, then turned the corner.

I released the brake, put the Renault into gear, and accelerated to the end of the street, looking south as I approached the intersection, seeing Sam following Lacey, who was crossing Perronet at a moderate pace, not drawing attention to himself. Sam was striding faster, closing the gap.

I rolled on into d'Inkermann without stopping. I had to hang back but I had to be near at hand when Lacey committed to his next move. Cyrus could be hidden somewhere near the hospital, within walking distance, and we'd keep up our little parade all the way there. Or Lacey was going to catch a fiacre as soon as he could, probably at the next intersection, the traffic circle on the Avenue du Roule. In that case, I'd pick up Sam and we'd follow. Or Lacey was going to soon turn east and head for the Porte Maillot Metro station. If that was his intention, I was done for the morning and I had to hope that Trask had hand-groomed Sam well.

Sam was across Perronet and it was only a short block onward to the circle. I had a clear intersection and glided through without shifting downward.

Up ahead, Lacey was approaching Avenue du Roule, and he was slowing. So was Sam. Lacey stopped, and Sam stepped into the door-way of a shop. I pulled up to the curb before him. I flashed him my palm as I kept my eyes on Lacey, who was standing with his back to us, ambiguously motionless.

The Renault idled.

I turned my face briefly toward Sam. We simply touched glances. He leaned a little forward to take a quick look to the traffic circle. I turned back to Lacey, who suddenly grew animated and raised his hand. He was hailing a fiacre.

Sam and I both recognized the gesture at once and he strode across the sidewalk and around the car at the rear and slipped into the passenger seat.

A fiacre with a swaybacked horse stopped before Lacey. He got in. I was happy for its classic, four-wheeled, sealed-up design, with a high back window the size of the cover of one of Lacey's Joseph Lincoln novels. A couple of spies could follow him with impunity.

Though slowly.

By this time I fully expected all of us to head north and then east on the peripheral road, following along the Thiers Wall to an entryway into the Zone. But instead we turned south and then entered the widest thoroughfare in the city, the eastward-leading Avenue de la Grande Armée.

At the pace of a marching band—though ours was invisible and silent and octogenarian—we paraded for a mile along this wide, straight, asphalt boulevard with its rows of horse chestnut trees all the way to the Arc de Triomphe de l'Étoile where la Grande Armée turned into a mile and a half of the equally wide, straight, and horse-chestnuted Champs Élysées.

We seemed to be making our swaybacked, second-gear way farther and farther from anything that could possibly hide Cyrus Parsons and his bomb making.

But at the Place de la Concorde we crossed the Seine.

We were on the Left Bank again. We followed the Boulevard Saint-Germain and then turned more sharply south onto the Boulevard Raspail, heading for the center of Montparnasse. Somewhere up ahead was La Rotonde, where nine days ago I was sipping a Bijou in the dark while Cyrus was walking out of the nearby café at the Hôtel Terminus, having left a satchel full of dynamite behind.

He stirred in my head.

I was getting close to him. Here on the Left Bank.

That thought had just occurred to me when the fiacre slowed abruptly and I needed quickly to apply the brakes. Though the horse did not fully stop. We continued carefully through an extended intersection of three streets, and ahead, to my left, at the crossroads of two of them, was a familiar sight.

Straight from the front page of yesterday's *Excelsior* was the grand Hôtel Lutetia. A twenty-five-yard facade on the crossing Rue de Sèvres, with a ground-floor bistro and patisserie, and the long run of it around the corner, for a full block down Raspail. The gendarmes in their capes and brass buttons and flat-topped kepis were already visible in force, a dozen flanking the front entrance halfway along Raspail, rifles across their chests. Expecting the big brass. A city truck was parked at the small *place* where Raspail and Rue d'Assas met, more gendarmes unloading the stacked, unassembled parts of wooden barricades.

We turned there, into Rue d'Assas, the old horse must have taken a few flicks of the whip, as I was able to upshift once again, from first gear into second.

The street was paved in brick, angling in the direction of the Luxembourg gardens, but we didn't stay on it for long. We passed the grounds of the old convent of the Carmelites and then the extended four-story, stone-and-brick building of the Catholic University of Paris. At its end, we turned left onto Rue de Vaugirard and tracked along another side of this papal Parisian block, glimpsing its centerpiece, the domed Church of Saint Joseph of the Carmelites, behind a passing, high, stone fence.

At the next corner the fiacre turned right into a side street that I could see was not quite wide enough to fit the Renault and fiacre side by side. I had a hunch and shifted down before I reached the turn myself. I stopped, but kept the motor running.

Sam looked my way.

I leaned toward him and said, loud enough only to be heard over our motor, "If that's the place, we're going to end up sitting right behind him when he gets out."

Sam popped a confirming forefinger at me. He said, "Mr. Trask didn't know to tell me that."

"Exactly."

Sam figured out what to do next, however.

He slipped from the car and up to the corner, which was edged by a building. He took off his hat and executed a series of cautious peeks, followed by an extended half-face gaze.

Finally, he pulled back and returned to his seat in the Renault. He said, "Got it. He went into an outer doorway, a wall of some sort, about a third of the way down on the left. The whole street is maybe a hundred and fifty yards long."

"Any vehicles?"

"Twenty yards down on this side. A Unic Landaulette. Probably a taxi. But it's half up on the sidewalk. Maybe a private one and the driver lives there."

"At least the Renault won't be entirely alone."

But I didn't like the setup.

I put the car in gear and we took the corner slowly. "These are close quarters," I said. "It's safest to watch in the rearview mirror." It was affixed just outside the passenger's side, on a rod at the outer edge of the windshield.

I passed the Unic.

A moment later Sam said, "That's it."

He nodded to a passing concrete wall, maybe ten yards wide and not much taller than a Senegalese company captain and his kepi. The wall joined a couple of two-story buildings at the sidewalk and a third building was recessed inside. Invisible was a small courtyard just beyond the metal door in the center of the wall.

The door, I noticed, had an easy ward lock, if and when needed. And a number above it. Nine.

I drove on, putting about twenty yards between the courtyard doorway and us. A couple hundred feet farther, Rue Jean-Bart ended at the cross street. I pulled to the right curb, going partly up onto the low sidewalk.

I turned off the engine.

"From that doorway they can't see you sitting behind the wheel," I said. "Let's do the mirror."

Sam began to adjust it.

He looked my way.

"There," I said. I could see the doorway.

I looked at my Waltham. It was almost ten o'clock. The pursuit took nearly an hour. "Goddamn horse," I said.

Sam laughed. "We slid out of the twentieth century."

Once again I felt oddly much older than Sam. I realized I was more or less a man when the century turned and he was a child. A time when you could not find an automobile on a city street.

"I should go," I said. "Right now I'm recognizable by either of these guys at a glance. Cyrus might not have arrived yet. He could come from down there." I lifted my chin in the direction of the cross street.

Sam looked. "Of course," he said. And then he turned to me. "I appreciate what you're doing. I hope to learn a lot from you."

One more role I found myself playing. I was a goddamn repertory company.

I said, "Then realize this whole morning has been sloppy. Because it was rushed. I should've been able to put you on the street now. On a doorstep dozing with a bottle, say. But you look like the embassy man you are, in your serge and trilby. We had no choice. You saw for yourself why we had to get straight to the surveillance."

"I understand. How long will you be gone?"

"I hope only a couple of hours. Don't try to take them both on alone."

"Good luck with the French."

"Right," I said.

I got out of the Renault.

Sam slid over under the steering wheel.

He reached back behind the seat and brought up a newspaper.

He opened it and laid it on his steering wheel. He said, "The moment anyone comes around that corner." He lifted his chin in the direction of the cross street.

"But hold the paper low," I said. "He doesn't know your face. If you cover up, it's a red flag. It could be anybody. Even me. Just don't look at him till he's in your mirror."

He nodded and said, "Jeez. "

I assumed I knew what he meant. "Yeah. Very complicated."

He shot me a little smile.

I turned and stepped to the back of the car.

The street was empty to the far corner. I walked briskly away toward Rue de Vaugirard. I pulled my hat down and gave a quick look to the passing wall and its door and the upper story of the house at the back of the courtyard. The windows were shuttered.

I had plenty of time to walk to Fortier's office.

I turned right on Vaugirard, glancing down the papal block to the left, the church, the Catholic University, the convent. I left it behind, thinking still of the Catholics and their tribulation under the Third Republic, which was born from the last big war with the Germans. And I turned up Rue Bonaparte. It surprised me almost immediately with the Church of Saint-Sulpice, with its facade of double-stacked colonnades and twin kepi-flat towers. All of which had me trying to get inside Cyrus's head again. Was he a clever man? An ironic man? Finding a hideout for a couple of anarchists in the middle of a seriously churchy neighborhood.

Half an hour later I was looking into the Seine on the Pont Neuf between the Left Bank and the Île de la Cité, trying to create the story of a couple of German saboteurs. Just another role to play. Christopher Cobb the novelist.

And then I was approaching Trask, who stood beside the Pierce-Arrow, which sat before Fortier's town house on the Place Dauphine.

He nodded.

I nodded.

We did not speak. He did not look at his watch.

A gendarme led us up to the second floor and through the open office door. It was precisely eleven o'clock. As before, Fortier rose from behind his desk at the far end of the room, his boar, his rifle, and his wolf hanging behind him.

27

We approached.

Two chairs were arranged before the desk.

Fortier circled around to greet us. No handshake test across the desk this time.

He even took a step toward me.

I thought: *Trask's lie must be a whopper.*

Which was a thought that made the lingering, firm handshake I was having with this tough old man regrettably unsettling.

Fortier said, "You are a special friend to France."

I thought: *Oh shit.*

And even as I was thinking as one Kit Cobb, I heard another Kit Cobb offer a gentle correction to Fortier, in French, "*America* is a friend to France."

I felt Trask's hand pat me on the shoulder at this and then guide me to one of the chairs. I obeyed. Fortier watched the process and smiled and took it as his cue to circle back behind his desk and sit as well.

We were already calling the shots, we Americans.

As we all settled into our seats I glanced at the wolf head on the wall behind Fortier. I was reminded of the first impression it had made, that it looked almost indistinguishable from an American farm boy's sheepdog. And I thought: *Indeed. Our ravenous wolf turned out to be a rogue sheepdog.*

Trask said to Henri, in slow, loud English, "I will recap what we know, Henri. I know you understand some English. But this is important, so I will have our man Cobb translate."

He looked at me and waited.

I dumbly turned to Fortier.

He was looking at me, waiting.

I translated.

And so it went for a few minutes.

Trask's words and my voice rolled out our fabricated explanation. How even after we all had at first fallen prey to convincing but bad information, I had never given up, even with no remaining leads. How America's friendship for France and our refusal to accept terrorism anywhere in the world sent me back undercover. How I returned to my sources in the underworld of German immigrants in Paris. How, therefore, when an ambulance was stolen from the American Ambulance Hospital of Paris, I was able to uncover a lead. How we were right all along. How the flow of war refugees brought a resourceful German saboteur to Paris. How one of my German sources had seen a fellow immigrant with the ambulance. How I was presently pursuing consequent leads to find the Hun—leads too sketchy yet to speak of but very promising—and I hoped to succeed within the next few days.

That was our story. And how.

Fortier had listened with a gaze focused on my face that did not waver for a moment, a gaze that one Kit Cobb fretted was a look of utter, damning skepticism but that another Kit Cobb—the main man at this moment and for however many necessary days to come—Kit Cobb the American spy—knew to be a look of tough-guy, fellow-spy admiration and approval.

The silence that followed lasted the exact few seconds that admiration required. Then Fortier said to me, with bona fide warmth, in English, "Thank you, Monsieur Cobb."

"Please call me Kit," I said. I wasn't sure which of several possible Cobbs felt it necessary to make that distinction at this moment.

But it pleased Fortier. He smiled. "Kit," he said.

Then he ignored Trask.

He spoke only to me, in French. "They are your sources. I respect that. I do not ask you to identify them. But tell me. Do you trust them?"

The bad taste was still in my mouth from the lies I'd endorsingly translated to an ally country fighting for their lives against some manifest bad guys. I felt compelled to mitigate those lies somehow. Even just operationally, for when Trask might have to undo them. I said, "I trust these sources as much as you trusted yours."

He flinched ever so slightly.

I also know tough guys of a professional sort. I had confidently wagered this little combination left and right, in its playful aggressiveness and its candor, would win his respect.

I saw him teetering between my hope and some degree of offense. I shot him a little smile and added, "But I won't say that."

And he gave me a little smile back. "Thank you," he said. "We both understand about sources."

I said, "But I can offer this. I do trust—and I am saying this with equal candor—that I will end the bombing within days if not hours."

"Very good," Fortier said. "And I must remember how you finessed your reply. We French love finesse."

Trask cleared his throat loudly.

Fortier and I both looked at him.

He lifted his eyebrows at us. He didn't know French but he recognized interesting body language and facial expressions when he saw them.

Fortier and I looked back to each other.

He said to me, "You may translate for us now."

This was a tough-guy old man who knew some finesse himself. I was translating for "us." He closed the loop between us and Trask. He knew I was *his* guy, not the chilly old man's in the other chair. For some reason I felt inordinately touched by this.

Fortier went on, "I am most worried about tomorrow morning and the conference. We have kept these explosions out of the press.

But tomorrow a bomb anywhere near the Hôtel Lutetia will be impossible to conceal."

I translated for Trask.

And I continued to do so as we went on to establish these things between us: The important people will be safe inside the Lutetia. The cordon of security around the hotel will be thorough and fierce. But the people of France must be free to see the efforts its government is making to find a winning strategy, to secure and engage its allies in a shared goal. President Poincaré himself made this public relations goal clear and urgent to Fortier. There will be impenetrable zones of security. But the eyes and ears of the French people must be quite near to the event. This was the basis of Fortier's overarching worry. This German bomber was very clever to steal an American ambulance. The deaths he caused were despicable. We must expect him to somehow be clever tomorrow, and he might be willing to sacrifice his life.

After all this went back and forth, though mostly forth from Fortier, the old tough-guy Frenchman leaned toward Trask and said, "I trust your man Cobb."

I translated.

"So do I," Trask said.

"So does he," I said to Fortier.

"As much as I?" Fortier said.

"Do you want me to translate that?"

With a small smile, drawn sideways toward me and away from Trask, he said, "No."

I said to him, "Most of what we do in this line of work requires finesse, doesn't it?"

"It does," he said.

"But the jobs themselves seem to succeed only with an act that is its opposite."

"Your understanding of this is why I trust you," Fortier said, and he immediately rose.

The meeting was over.

After the handshakes and au revoirs, as Trask and I walked the length of Fortier's long office, I suppressed a smile. The tough old guy had not missed Trask telling us all when to sit. Fortier had just made it clear, with finesse, that he was calling the shots.

With the last au revoir, he wrung from us a solemn oath to stand side by side on the barricades with him at the hotel in the morning.

Once Trask and I were approaching the Pierce-Arrow, he said, "We did what we needed to do."

"Good," I said.

"What was that last part? You didn't translate."

"He told me to go kill this guy."

"Good advice. Back to the surveillance?"

"Yes."

"Where is it?"

"Number nine, Rue Jean-Bart."

"You'll guide me. I'll drop you around the corner."

"My hotel first. It's right on the way. I need a couple of things."

I'd decided not to put on an elaborate disguise. A convincing theatrical beard would take too long. Now that we were clear of our obligation to the French, I regretted each further moment away from Rue Jean-Bart. But my hotel was right on the way and what I needed would take only a few minutes to gather up.

It was only a few minutes later that I brisked into the lobby of the Hôtel de Seine. The concierge hailed me at once.

I stopped.

He lifted a hand and opened a drawer in the front desk, saying, "A very insistent young man."

I strode to him, plucked the envelope from his hand. "When did this come?"

"Perhaps an hour ago. Perhaps somewhat more."

I turned my back on the concierge, took a step away.

I ripped open the envelope.

I went straight to the signature.

Cyrus Parsons.

And the note, written in a cramped, upright hand, said:

Perhaps you have not had time to write our first story. It was no doubt too late for the morning editions. I still hope you are the man for the job. With your own driver and a ruling class automobile, I worry, however, that I have misjudged you.

Cyrus Parsons

I took the stairs two at a time and burst into my room. I pulled a leather courier bag from the wardrobe and packed in my pouch of lock-picking tools, my flashlight, and some additional firepower—a Luger, which I'd appropriated without finesse in Istanbul this past spring.

My urgency had kept at bay a full consideration of the note's implications. This much, only sensed downstairs, now flared fully in my head: *Cyrus was watching early this morning outside the gate of La Chapelle. He'd gone nowhere except into the dark across the road to wait. We had parked perfectly to give him a good show. And a good look at Sam.*

I shut the bag, slipped the shoulder strap over my head and across my chest, and I beat it down the stairs, thinking: *Sam is a big boy. He's armed.*

Trask was sitting behind the wheel.

I circled the Pierce-Arrow, my mind sorting through things quickly. I knew at once that Trask should come nowhere near the scene of the surveillance in our ruling class automobile. But I needed to get to Rue Jean-Bart fast, so I was reaching in for the passenger door latch. How much to tell him at this moment was the big question. If we feared for Sam, he might want to intrude. Trask had never been an on-the-ground operative. I saw him as an operational liability. I slipped in beside him and kept my mouth shut.

Except to say: "Don't spare the horses. The longer Sam works this alone, the more risks we take."

"Agreed," he said.

We took off down the Rue de Seine, and when we turned and started to barrel west on Vaugirard, I told him to pull over just past the high back wall of the Luxembourg Palace, short of Rue Bonaparte. He did, sliding up to the curb across from the Musée.

"You'll be at your office?" I asked.

"Yes."

I started to open the passenger door but he put a hand on my arm to stop me.

He said, "No finesse."

I'd skipped that whole remark in my translation. It did not surprise me Trask knew more French than he let on.

"No finesse," I said.

I got out and strode off west.

Trask did not pass me in the car, but turned onto Bonaparte behind me. I figured that I had to try harder to set aside the Cyrus in my head when I considered Trask. I needed to give my ruling class boss a bit more credit. But I also needed to keep connected to Cyrus. He was no hayseed. He was shrewd and aggressive beyond the dynamite.

I was approaching the corner of Rue Jean-Bart. Staying alert. I could well confront Cyrus at any moment. He could be walking this way, intending to turn at the same corner. It was one of those moments when I found myself naturally aware of the weight of the Mauser against the small of my back. I strode harder and made an anticipatory decision. The simple thing—the only thing—if I found him before me would be to kill Cyrus immediately, on the street. Then Sam and I would go into the house on Jean-Bart and take care of Lacey.

But now the corner was a few steps away and Cyrus was nowhere in sight.

Fine.

I turned the corner.

The street was empty.

The Renault was gone.

28

I stopped.

Sam would not have driven away if Cyrus hadn't shown up. Even if Cyrus appeared, Sam would have waited for me unless they'd gone out together carrying a satchel. Or unless there'd been an unexpected confrontation. And given the timing of the note and the revelation in it, I did not like the possibilities of a confrontation that made Sam vanish before my return.

Either explanation told me what to do next.

Go in.

I hustled down the street.

Before the metal door, I opened my courier bag and pulled out my lock-picking tools. I found the right skeleton, inserted it in the keyhole. The bolt moved. I edged the door open only enough to keep the lock undone. I put the tools away and took out the Luger. I released the safety catch at the top of its grip.

I threw open the metal door, stepped in, quickly scanned the space with both hands on the pistol.

No one was in the arc from one corner of the house in front of me to the other. All the windows were shuttered. Then on around to my extreme right. No one. Back to my extreme left.

No one.

A trash bin there. A rake behind it, some other tools sticking up. Close to the wall was a manhole with a drainage notch, laid into cobbles. The whole courtyard was cobbled. Like a street. A very old street.

I closed the door behind me, thinking this space had not been designed as a courtyard. It might, indeed, have once been the street, or part of it, or a side street. A long time ago. That would explain the manhole. This was never a Haussmann neighborhood. Buildings just sprung up. The two that formed the sides of the courtyard had no entry into it.

The only door was into the house before me.

I stepped to it.

A latch lock. But before I set to picking it, I tried the thumb lever. The door yielded.

I carefully stepped through, into silence and darkness. I pushed the door closed without letting it snap shut.

I did not move.

I waited and listened, the Luger poised before me in the dark.

I heard only faint familiarities. The buzz of silence. The ticking of timbers.

The background smells were familiar as well. Mildew. German cockroaches. French, to the Germans.

I pulled the flashlight from my bag and sent its beam down the corridor. It went ten or twelve feet and found a staircase to the right and a doorway across from it. Nearer to me, a couple of steps along, were facing doorways. I moved to the one on the right and the beam scanned an utterly empty parlor. The space opposite was larger, the sitting room. Also empty. In its back wall a doorway into darkness.

I hesitated again. No sounds.

I proceeded through the house, both upstairs and down, and I found very little. There were a few objects that might be left by a family thoroughly abandoning this place as the war came on and the father and the son went off to the trenches. A book, a shoe, a broken plate. A dozen other bland bits and pieces.

In three rooms there were traces I tried to read.

In two chambers upstairs, the dust that uniformly coated all the other floors was greatly disturbed, wide paths swiped and scuffled through, exposing the wood beneath. In each of the two was a clearing of dust that defined a space large enough for and vaguely in the shape of a sleeping bag. I thought: *At least Cyrus escaped Lacey's snoring*.

The third room was at the back of the first floor. The floor had been scuffed nearly clean. There was a woodstove and in it was ash with bits of charred hardwood. Recent embers. A large worktable sat in the middle. No smells. There wouldn't be unless the dynamite was ancient and sweating nitro. But there was no dust. None.

That was it.

Not much.

I was risking the usual. Seeing what I expected to see. Coming to conclusions that were, in fact, imaginings.

Lacey did come in here.

He was not here now.

In that regard, one possibility was just off the room with the stove and the table. A door that led out back. I opened it. In the clouded afternoon light was a ragged space of grass and the rear of the buildings on Rue Madame.

I'd seen enough.

I retraced my steps down the central corridor and went out the front door and through the courtyard, trying to understand. The house might have been a staging area for bombs. Assembled there and then taken off to do their work. The two bombings that had begun this whole thing were within easy walking distance of Rue Jean-Bart.

I stepped from the courtyard.

The street was still empty.

I closed the metal door and relocked it, in case nothing had changed, in case the surveillance would somehow resume.

Maybe our Yankee anarchists did go out with a satchel. Sam had to improvise. If he didn't have a clear shot, or if only one of them went out with the satchel—Lacey, with Cyrus still not having shown up, still off somewhere, vanished in The Zone or wherever—maybe Sam had to make a quick decision. Stick with the surveillance like Trask wanted so we could be sure to take them both out at once, even if that meant letting the bomb get delivered and detonated. Or follow the bomb and stop it.

Maybe that's how it went.

Maybe Sam was safe, off being a hero.

Or maybe Sam was dead. Maybe Cyrus arrived and recognized him at once and kept it to himself and went in and made a plan with Lacey and they went out the back and circled around from Rue Madame and one of them diverted him while the other killed him and the two of them took the body and the Renault away to dump them far from their hideout.

Whatever happened, I could not afford to wait here and see.

I needed to talk to Trask right away and the closest post office I knew of was on Saint-Germain near my hotel. But then I thought of the nearby Lutetia. The brand-new luxury hotel would have a telephone cabinet.

I took off along Jean-Bart and then around the papal block once more and up Rue d'Assas. As I emerged onto Raspail just below the hotel, the first thing to see, west across Raspail, past the wall of a military prison and facing north on Rue de Sèvres, was a large loaf of neo-Gothic bread, still another Catholic church.

I thought: *If a great battle plan to defeat the evil Kaiser Wilhelm does not emerge from the Lutetia tomorrow morning, God does not exist. If He exists, He has the place sufficiently surrounded to get the job done.*

The police had been busy since this morning. A barrier of wooden saw-horses and attending gendarmes already controlled sidewalk access along the hotel. I approached the checkpoint and showed Fortier's give-this-guy-what-he-needs letter from the Préfecture de Police de Paris. It got me through the saw-horses and, presented once more, through the front door of the hotel.

Pairs of gendarmes, rifles across their chests, flanked the way from foyer to reception area, where the floor tile was laid out in a vast, slanting black-and-white chessboard with no edges, spaces proliferating outward, colliding with walls. A fitting comment on the task of the coming morning.

The reception desk sent me through a wide doorway into the lobby lounge and an alcove in the corner containing a *cabine téléphonique*.

I closed myself in.

I rang through to Trask.

"It's Kit."

"This is too quick to hear from you on a telephone."

I said, "That's right. And I want to be mindful, but you need to do something right away. You and the people you can marshal."

"All right."

"Our man and the car were gone."

"Gone?"

"Vanished."

I heard Trask grunt, as if he'd just taken a right hook to the body. He knew all the implications.

I said, "I went inside."

He took a moment. "I understand," he said.

"No one. Nothing. An empty place with a bare few vague indicators. The two were there, I believe. But now, they and any clear trace of them are gone."

He grunted again.

"No word from our man?" I had to ask but he'd have said already if so.

"None."

A few moments of mere line static commenced. I tried to think of a mindful way to speak the thought that arose in me now and that I felt surely was rising in Trask.

"You and your French friends should look. Quickly." I hesitated to say it, but I added, "Look where an automobile can go nearby and be seen by no one, or only by the indifferent."

"Yes," he said, and though it was brief and a single simple syllable and passing through the scrim of a telephone line, the word was filled with something I had not heard in Trask.

More static and thinking and then Trask said, "We have our duty tomorrow. You know what's crucial now."

"I do," I said. The Hôtel Lutetia.

And that was that.

I hung up the telephone.

I turned and put my back against the side of the cabinet and leaned heavily there.

What I felt seemed simply to be exhaustion.

I had plenty of reason to feel that, though the afternoon was barely an hour old. It had been a long night and morning. I knew it wasn't that simple. But for now exhaustion was sufficient.

I returned to my hotel, went up to my room, and without undressing lay down to rest.

For the second time on this day I was awakened by a banging at my door.

I wobbled awake.

The room was dim. The shutters were closed but the cracks were dark.

More heavy knocking.

Trask's voice. "Kit. Are you there?"

"Yes," I said. "Yes."

I rose and crossed the room. I turned the switch to ignite the electric light and opened the door.

His face was jaundiced by the light.

We stood facing each other unmoving, unblinking, for an oddly long moment. I was still groggy. He was apparently dead from a bad liver. Or so it appeared. My mind was putting the scene into wry headtalk as I tried to clear away the residue of an exhausted afternoon nap.

And then I understood.

"Sam," I said.

"Sam," Trask said.

29

Trask and I did not move.

We let the details that should probably have been spoken remain unspoken for now, giving them time to dissipate in the fraught silence between us.

Then Trask said, "I woke you. Do you even know what time it is?"

"I do not."

"Half past six."

"That's why I'm hungry. I don't think I've eaten for a long while."

So Trask and I walked together down Rue de Seine, and at the Boulevard Saint-Germain he said, "This way," and we went along the full Gothic length of the Church of Saint-Germain-des-Prés and turned in at the Brasserie des Bords.

German food. Made tolerable in Paris because it was, strictly speaking, Alsatian.

After we sat, I with my back to the mirror on the wall and he across from me at the small table, we two men devised one more lie between us on this day. That we were full of regret was a given. That we understood the risks of the secret service. That we understood the hard political realities of this world. The lie was that we were not as saddened, as unsettled, as we actually were.

So before we said what we knew we must, Trask lifted his menu a little. "From the banks of the Rhine."

I said, "Did I miss something in you I should've seen? A sense of irony?"

"I keep it hidden," he said.

"Bismarck annexed Alsace for its superior sauerkraut," I said.

"Not ironic, really," he said. "You and I aren't gunning for Germans."

"No we aren't," I said, though it was barely audible.

"We're gunning for our own." Trask's tone could hammer a horseshoe.

The waiter was beside us. We ordered the *cervelas*, the wurst, though these were made in France or Switzerland; and the sauerkraut, transformed in Paris long ago into *choucroute*.

With that done and with a *demi* of beer in front of each of us, which tasted like good German beer, we drank for a time, and then the food came, and we ate.

All of this in carefully nurtured silence.

We each ordered another half-liter of beer, and it wasn't until those *demi* glasses were before us that Trask said, "I liked that boy."

"I did too."

"One of them cut his throat."

"Cyrus," I said.

I thought of his Abercrombie sheath knife, left behind in their room. Lacey brought it for him in his Gladstone.

I told Trask about the note I'd gotten just after he'd dropped me off at the hotel. Just the facts of it. Flatly.

"Bad luck," Trask said.

That I hadn't been there for the note before we had to take up the surveillance.

"Bad luck," I said.

He said, without hesitating, "I still have some muscle at the embassy. We slipped into the hideout. An hour ago."

He should have come and gotten me. I kept quiet.

"It was still as you said."

I didn't answer.

He picked up on my silence.

"It was a snap decision," he said.

I wondered if he'd admit to the real reason.

I still didn't help him out.

"We *expected* it to be as you said."

He took a drink of beer. Leaned back a little in his chair. As if that was all he'd offer.

I said it for him. "You liked the boy."

Trask showed me nothing. Not in his eyes. Nowhere on his face. Not with his shoulders. But he said, "It was a hasty decision."

The decision to go in without knowing they were both there. "I understand," I said. *You were grieving furiously.*

He said, "Tomorrow we can only stand and wait."

"They also serve," I said.

"Written by a blind man," Trask said.

He knew his Milton. He knew how little we presently had to go on.

"I hope they try tomorrow," he said.

"I'm afraid if they do, it will be somewhere else."

Trask nodded.

I said, "While we wait at the one place we know to look, they've got the rest of the city. Carnage on the very day will be good enough for them."

"And that can be anywhere," he said.

I had nothing to add to that. I thought to simply drink my beer and was surprised to see it hanging in the air before me. I'd lifted it along the way but I couldn't recall when.

I put it down.

I finally asked, "Where did you find Sam?"

"On the Saint-Denis Canal."

The canal ran through The Zone. After we fulfilled our obligation to Fortier in the morning and covered the best bomb target in Paris, we needed to search among Cyrus's oppressed.

"He was in the backseat."

I returned my mind to Trask. The backseat.

"On the floor," he said.

I didn't quite get it, since they cut his throat. "He seemed a tough guy," I said.

"One of them slugged him from behind. Knocked him out. They cut his throat sometime after he was on the floor."

With that fact laid out between us, we both tried to steel ourselves again. But I saw the struggle in Trask. I felt it in myself too. I said, "Did you know him for long?"

And Trask said, "He was my nephew."

Then we simply drank.

Rather slowly. Drank enough. Though not so very much, given the circumstances, but we were neither of us that sort of man.

What we did do was say nothing more.

30

I entered my room, closed the door with meticulous care, and I sat down on the side of the bed in the dark.

It was nearly ten o'clock.

I would make the short walk to the Hôtel Lutetia on my own in the morning.

But sitting now, slumped a little, my palms splayed on my knees, I found one thing on my mind. I wanted to go to Louise.

I'd been wordless long enough tonight.

I'd understood the hard realities for long enough.

But I did not move.

I would sleep and gather my strength and stand with the tough old Frenchman on the barricades for whatever hard reality he understood about his job and about his countrymen and their war, and then I would go to the other side of the Thiers Wall and try to hunt down a couple of my fellow Americans in order to kill them. Only then would I go to Louise. And I thought: *Only then, my darling. But certainly then.*

So I slept.

And I woke.

I shaved.

I looked at the scar on my face.

To my courier bag I added an extra magazine of cartridges for the Luger and one for the Mauser at the small of my back.

I went out.

The day was almost mild, as it was when this all began, the night of Cyrus's first bomb.

I strode toward the Hôtel Lutetia and did not slow down till I approached Raspail. The time was just past nine o'clock. The meeting would begin in less than an hour.

The saw-horse barricade began at this near end of the hotel. I showed my letter to the gendarme and went through.

The barricade swept outward from the lower edge of the hotel to block off Raspail all along the building's length and took the turn up ahead at the crossing of Rue de Sèvres to cordon that street to the Lutetia's farthest end. The opposite sidewalk, however, was open and people were already gathering there. Every half-dozen yards a gendarme stood at the edge of the near sidewalk facing the people who were taking up positions at the barricade across from them, the street itself becoming No-Man's Land.

Up ahead I saw Trask and Fortier together on the sidewalk directly before the hotel entrance. They were smoking, not quite shoulder to shoulder and turned very slightly away from each other, looking in opposite directions, like a couple of brothers having just quarreled at a family reunion.

Fortier was slightly angled in my direction. He didn't see me. As I drew near, I figured out from his face, his eyes, what he and Trask were actually doing. They were intently watching the people across the street.

All three of us were in for a bad few hours. Trask was right. This was what we were reduced to doing. Standing and blindly waiting. Watching for something we had little chance of seeing, much less preventing. I still thought our anarchists were far away, off in one of a countless number of possible unsuspecting public places in Paris, poised to strike. Even if they intended to make a splash in the vicinity of the conference, they could just let the crowd gather over a hundred-yard stretch on two streets and then elbow their way in anywhere at the back, set a satchel down, elbow back out, and walk away.

Trask and I were the only ones who knew the threat wasn't an anonymous German agent. I alone among us knew what they looked like.

We had no photographs of our two anarchists. I did have an image of Parsons's vaguely similar uncle. Possibly useful door-to-door in The Zone, but worthless in a crowd hunt. And if Parsons and Lacey planned to strike somewhere else today, the French simply knowing the threat was from two Americans would have done no good anyway.

I let these thoughts go.

It wasn't my decision to make, to turn them into Germans.

I was close enough now to Fortier for him to see movement. He glanced and took a step to greet me. We shook hands.

I said, "We should at least be watching from the rear of the crowd, don't you think?"

"Yes of course," he said. "Patrol behind the lines. You are free to do that. Monsieur Trask and I are here for show."

Monsieur Trask himself was now a physical presence in our conversation. All this, however, had been in French. I said to him, "We think I should patrol the back of the crowd as best I can."

"And you and I should have breakfast tomorrow," Trask said.

We looked at each other a moment. His eyes were red and faintly puffy. "Are you okay?" I said.

"Not till it's done," he said.

I turned to Fortier. "You thought yesterday that this German might be clever again, as he was in stealing the ambulance."

"Yes."

"Are you letting any vehicles inside the barricade from this time on?"

Fortier said, "In less than an hour President Poincaré will arrive for the sake of the front page of tomorrow's *Excelsior*. But it is a fact no one has known until this morning's newspaper. In the night, every street for a hundred meters beyond our hotel perimeter has been forbidden for any vehicle."

"His carriage will come through alone?"

"Preceded by his mounted guard and followed by a wagonload of troops for his defense."

"More show?" I said.

"But of course," Fortier said.

"He will come from the Élysées Palace?"

"Yes."

"Along Boulevard Saint-Germain?"

"And then Boulevard Raspail, from the north."

"A better place for me to patrol," I said.

Fortier put a hand on my arm. "A good thought," he said. "Better than here."

I left the perimeter at the point where I came in, and I began to circle the growing crowd, which was becoming substantial opposite the hotel's front entrance and gathering two and three deep elsewhere up Raspail and across the intersection and along the Rue de Sèvres. I understood why the crowd was growing. The big conference. Joffre and the British general. And now the president arriving.

I hustled on past the turn of the crowd into Sèvres and north on Raspail. People were flowing this way. The citizens of Paris. Photo fodder for the *Excelsior*. Vehicles were prohibited a block beyond the hotel's perimeter, but the crowd was not. The authorities, anxious for the show, thought it was enough to have troops and saw-horses and to let the populace accumulate to gawk from afar at the war leadership at work.

Cyrus was resourceful. No doubt. How precisely could all the gendarmes have been briefed? The same impulse to censor the newspapers would make the authorities stupid about how much they told their foot-soldier gendarmes. Did the gendarmerie even explicitly understand that they were looking for a bomber? If they did, these men would go off to their wives and buddies and help widely confirm the inevitable current rumors of sabotage bombings in the city. They would help stoke the fear and discontent of the home front.

The gendarmerie knew nothing. I was striding along now with a courier bag over my shoulder. A roll of half a dozen sticks of dynamite with a cap and fuse could easily be stuffed inside. No one was stop-ping me.

And so I strode on, glancing into the doorways and scanning the overlooking windows as I passed by, not really expecting to see Parsons or Lacey lurking or looking, but feeling that I myself, in my role as a spy, was as stymied as the troops and the press in this so-called Great War.

And then, up ahead, I saw the president's guard on chestnut light-cavalry horses, high-stepping this way. Half a dozen *chasseurs*—the "hunters" of the French army, trained for rapid action—in dress red pants and blue coats with gold-brush epaulets and gold helmets crested with horse-tail manes. And behind them, the president's coach pulled by a massive white horse with a docked tail. And behind the president, the open transport cart full of troops and rifles.

I turned to face the street.

But though my eyes were open, I was no longer seeing anything.

Because of a sound. A sound I'd stopped really noticing, as it was so common in this part of the Left Bank where I lived, where I ate and drank, where I slept, where I'd heard a bomb and saw its work and followed an anarchist and searched an empty hideout. I'd heard this sound so often it no longer registered on me.

But now it did. Amplified in this little parade.

The sound of the iron-shod hooves of six chestnut horses and the iron-rimmed wheels of a presidential carriage and the iron hooves and the iron wheels of a squad of gendarmes in a wagon. The prancing tramp and the lumbering roll of metal on cobble.

And beneath the iron-on-stone sound was an associated sound. A hollow sound, a deep, cavernous, resonating hollowness welling up from below the street.

And I understood.

I understood that hollow sound and I understood all the churches around us. Long ago, these churches were built with quarried lime-stone. And long after that, their cemeteries were systematically emp-tied. Emptied into that same vast rock quarry. A quarry that made the earth beneath my feet, beneath much of this city, a maze of tunnels.

The Catacombs.

And I thought of a thing that had been odd but I'd let it pass, explained it away. A manhole in the cobbles of a small, very private courtyard before a house that was surprisingly empty.

I turned around and faced south.

And I began to run.

Toward the Hôtel Lutetia where the president of France was heading and would enter and where he would join the allied generals for the beginning of their conference. The Hôtel Lutetia, which sat, it now occurred to me, over the Catacombs.

I circled the crowd and beat it down d'Assas and it wasn't until I'd turned into Vaugirard and was approaching the Carmelite church that I thought of the alternative. Dashing into the Hôtel Lutetia and clearing the joint. But I realized who I was by instinct. A *chasseur.*

A hunter.

31

Though that was a notion of myself that I knew was about to be tested, as I put my hand on the crowbar I found leaning with the other tools against the wall bordering the courtyard in Rue Jean-Bart, and I stepped to the manhole. I slipped the tip of the crowbar into the notch on the cover. I lifted the metal disk and swung it away and looked down the dead dark hole leading into the Catacombs.

As a kid playing a game I'd put myself in a box. As an adult, I found I had a whole shelf of boxes that I was jumping in and out of. Spy and newsman and lover and fatherless son and son with a mother of a certain sort and mentor to a doomed young man. And this country and my country and the whole goddamn world had put themselves in boxes and me along with them. Every box tight and dark and you could kick at the sides and they would not yield.

But there was only one way out that I could see. Out of all of them. And that was at my feet. Down into this tight dark space that at least you could walk around in and at least you had the company of the legions of the dead and at least there were a couple of killers at the other end that you could shoot dead.

Notion confirmed.

I was a fucking hunter.

And I went in.

Down the step irons, down ten feet, twenty, thirty, and the dark surrounded me now in the tight, vertical tunnel of this entryway, and I gripped the irons with my hands and felt fast with one foot and groped downward with the other and held fast on that step and groped on, doing this over and over, making it all rigorously precise, and down I went.

I looked up only twice at the circle of blue sky. Blue and bright and inexorably diminishing. I thought: *This is how death comes, dying in your bed. The light bound in a circle, contracting upon itself, growing smaller and smaller, moment to moment.* I knew these were dangerous thoughts for me. And so I thought this: *Cyrus Parsons and James Barrington Lacey won't die like that. For them it will be far more abrupt.*

And I was fine.

I sensed, at my back, the downward tunnel suddenly gaping open, and my foot stretched downward and there was no iron step but stone surface.

I was standing now. The light from above was faintly still with me, but I did not look up. I was here now. I knew my eyes needed to adjust. I turned. And I had to pause in order to plan, to anticipate, to prepare.

I'd entered a passageway that went both to the left and to the right. My back was against the steps, which were on the street side of the entryway. So my back was turned to the west. The hotel was north. I would go left.

I held a breath. Let it out slow.

It was all about the hunt.

And then the larger challenge suddenly rushed over me. Time was very limited. I took out my Waltham. Nine-forty-five. The conference would officially commence in fifteen minutes. From that moment on, the blast could happen anytime. The straight path from this spot to the hotel was perhaps five hundred yards. But the passage was unlikely to be straight.

And the problem that had been gnawing like a rat in the center of my chest lifted its face and stared me in the eyes. How was I going to dash off and find the bomb in the rat's maze that lay before me? How would I choose a direction when I confronted the first fork in the path? And the next and the next.

But it struck me: Parsons and Lacey had to find their way as well. Their way in. And they had to mark their way out. I didn't have to find my own way. They found it for me. I simply had to recognize and follow the return trail they left for themselves.

Though now I felt confident the path would be open to me, and though I was keenly aware of my ticking Waltham, I still held myself in check. There were other issues I needed to work quickly through before plunging into the dark.

I had to get as close to Parsons and Lacey as I could without them knowing I was there. In a tight underground passage with stone underfoot they'd hear my shod footfalls from far off. Furthermore, with groundwater finding its way into these tunnels, all of the footing, stone or not, was going to be slippery.

So I crouched down and I took off my shoes and socks. In my bare feet I could be quieter in my movement, and I could also be surer in my footing on a slippery surface. I stuffed the socks into the shoes and set them aside.

I stood. Another measure for the sake of silence: I took the courier bag from my shoulder. I opened it and removed my flashlight and put it into a coat side pocket. I put the extra Luger magazine in another pocket. I took out the Luger itself and tucked it into the strap of my Mauser holster at my waist for now.

I put the courier bag beside my shoes.

I put my trilby on top of it.

I stepped into the center of the passageway.

The stone beneath me was smooth and chill. I shuffled my feet a little, rubbed the stone, told my body to be fully present on this path. I didn't need to kick against the side of this box. It was a natural thing to be here. My feet knew that.

And one more natural thing. I put my hand to the Luger and drew it out. I liked the little Mauser in the small of my back but I was very happy to hold the Luger, my palm swaddling the walnut grip, the crotch of my thumb and forefinger wedging into the deep curve at the top of the grip beneath the breech toggle. Hand and pistol each fit the other precisely and fully. I would carry it with every step. It was true I might have to use it suddenly. But I was also happy for its heft and its assurance and its reminder of why I was feeling just fine down here.

I took a step into the darkness.

I stopped.

Even this short separation from the entryway rendered the darkness absolute.

One last moment for problem-solving.

I took out my flashlight. It was too bad. Going quietly was meaningless if I shone a heralding beacon of light before me. But if I could catch Parsons and Lacey at work, their work space itself would be lit. I'd see them first. And if they'd left it, they would be lighting their own way.

I was ready.

These moments of thought had allowed my eyes to adjust as much as they could to the dark.

And I saw a thing that drew me up sharply.

A light.

Small. Low. Up ahead.

It was not moving.

I figured I understood.

I turned on my flashlight.

The limestone walls were a foot or so more than an arm's length away on either side. Empty at this point. Just walls. I strode forward.

Fifty yards along was a fork in the path. A gentle divergence but a choice. Two tunnels. That's where I found the small, low light. Parsons and Lacey had lit two four-inch coach candles and placed them beside each other at the mouth edge of the tunnel to my right.

They'd planned carefully. Perhaps for a long while. There were maps of the Catacombs. They could blow any target beneath the Latin Quarter. The ceilings above were notorious in the city for their weak spots, even for their occasional cave-ins. These two were ready. Maybe they'd just gotten lucky with the conference being at the Lutetia. It was a prime target even on its own.

I took the turn they'd marked. I shone my flashlight out ahead of me and I broke into a careful jog, the beam bouncing before me, my mind focused only on the ever-changing few steps ahead, my feet focused only on the footing, toes gripping and releasing, bidding me to slow when the footing got damp, shifting my center of gravity lower or higher to keep me steady. And I counted my strides. A yard per stride, roughly. Not precise. But I'd get to a given number without worrying about anything but speed.

Four hundred, I decided. If they'd already set the bomb and were coming back this way within the four hundred strides, we'd have a sudden confrontation. At least I knew they could be coming, while I would be a surprise to them. But I was afraid that beam ahead of me obscured any similar beams beyond its reach.

A risk I had to take.

And the risk was probably even greater. Surely they had firearms. This was too important a bombing to chance anyone happening upon them. Their planning had been careful. They were ready and eager killers. I had to be prepared for a shoot-out.

I pressed on as fast as I could.

Another fork at just over two hundred strides.

I slowed and paused briefly.

A turn to the left. Not severe. Four hundred was probably still the right count. Only darkness down the marked tunnel. No approaching lights. I shone my beam, preparing to resume the run.

And movement before me.

I reared back.

Low. Scattering forms.

Rats.

I walked on for a time, focusing the beam a little closer to me. Keenly conscious of my bare feet. But the vermin were gone, it seemed. I didn't like my chances with the rats if I fell and knocked myself out for a few minutes. But moving, with light, at my size, I was okay.

I took up the jog again.

The rats made me aware of smells. Their odor. Their shit. And then I was past their hangouts. And the smells were simply of mold and damp clay soil.

Then those smells suddenly ceased.

And a smell of something else came upon me, something old, like old stone or old wood but neither of those, a smell with perhaps a trace of quicklime. And then something rolling past me beyond the edges of my tungsten beam. A profusion. Faces. The walls were watching now, from floor to ceiling, large empty eyes, a crowd of thousands and thousands, the faces densely surrounded by the knobs and condyles of femurs and tibias, my first encounter now with the denizens of these tunnels, the legions of the dead, the disarticulated bones of millions. There were two of these Parisians of the Catacombs for every one Parisian walking around above us.

I'd seen enough of them. I kept my eyes ahead and focused on running and I gave myself to the rhythm of it. My legs moved as if on their own and my feet gripped and I held tight to the Luger and the light went before me and soon I was at four hundred strides.

I slowed to a walk. I stopped. I turned off my flashlight.

I was breathing heavily. But only from fast movement in heavy air. I was a denizen myself now of the Catacombs. I took a moment to let my breath abate and I peered carefully into the dark before me. No distant signs of light.

I turned my flashlight on.

I took out my watch.

Two minutes to ten.

Speed now. But quiet too. Before I'd begun to count I'd taken a number of steps at the start of this journey. And my strides were probably often longer than a yard. Perhaps many. I was surely drawing near.

I walked as fast now as I possibly could while putting each foot down with restraint, keeping the beam angled sharply before me. When finally a turn led directly to their work area, surely it would be visible from farther off than my beam. Silence was paramount now.

Almost with that thought the surface changed from stone to clay. This variance of footing had been common through these past fifteen minutes. I thought: *This is good.* I felt emboldened to go faster with the quieter footing.

I let my beam go out a little farther ahead to light a faster pace.

I'd been thinking too much. And I'd gone too long without turning off my light to look ahead for marker candles. So now my beam traveled before me and I was moving fast.

And by the time I noticed the pair of candles just a few feet ahead, my beam had already breached the mouth of the side tunnel where the candles sat, and my momentum carried me on even as I thought to turn off the flashlight and I began to move my thumb to the switch.

This transition from light to dark had gone fine before only because no one was there.

But now there was.

My flashlight had barely switched off when I arrived before the tunnel mouth where my light had already gone, and the two lights about ten yards down the tunnel vanished as fast as I now saw them and Lacey's voice said *Shit* and I was diving forward and downward in the total dark, angling off center toward the right-hand wall and I was landing, breaking the fall with my knees and my left hand and the tunnel clanged and a muzzle flashed in the direction of the space where I'd just been standing, and then another flash in the same direction.

Parsons and Lacey both had guns.

The echoes were still clanging in my head—and theirs—and I rose up to my knees and twisted my torso against the wall and extended my shooting arm to aim into the space of the muzzles and my thumb went to the safety catch and released it even as I heard Parsons and Lacey scuffling sharply and then going silent.

The shooters were no longer where they'd been.

The two of them were also pressed somewhere along the wall.

The blackness was absolute.

I held my breath.

I held my shooting pose.

I did not move.

In my head was an impulsive thought: *Well, thank God they have guns.*

I knew what I meant by that, but in these moments now, in the dark, deep under the ground beneath Paris, playing the role of Kit

Cobb the unperturbably deadly American spy, with a bomb obviously set and its fuse burning an unknown distance down the tunnel, with my shooting arm stretched out toward two invisible men with their shooting arms stretched in my direction, I knew what I meant but it surprised me. I was glad I didn't have to assassinate two unarmed men. Americans even. I was glad they were shooting back. Part of me insisted that was a stupid first thought and I had better things to consider.

I certainly had better things to consider.

In this hiatus I suspected we all three were arriving at the same conclusion: the next man to shoot, thus exposing his position, would himself be shot.

One against two, I had the worst of that deal.

Even if I outfoxed one of them and plugged him, I'd give the other a clean chance at a kill.

But Parsons and Lacey had a tough negotiation to pull off between them to make that work as a strategy. Very tough, under the circumstances.

I rested my shooting arm for a moment.

And I found something in my other hand.

My flashlight, clenched tight.

I slipped it into my pocket.

I listened.

One of them was breathing very heavily. Very fast. But the distance between us and the acoustics of the place made it impossible to turn a sound into a reliable target.

Suddenly Cyrus's voice: "Go."

And Lacey's: "You."

Negotiations had begun.

They had the pressure. Down the tunnel the bomb was ticking or burning. Probably a ten-minute fuse. They needed to haul ass far away. I had a much closer goal. The bomb and its fuse.

"Shoot," Cyrus hissed.

"You," Lacey hissed back, employing his Harvard debating techniques.

They both scuffled, but in place, no sound coming closer. They hadn't gotten braver. They were simply shifting around, afraid I'd draw a bead on them from their echoing voices.

And I thought: *I need to induce at least one of them to shoot, then make a kill, and at the pull of my trigger move smartly in an unexpected direction.*

Right. Just that.

And then: *There are two of them but I have two guns.*

I knew a quiet sound was more localized than a voice. So I was very very gentle in leaning forward and squaring my torso around just enough to let my left hand go inside the back of my coat. I put my hand on the Mauser. I was trying to draw it from its holster backwards.

I waited.

Somebody down the way scuffled again and I took the sound-cover to draw the Mauser and bring it out.

More scuffling, going from low to the floor to higher up a wall, generally from the direction of the left side of the tunnel, and I arranged the Mauser for shooting from my left hand.

This whole stand-off was spooking one of them, probably Lacey. I didn't blame him.

The Mauser was ready.

I turned my torso gently again and pressed flat back against the wall. From where I was pressed I extended my Mauser hand as far as I could into the middle space of the tunnel. I didn't have to hit anything. Just imply a body in space.

I sharply angled my hand toward me at the wrist, so the muzzle would face directly down the tunnel. As if I'd stepped out squarely into the path.

More scuffling down there.

I squeezed the Mauser trigger and let the pistol go and twisted my body back around while falling forward along the wall, getting lower, and I was falling and watching down the tunnel and whipping the Mauser hand back toward the Luger and my head was ringing as I was falling and before me now on the right was a bang and flash and I was on the ground and my Luger arm was straight and my left hand found my right and I fixed on the flash and I adjusted a little upward and I squeezed one round and instantly another, and I rolled to my left and a second muzzle flashed from the left side, aiming at where I just was, and my Luger came up and I put one round into that space and another, and I rolled onward and fired one more round to the right and one to the left and rolled back right even as all I heard was the echoing blare of my gunshots, and I aimed low and shot my last two rounds about six inches off the ground, one to the left and one to the right.

Hoping I was shooting dead or dying bodies now.

My eight shots done.

My hand went into my pocket instinctively, pulling out the other magazine, and by the time I realized what I was doing, my head started to quiet down and everything else was quiet too.

Very quiet.

I realized there had been no more muzzle flashes but mine from my second shot onward.

But I went ahead and rolled back left, popping the spent magazine and loading the other.

Still quiet.

I lifted the Luger and waited.

And listened.

I thought: *It's done.*

To which my body replied with an abrupt clenching in my chest. *Not done.* There was the unfinished business of a bomb.

I dipped into my pocket and pulled out the flashlight.

One last precaution.

I rose to my knees, aiming the reloaded Luger into the space before me. Then I turned on the light and scanned the tunnels quickly.

Two sprawled assemblies of shoe bottoms and knees and arms.

I stood up.

I moved to them.

I shined the light on Lacey's gaping mouth, his fixed and empty eyes.

Then on Cyrus.

His eyes were closed. His mouth was closed. As if he were peacefully sleeping.

I put a bullet into the center of his forehead.

Now the bomb.

But I paused.

The thought of the bomb presented the details of what was ahead.

"Shit," I said. So softly there was no echo.

I had overlooked one tool.

But I figured I knew where to find one.

I knelt to Cyrus. I felt inside his coat, along his belt line, and I found his sheath. I had to get going. I almost grabbed the knife from the sheath. But I was about to run. It would do no good to fall on the wet stones and stab myself. So I took time to unbuckle his belt and remove the sheath and put the whole thing into my inner coat pocket.

And now I was moving fast.

I did not try to figure the chances. How many minutes ago they'd set the fuse. How long the fuse would burn.

I just focused on the ground ahead.

Clay.

I pushed on fast. Too fast. Wet clay. My foot slipped, I pulled up, throwing my balance lower, stumbling, going to one knee.

I had to stay calm.

A slower pace to avoid a greater delay.

I rose back up and moved off. Quick but precise.

And all that I saw was the flow of ground into my light. Stones again now under my feet and more ahead and more.

Minutes were flowing too. My mind wouldn't let go of a sense of that. One minute. Two. Three, I guessed.

Then suddenly I was upon a pair of candles and another turn and I took it, and thirty yards ahead was light. A bright white light. I approached. The white glow of the gas mantle of a Coleman lamp, casting its radiance far into the tunnel. Parsons and Lacey had left it behind. Less to carry. It lit the start of their escape. The end of their lives.

Too bad, boys.

I strode now into an abrupt expansion of the tunnel. A chamber held up by four pillars of massive stone blocks. Three dark entries—other tunnels—converging here.

And in the center were the stacked rolls of dynamite. Dozens of sticks. From the center bottom stack ran the long, looped fuse, twenty feet long and smooth white. A Bickford fuse. Inside its tar-varnished exterior the jute yarn was burning unseen. No sparks. Safe as hell. Only a hiss. I had no time to figure out where the fire was. The fuse burned at two feet per minute. A ten-minute fuse. Not much time left.

I plunged to the starter stick and its blasting cap, pulling the knife from my inside pocket, ripping the blade from the sheath.

And now I could hear it.

A hissing.

Very near.

Coming this way.

I crouched to the fuse, grasped it near the cap, put my foot on the fuse about a yard along. In between foot and hand I laid the upturned blade beneath the cord and I sliced upward.

Not quite enough.

Upward again and the cut went through and the loose end held down by my foot thrashed away.

The hissing was very close, somewhere in that length of fuse flailing back toward its blasting cap, the flame about to arrive at the cut end.

It was going to spark into the air.

I grabbed the fuse and lurched away from the dynamite and pressed the exposed jute squarely against the stone of the floor.

The flame arrived, sizzling, the spark pressing to escape.

I stubbed it out like the butt of a Fatima.

Then silence.

32

I carried the Coleman lamp through the Catacombs of Paris making the joint seem bright and big and a swell place to take a stroll in your bare and battered feet. Even as my knees and my hands felt a little bit shaky.

But it got me through, and so I climbed out of the ultimate box and made my way to the Hôtel Lutetia, leaving my Coleman lamp behind, and I found Trask sitting alone at a table at the hotel's street-side bistro. He was, no doubt, busy saving our country's reputation. He looked me over, knew something was up, rose and put his hand on my shoulder, and he said, "Tell me." I told him where the bodies were and, incidentally, that I had just saved his life.

"Thank you," he said. An intense whisper. Which was about the bodies, and about Sam.

Then I turned and walked away.

I went straight to the Rue Perronet.

Louise answered the door, and as I saw her go a little bit wide-eyed at the look of me, I recalled that I was still dank and dirty from my morning's work. But she regularly saw worse, so she drew me into the room at once and closed the door and readily initiated our embrace.

Which I was reluctant to end.

But we had not spoken.

We needed to.

I pulled back a little, and we embraced for a few moments more with our eyes.

Before I could speak, she said, "Let me bathe you."

And she spread out towels on her bed and she laid me down and she removed my clothes and she bathed me with a sponge. As if I'd been carried from a train car at La Chapelle and put into a bed at the American Hospital, wounded by the war. And she found my wounds, the bruises and abrasions. Of my feet, of my knees and elbows, of my shoulders and chest. She found the places that hurt that I did not realize hurt until she found them, and she cleaned them and dressed them.

And when this was done, Louise removed her own clothes and lay down beside me, and we talked. She found the other wounds in me. I told her the ending of the story I'd begun in this bed night before last. I told her how wrong I'd been, over and over, all along, until finally I was right. How it had ended with Americans. Only Americans. Trying to kill each other in the dark.

She listened staunchly. Like a nurse who'd become accustomed to seeing the wreckage of men. And when I'd done, she took me in her arms, and we simply held each other close.

We lay like that for a long while, even as the late-autumn day faded into night.

And just before we slept, she asked, "What will you do now?"

I did not know.

So I answered her with a kiss.